MURDER IN THE COMMUNITY GARDEN

Designing a community garden as part of a new condo project seemed like a no-brainer to landscape architect Tory Benning, since it would bring people together and enhance the environmental profile of the property. But soon members of the garden begin squabbling and even leveling accusations of sabotage against each other in a friendly growing competition. Then one of the gardeners is found murdered at the grand opening, and Tory realizes she'll have to weed through some damning false evidence to help prove her implicated friend is innocent.

It's a daunting challenge given that her friend was seen threatening the victim on live TV and all the clues point to him as the culprit, but Tory is certain someone is behind a devious plot to set him up. As she starts looking into the backgrounds of those closest to the victim, secrets begin to emerge about marital infidelity, a sizable inheritance, and estranged children. Fearful now that she might be going up against someone far more cunning than a garden-variety killer, Tory will have to stand her ground to bring the culprit to justice—and be careful not to dig her own grave . . .

TITLE PAGE

Murder in the Community Garden

Judith Gonda

Judith Gonda Books

Copyright

Murder in the Community Garden
Judith Gonda

Cover design and illustration by Dar Albert, Wicked Smart Designs

Judith Gonda Books
are published by
Judith Gonda Books
www.judithgonda.com

ISBN: 979-8-9941464-5-3

Dedication

For my grandson, Benny, born the same year I wrote this book

ACKNOWLEDGMENTS

Thanks to my wonderful family for always being there for me and cheering me on: my husband, Victor; my daughters, Jennifer and Heather; my son-in-law, Matt, and my grandson, Benny. I'm also grateful to my two Pomeranians, Izzy and Ollie, for providing loving companionship and inspiration.

Thanks also to my great agent, Dawn Dowdle, for her wisdom and counsel, and to my amazing editor, Bill Harris, who always gives wonderful suggestions and insights. I am also grateful to the talented artist Dar Albert for the cover, and to Beyond the Page Publishing and staunch writer advocate Jessica Faust for their support. I feel very fortunate to have such smart, creative, and kind professionals to guide me.

As always, I'm immensely grateful to the readers, writers, and reviewers who support me and leave reviews. Your time, generosity of spirit, and positivity are truly appreciated! Love you all!

CONTENTS

CHAPTER 1

I propped myself up on my elbows, trying to figure out whether I'd been awakened by someone ringing my doorbell or whether I'd dreamt it. I reached for my phone on the bedside table and tilted it toward me. Nearly one o'clock in the morning. The time flashed on the screen for a second and then went dark. Darn. I needed to charge my phone. I plopped back down in bed, thinking it was a little late for a courtesy call. It must have been a dream.

A few seconds later, a violent banging sounded on my front door. I jerked to attention and blinked a couple of times, adjusting to the dark. I caught sight of a white ball of fur speeding across my bedroom floor. I tumbled out of bed, grabbed my phone, and hurried after Iris, my cream sable Pomeranian, wondering who on earth would be knocking on my door at this hour.

Must be something bad, though—nothing good ever happened after midnight, at least according to my aunt Marian, my late mother's sister. Neither my BFF Ashley, nor Jake, the PI I'd been seeing, would have come over without texting first. Same with my uncle Bob and aunt Veronica, relatives on my late father's side—unless there was a catastrophe.

Great. Just what I needed. My heart pounded harder as I stumbled shakily down the nightlight-illuminated hallway after Iris. My phone wasn't the only one running on empty. I was in low battery mode too, barely able to defend myself against an uninvited visitor my vivid imagination had already molded into the spitting image of Freddy Krueger.

When we got to the front hallway I stood like a squirrel on full alert, pricking my ears and trying to assess the risk level, my heart racing as Iris darted back and forth from the front door to the living room, pausing only to sniff at the threshold or press her nose against the picture window. She barked incessantly, drilling her gaze into mine, her whole body jerking with each bark. I peeked out the living room window. Parked out front was what looked like a late-model luxury car of some kind. Maybe a Mercedes. A well-heeled villain, apparently.

I gave Iris the stink eye and pressed a trembling finger to my lips. “Shush!”

She yapped louder, her tail wagging hard, her gaze never leaving mine, apparently convinced a masked marauder was ready to break down the door. Since Iris often erred on the overdramatic side, I hoped this was one of those times, and told myself that bad guys typically didn’t knock first before breaking in, or did they?

I tiptoed closer to the door, straining my ears to hear anything other than Iris’s barks. Was someone still out there?

Boom, boom, boom. I flinched hard. The heavy pounding on the door answered my question. Iris flung herself against the door, seemingly under the impression she could break it down the way cops do in movies.

An angry male voice shouted through the thick wood of my Mediterranean bungalow’s front door. “Open up. I know you’re in there.”

I gulped, frozen in place, my heart beating at full throttle. Options for my next move flipped through my mind. Call nine-one-one? Ask who it was? Grab Iris and run out the back door?

A voice pierced through Iris’s racket. “Tory, can you hear me?”

They knew my name?

“It’s me, Mac. I need to talk to you right away.”

Mac? I stared into space for a second, still foggy-brained and half asleep. Oh. Mac.

“Hold on.” I slid my phone onto the hall table and stretched out my arms to Iris, who sidestepped my reach. “I’ll be right with you.”

I slow-jogged after Iris, popping into my office, where I pulled a long hoodie off the back of a chair. I wrestled it over my tank top and skimpy shorts while disabling the security system on the panel near the door. Iris skipped past me, still barking her lungs out, taunting me from afar. I bounded after her again, this time corralling her in a corner with my leg. I scooped her up, unhooked the chain, and opened the door.

Before me stood Mac McGregor, who chaired the Hotel Santa Sofia Corporation board and was also currently running for mayor of Santa Sofia. His six-foot-plus frame filled the doorway and loomed larger than I last remembered, probably because I was barefoot and he was wearing trendy thick-soled combat boots.

"Oh, my goodness, Mac, what's going on? You scared the living daylights out of me."

"Trouble in the community garden. That's what's going on." He pushed past me and stepped inside. His scowl softened as he studied my face. "Sorry, didn't mean to scare you. She just made me so mad."

"Who?"

"Bunny!"

"Bunny? Bunny Hare?"

"Yes, Bunny Hare. Who else do you know named Bunny?"

No one. And certainly no one with the ridiculously cartoonish name of Bunny Hare, a moniker she had chosen to keep when she married her second husband, Hollywood director and producer Peter Yusem. Keeping her own name was totally on brand for the publisher and editor of our local weekly, the *Santa Sofia Sentinel*.

"What did Bunny do now to get you so mad? I know she spelled your name wrong in the *Sentinel* last week, but she said that was a typo."

My most recent project as a landscape architect had been the Jacaranda Gardens condominiums, and I'd selected both Mac McGregor and Bunny Hare as inaugural members of its community garden. Adjacent to the condo grounds, the community garden was the feature that had cinched the win for Benning

Brothers Landscape Design and Nursery, a company I'd inherited from my father and which I now headed as president. Bunny was an easy choice, not only because of her standing in the general community, but also because of her outspoken environmental advocacy and substantial influence with anti-development activists, whose opposition to the condo had been somewhat placated by the community garden addition.

Mac glowered at me. "Something far more sinister, I'm afraid, aimed at making a mockery of me, my campaign, and your community garden."

Now he had my attention.

"What do you mean?"

"She's the one who took it."

"Took what?"

"My prize cabbage."

For crying out loud. He woke me up for a cabbage?

This was the second time Bunny Hare drama had disturbed my night's slumber. Earlier Bunny, who was also a Santa Sofia city council member in addition to being Mac's main opponent in the upcoming mayoral race, had called me to claim someone had stolen *her* prize cabbage, and she wasn't shy about pointing to Mac McGregor as the culprit.

I breathed in and exhaled softly. "Why on earth would she do that?"

And why would it be timed for the eve of the garden's official opening day? After pandemic-related building construction and landscaping delays, the official opening of the Jacaranda Gardens condo project was finally going to take place tomorrow afternoon with a ribbon-cutting ceremony at the garden followed by the unveiling of the best harvest contest winner, the title both Mac and Bunny were vying for.

Mac harrumphed. "Obviously because then she would have the largest cabbage and win the competition."

Bunny's exact answer when I'd asked her the same question about Mac hours earlier.

The community garden opening had originally been scheduled for Easter, with an egg hunt, but the delays pushed it to June. But at least we still had the pairing of Bunny Hare and Mr. Mac McGregor as inaugural gardeners to evoke bucolic Beatrix Potter vibes. We'd chosen ten community leaders and civic representatives to start their garden plots months ago in anticipation of the official launch, since actual flowers and plants were a much better visual selling point than dirt plots, which was especially important since not all the condo units had been sold yet.

I rubbed my eyes and wondered whether I should share Bunny's story, painfully aware that every minute wasted talking about cabbages was one less moment of beauty sleep before my TV interview at the community garden with anchor Melinda Yang on *Good Morning, Santa Barbara*. Being featured on their midmorning segment was a big deal. Neighboring Santa Barbara was a much larger market, so we were grateful for the additional exposure.

"You know what's odd, Mac? Bunny called me earlier tonight to tell me her prize cabbage was stolen."

He braced himself against the living room doorway. "What? Are you kidding me?"

I looked down and fidgeted with the zipper on my hoodie. "Nope. Maybe someone is playing a prank on both of you?"

"Hardly a prank when a mayoral race is at stake too."

I raised my head. "You really think the cabbage competition is that important to the mayoral race?"

He glared at me.

"For Bunny, I mean."

I'd always been competitive so I could relate, but I drew the line at vegetable contests.

I shifted my weight. "You think she'd actually steal yours so she could win? Then who stole hers?"

He smirked as he adjusted the blue-framed designer glasses that highlighted his blue eyes.

Iris squirmed in my arms, and I set her down on the floor. "Wait. You don't think she stole her own cabbage, do you?"

He nodded his head. "I do. And I know what you're thinking,

Tory. They're cabbages."

He was a mind reader.

"But do you know how long it takes to grow one?"

It was early for math. I paused to count on my fingers. "Since we opened the garden up for you guys in March, and it's June now, I'd say about three months."

He snapped his fingers. "Exactly. And she plucks it up tonight in less than a minute."

I still wasn't all that sympathetic nor on board with his theory. Especially at one in the morning.

"Okay." I pulled my long hair back from my face, wishing I had a hair tie handy.

"But it's far more than that. The cabbage is her simply thumbing her nose at me. The real damage is the leaked *Sentinel* editorial on Twitter."

"What leaked editorial? What are you talking about?"

"If you'd bothered to answer my calls or read the texts and emails I've been sending you for the last hour, you'd know."

"You called me?" My face heated up. "I must have shut my phone off after Bunny's rant."

I hated to lie, even white lies, but sometimes it was necessary. Frankly, I was a bit embarrassed to reveal to Mac that the real reason I didn't hear his call was because of my newfound obsession with K-pop. My phone's battery was running low after I'd binge-streamed the boy band Stray Kids' latest music video on YouTube for an hour—I was answering a call to duty to help them win a Korean TV competition where the number of streams, even from international fans, counted toward their win—and I was too tired to get out of bed to charge it afterward. I blame my friend Ashley. During the pandemic, in addition to binging the TV comedy *Schitt's Creek*, she'd gotten me into Stray Kids. The only problem being, once I'd gone down that rabbit hole, there'd been no turning back.

Mac tilted his head. "Yes, and it went straight to voicemail. I also sent you texts and emails."

"Wait." I turned on my phone.

The battery icon was black except for a thin red line.

"Oh, sorry. My phone died."

Mac furrowed his brows. "Well, better your phone than you."

I bent down to pet Iris. "What's that supposed to mean?"

He raised one eyebrow. "You'll see when you read my texts."

I shook my head slightly. "Okay. I can take a few minutes to go search for my charger, plug in my phone, and then wait for it to be charged enough to read them, or you can make it a lot easier, and just tell me right now."

Mac ran his hand through his wavy gray hair. "Someone apparently leaked an upcoming *Sentinel* editorial on Twitter. Supposedly written by Bunny, it said you were the mastermind behind the community garden, and it was part of an evil plot to normalize people's acceptance of big developers and urban renewal in Santa Sofia, the first step to gentrify the less-prosperous sections of town."

Let me set things straight. The last thing I would want for Santa Sofia would be to push residents out of their neighborhoods. I loved everything about my hometown, from its posh art galleries, resorts, and renowned restaurants to its more modest, blue-collar neighborhoods with a Western influence, where many workers from nearby ranches and vineyards in the neighboring foothills resided.

I gave Iris a squeeze and stood up. "What? That's absurd and dead wrong. We replaced one dilapidated strip mall that had been abandoned years ago with a beautifully landscaped project, if I don't mind saying so myself. Not to mention a wonderful community garden for everyone to enjoy. But she's entitled to her opinion, I guess."

Mac crossed his arms. "Is she entitled to threaten you and me in the process?"

I stood up straighter. "What?"

"Yeah, Bunny's editorial said one way to fix urban blight is by getting rid of the root cause, and I quote, 'like Hotel Santa Sofia condo backers and enablers Mac McGregor and Tory Benning.'"

I gasped.

Mac made air quotes. "She said that 'getting rid of these two developers would fix the problem fast.' And that if she won the mayoral race, she'd put a stop to gentrification and further development."

My head was reeling. "No! She singled us out? She actually wrote 'getting rid of'?"

Mac nodded.

"Why? I'm not even a developer. I'm a thirty-five-year-old landscape architect who designs gardens and outdoor spaces, for goodness sakes. I can't imagine Bunny saying that. It can't be real. It must be fake."

"That's what I thought at first too. But then Twitter removed the link, citing copyright restrictions. Would they do that if the article was fake?"

"Maybe? I don't know." I swayed a bit, stunned that Bunny could be that harsh and unprofessional. And menacing. Was this payback because I'd dismissed her stolen cabbage complaint too readily? I couldn't imagine her being that petty.

Bunny Hare wasn't your typical small-town newspaper editor who only focused on local garden club activities and posting seasonal recipes. She was a highly respected journalist with impressive writing credits, which included the *Atlantic* and the *Washington Post*. Most recently, her series in the *Sentinel* on the pandemic, drawing heavily on her own Covid-19 struggles and the lingering long-term effects, had been critically acclaimed and had received several prestigious award nominations.

"I honestly can't believe this is real. Bunny's always so nice to me."

Mac put his hands on his hips. "She can be a good actress when she wants to be."

I picked up Iris. "When did this happen?"

"A few hours ago. Someone texted me to ask whether I'd seen it yet."

"So that's when you started trying to contact me?"

Mac nodded.

Iris started to pant, signaling she wanted down again.

I lowered her to the floor. "Well, I guess I'll just have to ask Bunny myself if the editorial is real. I wonder if she knows it was leaked."

Mac's upper lip curled into a sneer. "I'm sure she does. Makes sense, since she'd already decapitated my cabbage. Talk about adding insult to injury."

"Well, better your cabbage than you."

His eyes sparkled. "Touché."

I leaned against the hallway wall. "How did you discover your cabbage was missing, anyhow? What on earth were you doing in the community garden at night? It closes at eight o'clock and gets locked up."

"I know. But I got a text message telling me that someone was trashing my plot."

My black cat Otis wandered into the hallway.

I reached down and stroked him behind his ears. "From who?"

"I have no idea. It was a number I didn't recognize. They just said it was from a friend."

"And how can you be so sure that Bunny is the culprit?"

"I have my sources."

"What sources?" I raised my eyebrows expectantly.

Mac made a zipper gesture across his mouth.

I sighed. "Okay. You can't tell me. So, then you went to your plot and then what?"

"I went to my plot. It hadn't been trashed, thank God. That's when I noticed my prize cabbage had been taken."

"So bizarre." I shook my head and pulled my hoodie around me more tightly.

I had to admit he wasn't wrong in thinking Bunny was totally capable of pulling a stunt like this, if only for the headline opportunity straight out of *The Tale of Peter Rabbit*: Mr. McGregor accuses Bunny of taking his cabbage. Even good journalists resorted to sensationalism from time to time.

I stifled a yawn. "Yeah, to me it seems like a stretch, to be honest. Bunny's a straight shooter. I can't see her stooping to cabbage theft. And I think she'd reserve the political theater for the *Sentinel*'s editorial pages. She thinks the pen is mightier than the sword, or the knife, or loppers, or whatever is used to cut a cabbage off its stalk. And she's smart enough to know better than to get herself and the *Sentinel* in legal trouble for making threats."

He shook his head. "I don't know. But since the community garden is your baby, I think it's your responsibility to protect everyone's plots from vandalism."

I moved closer to the front door. "I think the community garden has been kept safe and secure, Mac. The condo's security team patrols the entire property once an hour, twenty-four-seven."

"Well, Bunny must have waited and stolen it after they'd made their hourly check."

I rested my hand on the doorknob. "That's a pretty strong accusation without any proof."

"Okay, don't just take my word for it. Check the security cameras. Photos don't lie."

"Great idea if the cameras had been hooked up already. But I'm afraid the cameras aren't working yet."

"I saw the guys installing them the other day."

I cracked the door open. "Right, but we're still waiting for some of the right components. They sent the wrong parts initially."

He sneered. "How convenient."

"Well, we do have the security guard."

"Then let's go talk to him. Fat lot of good they'll be if they only make their rounds once an hour though."

"Now? Can't it wait till the morning?"

He cleared his throat. "I guess."

I opened the door all the way. "Look, it's late. Why don't we sort this out tomorrow morning before the opening? Who knows? By then the leaked editorial might turn out to be a fake and your cabbage might have even turned up."

"Oh, it's probably already coleslaw by now."

I chuckled.

"Oh, I almost forgot." His face tightened.

"What? Don't tell me your carrots are gone too?"

He reached into his jacket pocket. "I found this in my plot." He held up a glove.

"What's that?"

"Evidence."

"Evidence?"

"Yes. It's Bunny's and I found it in my plot."

"How do you know it's hers?"

"Look at it! It's a small gardening glove, one worn by a woman. My gloves dwarf this one." He placed the glove on his outstretched palm.

"But how do you know it's hers for sure? It could belong to any of the other female gardeners."

Mac nodded. "True. But at least we know a woman took it."

"This is all circumstantial, Mac." I tried to suppress another yawn.

"To you, maybe, but I know what's going on and I won't participate in any press conference based on lies and theft."

"Okay, it's not a press conference, Mac, just a short segment on *Good Morning, Santa Barbara* to promote the community garden. The exposure might attract buyers and would improve the public's perception of the condo project and the Hotel Santa Sofia Corporation, for which you still work, correct?"

Mac shifted his weight and nodded.

"So please show up. We need to present a united front and promote how the community garden is beneficial to everyone in Santa Sofia, not just the condo residents. Let's play up the positive aspects, like the organic produce that will be sold at the weekly farmers market sponsored by the condo association."

He sighed. "Oh, okay, when you put it like that. I'll try to channel my old acting chops and play the role of a happy gardener. Sorry to have bothered you. I just needed to tell you as soon as I discovered it missing, especially given the leaked editorial."

"Thank you. No problem. Talk to you tomorrow."

As soon as Mac left, I went to my kitchen counter and jumped on my computer to see if I could find the leaked editorial on Twitter. Otis, most likely interpreting this as a sign for a possible early breakfast, rubbed against my legs. When I couldn't find anything on Twitter, I tried googling. Nothing came up there either.

I stared into space trying to reconcile this with what Mac had told me. I concluded that, regardless of whether it was a hoax or real, its existence had been wiped clean. Or perhaps it had never existed in the first place, and Mac had lied and made the whole leaked editorial story up. But why would he lie? It didn't make any sense. I shook my head to try to clear the confusion I felt. It was nearly two in the morning. My mind was mush. Time to try to catch a few more hours of sleep before I had to get up. I headed back to bed with Iris trotting beside me.

CHAPTER 2

The next morning was rushed. After feeding Iris and Otis I took a quick shower and threw on the go-to outfit I wore to feel comfortable yet look professional, a black blazer and slim black pants with black heels. I wore black a lot because it was simple, elegant, and made matching easy. I slung my quilted black Kate Spade tote over my shoulder, bid adieu to the pets, and hopped into my Lexus SUV. I also favored black because, like many architects and landscape architects, I wanted the outfit I wore to take a backseat to the design solutions I presented. Plus, when I was out in the field, it didn't show the dirt.

Jacaranda Gardens was a five-story condominium project in the north part of town. The complex was inland but, like many parts of Santa Sofia, had ocean views from the upper floors. I took the Promenade, the coast route, north. It was a typical "June gloom" day in Santa Sofia, with low coastal clouds that made the ocean look gray. I turned east on Olive Branch Road toward the foothills, and as I got farther inland and up to a higher elevation, the sun had already broken through and was burning off the moist morning marine layer, a good omen for my frizz-prone hair.

After about a mile or two I turned left and drove up the circular drive leading to the sleek white condo building. The drive was lined with arching jacaranda trees (*Jacaranda mimosifolia*) that I'd specified both for their beauty and because they were recommended by Santa Barbara County for their drought tolerance. The small center island was also planted with blooming jacaranda trees, their lovely violet, trumpet-shaped flowers forming a dense umbrella and their fallen petals a luxurious bluish purple carpet.

I spotted my friend Philip Shoshani's Kia in the small front parking lot. He'd graciously volunteered to do my hair and makeup for the TV interview. Jacaranda Gardens had already received a lot of press, partly due to the *Sentinel*'s extensive coverage and Bunny Hare's media connections. In fact, it was Bunny who'd arranged to have the *Good Morning, Santa Barbara* team trek up to Santa Sofia for the segment today. As I got out of my car, I admired the clean, curved lines of the condo's wide balconies, some of which had smaller jacaranda shrubs hanging over them. Out of the corner of my eye I saw Mac drive up in his shiny silver Mercedes. I hurried ahead, eyes front, hoping to get a jump on him to avoid getting cornered into another venting session.

The condo entrance was modern and airy, with white marble floors and glass walls. I walked across the lobby, empty except for its leather and metal furnishings, to a hallway that led to the manager's office. Joey Hernandez, our newly hired manager, wasn't around. The first thing I did was check the whiteboard calendar that hung on the near left wall to see who was currently on security duty. On my way back from the office to the lobby I was intercepted by Mac.

"Hi, Mac, how are you today?"

He stood in front of me blocking my way. "She's here."

"Who?"

"Bunny."

I nodded. "Okay—"

"Aren't you going to talk to her?"

"Yeah, I will in a minute. I'm a little busy right now making sure everything is ready for the TV crew, who will be here soon. She's on my list. But first I want to talk to the security guard."

"Great. I'll come with you. Maybe he saw something at the time that didn't seem out of place, but once he finds out a crime has taken place it might seem suspicious."

"She."

"Excuse me?"

"The guard on duty right now is a female. Why don't you

let me talk to her first? I'll let you know if I find out anything relevant."

He scowled at me. "Suit yourself. I'll be at my plot."

The security office was located on the other side of the lobby. The door was open and at the desk sat a security guard in Hotel Santa Sofia's signature dark green uniform with their back to me. When they twirled around in their chair a familiar face greeted me with a big, authentic smile—Officer Barb Brockett, a stocky woman with tight blonde braids bobby-pinned in a tidy crisscross fashion across her head. I'd first met Brockett about eighteen months ago when she worked security at the Hotel Santa Sofia resort. After we found out we had a mutual friend in Adrian Ramirez, a lieutenant in SSPD's detective division, any time we'd run into each other at the hotel she'd always ask if I'd seen A-Ram lately, as she affectionately called him.

"Good morning, Tor-nado. How are you today?" Brockett's eyes twinkled.

I laughed lightly, touched that she'd created a nickname for me too. "Great, thanks. Getting ready for my TV interview with Melinda Yang from *Good Morning, Santa Barbara*. She and her crew will be here soon to film a segment about our community garden."

She smiled. "So I heard. What can I do you for?"

"I saw on the schedule you worked until five yesterday. Have you seen anything out of the ordinary? Like people hanging around the garden that didn't actually have plots?"

She scrunched up her mouth. "Let me think. Nope. Nothing unusual on my watch. I don't recall anything like that."

"What about the other guards? Do you know who was on duty last night?"

"That would be Jimbo's shift."

"Did he mention anything out of the ordinary to you?"

"He didn't mention anything in his notes. I believe Jimbo works tonight too. If you're around later, you can ask him yourself. His shift starts at five."

"What about people you see all the time, the gardeners? Any

of them reluctant to leave at closing?"

Brockett shook her head. "Not that I recall—"

At this point a scream pierced the morning calm. We both snapped our heads in the direction of the community garden, from where it seemed to be coming. Brockett sprinted toward the garden. I trotted behind her, hampered by my high heels, as I hoped and prayed Mac hadn't started some drama. Had he and Bunny clashed again? Or had the same weirdo who'd taken the cabbages returned to the scene of the crime, this time wielding a pipe or a machete? I really needed to turn off the notifications on my Santa Barbara County crime watchers app. Their practice of reporting every single incident of mischief and mayhem in the area was making me a nervous wreck.

Brockett reached the garden several seconds before me. A small group of gardeners was clustered around Bunny's plot. Judging by Brockett's reaction as she turned to me and smiled, my worst fears were unfounded. Peering over the shoulders of the onlookers I soon saw what everyone was watching: a standoff between Bunny, impeccably coiffed and outfitted in light-colored, casual designer clothing, and a possum. A big possum, much bigger than Iris or Otis.

Bunny, her silvery white hair pulled into a low ponytail, was holding a tall paper smoothie container with a straw stuck in its lid and was waving it at the possum. "It won't let me pass."

The possum wasn't moving and stared blankly at the ground. Maybe Bunny's shriek had stunned it. It looked one shriek away from falling over and playing . . . well . . . possum.

Brockett extended her arms. "I think if everyone moves back and gives it some space it will be able to make its escape."

I backed up. "It's kind of weird for it to be out in the morning. Maybe it's sick."

My observation sent Bunny into hysterics. "You mean rabid?"

Brockett clicked her tongue. "Not necessarily."

Bunny's eyes grew wider. She started to hyperventilate.

Another female gardener in a straw sun hat, gardening smock, jeans, and Crocs hopped over the low picket fence separating the plots and threw her arm around Bunny. "Just take a slow deep breath and then exhale slowly. Calm down."

With the commotion shifting to Bunny, the possum turned on its heel and waddled away in the direction of the street gate.

Mac, who had been watching along with everyone else, drifted over to me, chuckling.

I smiled back. "Maybe the possum took your cabbage?"

Mac whistled. "I never really thought of that. But of course, animals are some of the biggest garden poachers around. But wouldn't there have been a mess with parts of the cabbage everywhere? No. I'm pretty sure it was a human perpetrator."

"Perhaps, but based on Bunny's hysterical response in broad daylight, I hardly think she would venture here after dark, knowing that many wild creatures are nocturnal. Like racoons. Or skunks. Or coyotes. Or even mountain lions."

Brockett nodded. "Yes, to all of that. I routinely see skunks at night and keep my distance. Same with coyotes. I even saw a bunny yesterday evening."

Mac's mouth dropped. "You saw Bunny last night?" He turned to me with a glint in his eye. "See, I was right. I told you it was Bunny prowling around."

I shook my head. "No, Mac." I turned to Brockett. "You meant a bunny, like a rabbit, right? Not Bunny Hare."

Brockett laughed. "Yeah, I saw a cottontail, I believe. Cute little thing, and fast as the wind once it saw me."

Mac's face fell. "I see. But that still doesn't explain what happened to my prize cabbage."

I checked my phone. "Yikes. It's nine thirty already and I still need to get my hair and makeup done for the show. Let's meet up after they finish filming and talk more then, Mac."

Mac headed back in the direction of his garden plot. I rushed along the concrete paver path that led to the condo building, breathing in the intensely sweet scent of the Hidcote Blue English lavender (*Lavandula angustifolia*) that grew along its borders. I bent down to touch the grass between the large square tiles to make sure it was the artificial grass I'd specified since it looked so realistic. Because of California's drought conditions, I'd been specifying more artificial turf lately. Interspersed with the lavender, succulents, and other drought-tolerant plants, it added a reliable ground cover that we didn't need to continuously re-seed.

I was pleased with how the neutral palette of greens, grays, and lavenders in the condo's courtyard had turned out, picking up on the purple and green shades of the jacaranda trees out front. The courtyard's subdued color scheme and minimalist styling had a calming Zen quality in contrast to the lively patchwork of colors in the community garden plots. There, flowers and plants in every shade of red, orange, yellow, purple, blue, and green reflected the diverse essence of a community garden.

As I crossed the concrete-tiled courtyard, I glanced at a serene side patio where the sun was shining through the delicate gray-green leaves of the newly planted dwarf olive trees (*Oleo europaea*). Seated there in a sculptural gray iron and faux rattan chair at a round, beveled-glass table was Philip, chilling and sipping his coffee in the filtered light.

He jumped up. "Tory! So good to see you. Oh my God, your hair is so long. And your blonde highlights that grew out look like ombre now. I love it."

Philip was ready for work, his thick black hair pulled back in a neat man-bun and his paisley shirtsleeves rolled up, revealing his hairy arms.

"I told you it was long. When did I last see you? A year ago Christmas? I haven't had it cut since then. But the good thing is the longer length makes it less frizzy."

"Definitely. The weight of the longer hair has a straightening effect." He inspected a lock of my hair. "Let me trim about an inch off to freshen the edges, darling. And let's give you a fashion ponytail today. I'm already set up in a room the new manager, Joey, showed me." Philip lowered his voice. "Joey's very cute, by the way."

I smiled. "Anyway, for today—"

"Just a quick styling and light makeup. Got it! You'll be good to go in ten minutes."

I checked my phone again. "Good, because the shoot starts at ten sharp, according to Melinda Yang."

"Yes, I ran into her. She's one of my clients, you know."

"Oh. No. I didn't know."

But I wasn't surprised. Philip's loyal clients followed him wherever he went. He worked mainly at Hotel Santa Sofia's Zoe Stella Salon, but he also traveled to Malibu once a month for his entertainment industry celebrity clients.

I hurried after Philip to a small conference room with an adjoining bathroom near the manager's office, where he'd set up shop. I pulled up a chair and he sprayed water on my hair until it was saturated. After he trimmed my hair, he cranked up the blow-dryer.

I told him in between blasts of the dryer about Mac coming over the night before and his theory that Bunny had taken his cabbage. Philip seemed to be listening, but I didn't know for sure. When he was in his creative zone he was in his own little world. In about ten minutes my hair was dry and smooth. He deftly styled a sleek fashion ponytail and then quickly applied makeup. In another seven minutes we were done.

He held up a mirror. "Voilà!"

"Wow. Thanks, Philip. Great job. And fast." I sighed with relief that today he'd been quicker than usual.

Philip danced around me pulling and poking my ponytail. "And then Mac just left? He didn't cause any other trouble?"

"Yeah. No. He's basically a good guy. I've known him for years. He does have a narcissistic streak though, and a quick temper. I think he got really upset because he's nervous about the mayoral race mainly."

Philip had his arms crossed and listened to me intently.

"The last thing I want to do is to become the community garden police. But until the condo project officially opens, and Joey moves in next week, I'm afraid I'm it. The security guards can't be expected to monitor personal spats."

"Joey told me he moved in last week." Philip gave me a sly

smile.

"Oh, he did? Good."

"You look beautiful, by the way. Ready for your close-up, my dear." He chortled.

"Aw, thanks, Philip."

We hugged.

There was a soft knock on the door. The door opened and Joey Hernandez, a baby-faced young man with big brown eyes and slicked-back, short brown hair with side undercuts, stood in the doorway.

He took a few steps inside. "Sorry to disturb you. Melinda Yang is here."

Philip smiled at him approvingly.

Joey, in his dark green blazer, white shirt, and khaki pants, gave Philip a little wave.

"Thanks, Joey. I'll be right there."

Philip put his hands on my shoulders. "You look great. Go knock 'em dead."

We locked gazes for a second.

Philip's cheerful facial expression dissolved into one of distress. "Oh, my goodness, Tory! I'm so sorry. It's a saying. Like break a leg."

I exhaled. "That's okay. I know what you meant."

The last thing I needed was any more dead bodies. My experience the last year and a half had already exceeded anyone's normal quota.

I took a deep breath and headed to the lobby, where the glass walls provided a good view of the front parking lot. The sight of Melinda Yang chatting with her camera crew outside their news van gave my stomach butterflies. Hoping a quick walk would relieve my nerves, I took the path that cut through the rear courtyard to the community garden to wait for Melinda.

The community garden had forty garden plots that measured about twelve-by-twelve feet each, bordered by a six-foot-high metal mesh fence around the whole perimeter. Individual plots were accessed from narrow gravel paths running parallel and perpendicular to the center path. The garden had two gates, one at the courtyard and one at the street entrance.

Ten plots had been allotted to our inaugural group of gardeners. Besides our two mayoral candidates, Bunny and Mac, other community gardeners included two each from the city council, the police department, the fire department, and an environmental group.

In addition to the gardeners, on hand for the opening were the retiring mayor, a handful of city dignitaries, and a few Hotel Santa Sofia executives I knew, as well as Simon Walker, a photographer I was acquainted with who freelanced at the *Sentinel*. In the distance, I spotted Mac's wife, Kaley McGregor, talking to him in an animated fashion.

Near the entrance to the garden, in a plot across from Bunny's, a brawny male gardener with golden brown skin, wearing sunglasses, a cap with a sun flap, and a mask, looked up from digging and smiled.

As I approached him, I realized he looked familiar. "Hi, there. I know you from the Benning Brothers Christmas tree lot, right?"

He stood up. "From the Hotel Santa Sofia. The Firefighters Fundraiser. The Secret Maze? You were with Ashley. I was with my bros."

"Oh. That's right."

He held out his hand. "Tate Robinson."

I shook his hand. He had a firm grip. I got a good vibe from him, but I could've sworn his name was Trey.

"Tory Benning. Nice to see you again. Your plot looks great, by the way."

Mention of the Secret Maze triggered mixed emotions, but it was good to see Tate under happier circumstances instead of in his EMT role. And I couldn't wait to tell Ashley that I'd run into her crush.

I wandered down the center path to the back of the community garden, where Mac's plot was located, to see how he was doing. He was alone, raking the soil near his cabbage patch where the headless stalk of his missing cabbage was conspicuous.

"Hi, Mac. The news team is here."

He continued raking.

"Still no cabbage?"

Mac rested on his rake. "No."

"Hope you'll be able to join us on *Good Morning, Santa Barbara.*"

His only response was a furrowed brow. It appeared he wasn't done brooding over his cabbage. I returned to the front of the garden, passing Bunny's plot.

She waved me over, still sipping from her smoothie container. "Tory, I was hoping to talk to you before the taping."

I checked the time on my phone. "Okay, but we only have a few minutes. Melinda Yang wants to start at ten." I followed her down a narrow path to an isolated part of the garden.

She whispered, "I'm assuming you've heard that Mac accused me of stealing his cabbage?"

I leaned back and studied her face, which looked paler than usual. "Yes. He came over to tell me personally late last night."

She looked at me intensely, perspiration glistening on her forehead. "Really? I hope he's okay. He's acting so strangely, obsessing over this competition. It's a promo for the garden and Jacaranda Gardens, for God's sake."

"I know, but I think the vegetable contest represents the mayoral race to him. He's afraid he'll be viewed as a loser and you the winner."

"What? That's absurd."

"That's what I tried to tell him."

Bunny frowned slightly and parted her lips, as if about to say something else.

I wondered if I should mention the leaked editorial to Bunny. But the TV interview was imminent. Best to wait until after it was over.

Philip jogged up to me. "There you are. I've been looking all over for you. Melinda asked me to find you. She's ready to start shooting. Follow me."

I trotted after Philip with Bunny behind me.

When Melinda Yang saw us approaching the entrance to the garden, she waved to Philip, who then introduced us. Melinda had typical news anchor good looks. Her shiny black shoulder-length hair swung when she moved, and her figure was like a model's. She was wearing an elegant navy pants suit with high-heeled beige patent leather shoes.

Melinda gave me a wide grin. "All set, Tory?"

I breathed in the cloud of light citrusy perfume she was wearing. "As ready as I'll ever be. You're going to start with an introduction about the condo and its community garden?"

"Right. I'll give a brief intro and then get into some more details by asking you questions about it. Then we'll move into the garden to see the progress of the first gardeners. And maybe interview some of them."

That had sounded like a great format a couple of days ago. But now, given the animosity between Mac and Bunny, I wasn't so sure. But before I had any time to think about it, Melinda's camera guy had started filming.

She had stationed herself at the garden's entrance gate and immediately broke into her vivacious delivery and introduction.

Melinda and her camera guy moved closer to me. "With us today we have Tory Benning of Benning Brothers Landscape Design and Nursery. Ms. Benning is the landscape architect who designed the landscaping for Jacaranda Gardens and, as I understand it, it was her idea to have a community garden."

She held a microphone in front of me.

"Yes, that's correct."

"What gave you the idea to have a community garden here?"

"We wanted to build a project that benefited the whole community, not just the new condominium residents. What better way than to provide a community garden for all to enjoy and participate in. This way the public can reap the benefits from gardening, such as physical activity, stress reduction, and access to fresh fruits and vegetables."

Melinda started to stroll and lead the way into the community garden, commenting on individual plots, which were separated by little picket fences.

Melinda spotted Mac and walked all the way to the rear of the community garden with the cameraman following her. "I see we have some well-known residents of Santa Sofia in the garden today, two mayoral candidates, in fact. Mac McGregor, chairman of the board for the Hotel Santa Sofia Corporation, the developer of Jacaranda Gardens. How are you doing today, sir?"

I held my breath, hoping he'd say *fine* and Melinda would then move on.

Mac McGregor gave a quick smile. "As a matter of fact, I'm not doing all that great today. As you might know, to kick off the celebration of the condo opening the community gardeners are having a harvest competition, like a county fair, if you will, to see who's grown the largest vegetables in various categories. Up until yesterday I had the largest cabbage. But it seems some people can't bear to see others succeed and had to spoil the competition by stealing my prize cabbage."

I inhaled sharply.

Melinda kept her frozen smile in place and remained unfazed. "Any theories about who might be the culprit?"

"Actually, I do. Bunny Hare took it."

Melinda didn't miss a beat. "Bunny Hare, the city council member and your opponent in the race for mayor? And the owner and editor of the *Santa Sofia Sentinel*?"

"Yes. That Bunny Hare. I don't think there's another, in Santa Sofia, at least."

Bunny darted past me. "How dare you! I did no such thing. My best cabbage is missing too. You don't see me having a meltdown over it." She turned to the camera. "For all I know, Mac stole his own cabbage so that he could then falsely accuse me of stealing it."

Mac laughed. "Oh, that's preposterous. Creative, but preposterous. You're just trying to tarnish my reputation again, like you did last week at our town hall debate."

I couldn't believe my ears. Bunny was accusing him of stealing his own cabbage, just as he'd implied to me that she had done.

Mac shook his fist at Bunny. "This isn't over."

My mouth was hanging open. I didn't know who to believe. I trusted Bunny since the *Sentinel* always covered issues accurately and fairly. But I knew Mac better, through work. He'd twice been instrumental in choosing Benning Brothers for major Hotel Santa Sofia projects.

The camera person panned to a third gardener and showed his cabbage entry.

Mac's gaze followed the camera's aim. "That looks like my stolen cabbage."

Melinda did a double take. "How can you tell one cabbage from another?"

Mac crossed his arms. "By its size. And for the contest, size matters."

Melinda blanched but kept on smiling. Mercifully, they'd run out of time, and she ended the segment.

My shoulders slumped. "Thank God."

A deep voice behind me chuckled. "Just when it was getting good."

I turned to see a tall Adonis-like man (standing at just under five foot four myself, most people seemed tall to me), with a lean frame looking understatedly cool in jeans and a crisp white shirt. He ran his hand through his straight black hair cut in long layers that framed his sculpted face, pushing it back to reveal high cheekbones and a sharp jawline. His wide lips broke into a smile and his brown eyes followed suit, forming adorable crescents.

My face heated up. "Sorry, I didn't mean to say that out loud."

He bowed his head.

When he lifted his face, he winked. "Neither did I." And then he smiled again.

Dimples. Lord help me.

My cheeks got hotter. Who was this guy? I was pretty sure he wasn't with Melinda. Melinda's crew only consisted of Melinda and her camera person, and a camera guy helper who doubled as her driver. This guy was hot enough to be on TV himself. His rolled-up sleeves revealed toned arms that were taking my breath away.

Calm down, girl.

His self-deprecating air reminded me of Jake, the PI I'd been seeing. We were in some type of relationship at the beginning of the pandemic, or at least I thought we'd been. But we hadn't given it a label yet, probably because neither of us had been ready for a relationship, both of us having been recently traumatized. I'd been widowed, and Jake divorced. For some reason this guy reminded me a bit of a cop, specifically Adrian Ramirez, aka Brockett's A-Ram, who my best friend Ashley was currently dating, and whose relationship status was also "to be determined."

But I didn't think he was a Santa Sofia cop. I knew most of the SSPD officers, unfortunately, because I'd found myself in the middle of too many crime scenes in the last year or so. He must be a private investigator. I knew the PI vibe, low-key, curious, affable, like Jake. But why would a PI be here? Mac hadn't taken it that far, had he? Or maybe Bunny had hired someone to investigate the leaked editorial? But that would have been a quick turnaround. Wait. I still needed to ask her about that.

I also doubted he worked at Jacaranda Gardens. I knew most of the Hotel Santa Sofia Corporation personnel. Perhaps he was a prospective condo buyer. Whoever he was, he'd gotten my attention long enough to make me momentarily forget about the disastrous interview.

Melinda's jovial laugh brought me back down to earth. She appeared undaunted, poised as ever as she strolled over to me. "Well, that's not what I expected but that's what made it good."

"Well, at least it wasn't live, and you can edit out the accusations."

"Oh, it was live, alright."

I turned around, expecting some wry reaction from the hot guy I presumed was a PI, but he had disappeared. Without any comic relief to calm me down, I started to stress. I thought about the consequence of bad press, not only in selling the rest of the condos but on my future job potential if my community garden idea backfired and resulted in major drama.

Melinda squinted in glee. “But don’t fret! The good news for you is our midmorning show doesn’t have a very large following compared to our noon and evening shows. And anyway, we’ll edit it down because we don’t have as much time to allot to it in those slots.”

“Phew. That’s some relief, at least. What are we talking about then, only a few hundred viewers?”

She threw her head back and laughed, her hair swinging back into its perfect shape when she turned to me. “We wouldn’t be on the air if it was only that few.”

I made a mental note to tell Philip how good her hair looked. He’d love to hear his work being complimented.

Bunny called out to me and waved me over.

I touched Melinda’s arm and told her I’d be right back, then trotted over to Bunny.

Bunny furrowed her brows, which glistened with sweat. “Tory, now that the taping is over, I need to talk to you about something else.”

“Are you okay? You look a bit queasy.”

“I’m fine. Just an upset stomach.”

“Sorry. That commotion over the cabbages would upset anyone.”

I wondered what Bunny wanted to talk about. Maybe she was going to bring up the leaked editorial herself.

“I just need to finish up with Melinda first. I’ll be with you right after that.”

She gave me the thumbs-up sign and returned to her plot.

On my way back to Melinda, someone tapped my shoulder. I spun around hoping it might be Adonis but, alas, it was Mac.

“Tory, can I have a word?” He was frowning again.

Now what? Between Mac and Bunny, I felt that I’d be the next one getting an upset stomach.

“Sure. I need to thank Melinda Yang first, though. Hold on.”

Melinda had already headed toward the lobby. I followed her, passing a masked maintenance worker along the way, being careful not to let my heels slip off the concrete paver we shared briefly and sink into the turf that surrounded it. Most of the gardeners and other people who'd been in the community garden to watch the TV spot had gathered for the refreshments being served on the patio. The branches of the olive trees and the grasslike leaves of the big blue lilyturf (*liriope muscari*) planted in shallow wells around the patio swayed gracefully in the gentle breeze. I couldn't wait for late summer, when the lilyturf's lilac-purple flowers would bloom.

Loud voices sounded behind me, but I couldn't let any more distractions prevent me from catching Melinda before she left. I had no time to check out another brouhaha. My heels clicked on the lobby's marble floor as my stomach churned. I was really over all the bickering.

When I reached the front entrance, I took a deep belly breath and exhaled as I peered at the jacaranda trees. Their soothing beauty calmed me down. The camera guy and his assistant were loading their equipment into their news van.

I caught up to Melinda as she was climbing into the van's front passenger seat. "Melinda, thanks so much for coming all the way up here today. Sorry it got a bit heated."

"Don't be. Those are the moments we live for." She chuckled.

"I bet." I twisted my mouth to the side.

Melinda flicked her hair. "Don't worry, Tory. Like I said before, that segment was live for the morning news. But for the bigger viewing audiences at the noon and evening news shows, it will be competing with more stories, and will get edited down to a few sound bites."

My chest heaved. "Okay. That makes me feel a little bit better."

Melinda broke into a wide smile. "Relax. All people will remember is the opening of this beautiful condo project and Mac and Bunny acting like campaign rivals do. Mission accomplished all the way around."

"You think? It wasn't a total disaster with them fighting? You don't think that will scare people away from our project?"

"Absolutely not. A lively competition is what's expected. And a bit of notoriety might actually work in your favor. Remember, there's no such thing as bad publicity."

I leaned my arm on the van's door. "Hope you're right. I guess we got the exposure we wanted."

Melinda buckled her seat belt as the driver and cameraman jumped in the van.

Someone called out my name.

Joey Hernandez was running toward me at a fast clip. "Ms. Benning, Ms. Benning, something awful has happened."

Melinda leaned out of the window. "What now? Another missing cabbage?"

I giggled. "Right?"

But as Joey got closer, his distressed expression told me it was something more serious.

I moved toward him. "What happened?"

"It's Bunny!"

I furrowed my brow. "What about her?"

Joey panted, "She's dead."

CHAPTER 3

Everything seemed like it was in slow motion as I processed Joey's words.

I stepped nearer to him. "What? I just saw her a few minutes ago. What happened?"

Joey widened his eyes. "I don't know. All I know is I found her unresponsive on the ground in her plot. I already called nine-one-one. Police are on their way and an ambulance too. But I don't think there's anything they can do. I'm pretty sure she's already dead."

I leaned in closer. "Are you sure it's Bunny Hare?"

Joey nodded emphatically. "Yes. I'm positive."

Melinda jumped out of the van. "Wait. Did I hear you correctly? Bunny Hare is dead?"

My mouth was still hanging open. "How can she be dead?"

Joey turned and jogged back toward the condo. I was so stunned I couldn't move.

Philip ran out of the lobby and rushed over to the parking lot, flapping his arms and breathless. "Bunny's hurt. One minute she's fine, the next minute she screamed, and by the time I got to her she was on the ground bleeding from the head. I think she was attacked."

"What?"

Philip let out a deep breath. "She has a gash on the side of her head."

"Oh my God. Did you see who did it?"

He shook his head. "No."

"Maybe she tripped and hit her head when she fell?"

He wrung his hands. "Someone had to have hit her with

something. I don't know how else it could've happened. You'll see when we get there."

Melinda stood next to her camera guy, ready to go. "Take us to her."

Philip took the lead to the lobby, through the courtyard, and along the path to the community garden. We followed him through the garden's open front gate and turned right onto the narrow path to Bunny's plot. There, Mac and the other gardeners stood hovering over Bunny, who was sprawled out on the ground. Tate Robinson, the EMT with whom I'd had a brief exchange earlier, and Joey were squatted down next to her. Tate's brow became increasingly furrowed as he checked each of Bunny's vital signs. Joey looked on in horror, his big eyes seeming even bigger than normal.

A siren's faint shrill became louder and louder then abruptly stopped. A minute later the uniformed EMTs took over, asking everyone to back off while they examined Bunny.

One of the masked EMTs stood up and glanced at me, the serious expression in his eyes momentarily replaced with what I took to be a glimmer of recognition.

He shook his head. "Sorry."

My heart sped up and skipped a beat or two. I felt light-headed and a sense of déjà vu harking back to our Christmas tree lot a year and a half ago. This couldn't be happening again.

"Tory! Are you okay?"

I turned.

Adrian Ramirez grabbed my arm. "You were swaying. All the color's drained from your face." He grasped my hand. "And your hands feel clammy. Take some deep breaths."

Adrian, an old high school friend who was now a lieutenant in the detective division of the Santa Sofia Police Department, looked the same as the last time I'd seen him, his dark good looks appearing to be unaffected by the lockdown. He was freshly shaved, with well-groomed black hair, as always, and he smelled like the clean scent of soap.

I did as he suggested and felt better. Seeing Adrian's tall, muscular body and hearing his familiar, confident voice made me feel instantly safer and more protected.

"Sorry, I can't believe this is happening. We were talking only minutes ago."

Adrian patted my shoulder. "I want to hear it all. But first I need to cordon off the area." He turned to everyone gathered around. "I need everyone to remain on the premises until we have spoken to each of you. My officers will be questioning people in the courtyard and lobby. We'll try to be as efficient as possible. Please move to those areas and give us some space here so we can do our jobs. Thank you."

Melinda and her camera person held their ground. "We're press."

"I can see that. You can remain on the grounds but please, right now, everyone has to take about five giant steps back." Adrian waved his arm for them to move back.

Melinda chatted with her cameraman.

When her eyes fell on me, she hurried over. "Tory, hon, are you okay? Do you want some water?"

I nodded. "That would be great. Thanks, Melinda."

She retrieved a bottle from the roller bag her camera assistant had hauled. "Here you go. We're going to go live in a few minutes with a breaking news segment. Sure you're okay?"

Philip came over and hung his arm over my shoulder. "I'll take care of her, darling." He waved Melinda away. "Do your breaking news."

I unscrewed the water's bottle top.

Philip bent his head. "Do you want to go sit down on the patio?"

I shook my head. "No, thanks, Philip. I'm fine."

Joey headed over to me. "What should we do about damage control? Issue a statement of some sort?"

I took a sip of water. Damage control was the last thing on my mind. "I think we have to see what the police are going to do first."

"Got it." Joey held up a finger. "But I think I'll give corporate a call anyway and ask our legal counsel what we should do." He scurried away.

Philip turned to me. "Will you be okay if I go with him? I'll let you know what they say."

I nodded.

He trotted after Joey.

Unfortunately, I'd been here before. I called my BFF, Ashley Payne, to update her on what had happened.

My call went to voicemail.

A couple seconds later she called me back. "Oh my God, Tory! I just got your message. How awful! Stay put. I'm on my way. Be there ASAP."

Hearing Ashley's calm voice and knowing she'd be coming soon comforted me somewhat. I moved closer to where Bunny's body was. I recognized her husband, the famous director and producer Peter Yusem, whom I hadn't noticed earlier. He was talking to Adrian, gesturing wildly and clearly agitated. I drifted closer so I could hear what they were saying. I knew his wife had just died but, judging from his frown and loud voice, he seemed to be more angry about it than devastated. But hey, if anyone knew that grief was handled in different ways by different people, it was me. I was still struggling with my abrupt transition from bride to widow, and it'd been about two years already. I was the last person to judge. I edged even closer, pretending to scrutinize a row of lettuce in one of the plots.

Peter raised his voice. "You've got to arrest him. I'm telling you, he had it in for Bunny. Falsely accusing her of stealing his stupid cabbage, as if she cared that much about some silly contest. The man is unstable. He left my wife a menacing note last night as well."

What? Unstable? My immediate response was to defend Mac. I couldn't imagine him leaving a menacing note, let alone murdering someone. But I bit my tongue.

Police officers and CSI personnel bustled around me. Some took photographs while others continued to secure the area with yellow crime scene tape. I strolled around, remaining within earshot of Adrian and Peter, feigning interest in the police activity.

Adrian had started to take notes on a notepad. "So, he threatened your wife last night? With a note? What did the note say?"

I could no longer keep quiet.

"I don't know anything about any note, but I would never call Mac unstable. He's a smart and successful businessman."

Peter glared at me through his tinted glasses. "And you are?"

"Tory Benning. I'm the landscape architect who designed this community garden . . . and a colleague of Mac's."

Peter crossed his arms. "You designed the space where my wife was murdered? Then maybe you can explain why the gate accessed from the street was unlocked, providing an easy escape for the murderer. And Mac McGregor doesn't strike me as all that smart. The man's leaving clues all over the place."

Already, what I knew of Peter Yusem, I didn't like.

I put one hand on my hip. "If you think Mac did it, then why didn't he run away through the gate you've identified as an escape route?"

Although as I said it, I realized I hadn't seen Mac around since Bunny's body had first been discovered. I felt light-headed again.

Peter ignored my question.

He turned his back on me and addressed Adrian, who'd been taking notes the whole time. "Anyway, Detective, you don't have to take my word for it, he went on live TV with his crazy behavior just minutes ago, threatening Bunny, saying it's not over, just like the note he left."

I sucked in air. I thought back to last night and Mac's agitation. Although Mac would never win a "Miss Congeniality" contest, I'd always known him as a straight shooter with a soft heart under his tough exterior. I couldn't imagine him hurting anyone over anything, let alone a cabbage. But his reaction to a missing cabbage was so out of proportion to the offense. Could he be capable of such violence?

Adrian looked down at his notepad. "I'll take a look at the TV interview later myself. I take it you were here for it?"

"I wasn't actually. But I came to pick up Bunny right after it was over." I wondered where he'd parked, because I'd been in the parking lot with Melinda and hadn't seen him drive up.

Adrian nodded. "Let's get back to the note. What did it say?"

"It said 'This isn't over.' Just like he said on TV today."

"Was it signed?"

Peter crossed his arms. "No."

"And where did you find it?"

"On our front doorstep. It was wrapped around a rock. Secured with a rubber band."

Adrian looked up. "Do you still have the note?"

"Yes. I don't have it with me. It's at home."

"Good. I'll send someone over to get it, see if we can pick up anything useful from it."

Adrian's face lit up suddenly. I followed his gaze and turned around.

Ashley, her statuesque figure dressed stylishly in her favorite Banana Republic short-sleeved white jumpsuit that popped against her light brown skin, ran up to me and squeezed my shoulder. "How are you doing?" She turned to Adrian and smiled slightly.

Ashley Payne was my closest friend and I loved her like a sister, or what I thought it would be like to have a sister, since I was an only child. We grew up together and were roommates in college and grad school. She had her own law practice in Santa Sofia.

Adrian raised his chin to acknowledge Ashley. "Okay, Mr. Yusem. And what did you do when you arrived here after the TV interview to pick up your wife?"

"I was curious about the condos, so I took a little stroll around the courtyard and lobby."

Ashley leaned closer, her soft black spiral curls touching my face as she whispered in my ear, "Love the fashion pony, by the way. It's a whole mood."

I laughed. "Thanks. I can always count on you to make me smile."

She flicked my ponytail.

Adrian finished writing his notes. "Okay, Mr. Yusem, that's enough for now. Why don't I have one of my officers arrange with you for a convenient time to take your statement and pick up the note. I know it's hard, but the sooner the better. Again, sorry for your loss. Don't worry. We'll catch the person who did this."

My phone pinged. It was a text from Jake Logan, the PI I'd been seeing.

I'd first met Jake at the Firefighters Fundraiser at the Hotel Santa Sofia and we became friends over the course of the investigation of my husband Milo's disappearance. We'd just started a romantic relationship when the pandemic hit. We hadn't been close to an exclusive relationship yet, at least in my mind, especially since he lived about twelve miles away in Santa Barbara. He'd been the only guy I'd been dating, but that was thanks to the pandemic more than anything. The lockdown had pretty much cramped the single lifestyle hard.

I drifted away from Ashley and Adrian a little and read Jake's text.

Single and ready to mingle? Can't wait to see you this weekend now that we're both fully vaccinated.

I chuckled at his silly humor. My phone pinged again.

I have something important to talk to you about.

I gulped. What did he mean? I hated when people said that and then didn't tell me right away what they meant. Dude, don't position it like it's a teaser for a new Stray Kids album, for God's sake. Oh, no. I hoped he didn't want to talk about a commitment. Not when Adonis, that other guy I presumed to be a PI, had just passed by and winked at me again. I hadn't seen Jake in person for such a long time. I didn't know how I felt about him anymore. I mean, I liked him a lot. But I didn't feel ready to commit again, to anyone, for fear of losing it all again, like I had with Milo.

I texted him back and told him about Bunny's murder.

Oh no. Are you okay? I'll come up right away. I need to reschedule a meeting first and then I'll be on my way. Take care.

I strolled back to Ashley and Adrian. "Jake's driving up from Santa Barbara."

Adrian nodded his approval. "When?"

"As soon as he can. He has a meeting he has to move first."

Ashley gave my shoulder another squeeze.

Adrian moved a little closer to me. "So, tell us everything. Take it from the top."

My phone pinged. I checked the new text. "It's my realtor, Danielle Murphy. She wants me to call her ASAP. She has a tenant for my dad's house."

Ashley looked at Adrian, who was writing in his notepad. "Call Danielle and tell her I say hi. I need to talk to Adrian really quick anyway."

Adrian looked up. "Sure. Go ahead."

I strolled toward the condo courtyard. Danielle picked up on the first ring. "Tory! I've got a great potential tenant for your father's house." She sounded breathless with excitement. "I just got off the phone with his realtor and he looked at your father's house online and loves it. They're driving up from Los Angeles to view it in person later today."

"Great. Los Angeles? What's his story? Is he relocating to Santa Sofia?"

"I can't tell you any details about him right now."

"Okay."

"Let me call them back right now to arrange a time to show it. I'll keep you posted."

I walked back to the community garden. Ashley and Adrian were in the same place I'd left them. They stood close to each other, practically touching, and their heads tilted toward one another. Before the pandemic they had just started to date exclusively, but, like everyone else, they kept their distance during the lockdown and height of the pandemic surges.

Adrian lifted his eyebrows slightly and smiled. "Ready? How do you feel about answering some questions now?"

"I'm fine. Shoot."

Ashley, her long-lashed light brown eyes filled with concern, touched my arm. "Are you sure you're up to it? Adrian mentioned you seemed a bit queasy earlier."

"Yep. I was. It was so unexpected. I'd just talked to Bunny, just like I'd done a year ago Christmas with . . ."

The Christmas before the pandemic hit, I'd discovered a body in the Benning Brothers Nursery Christmas tree lot. Seeing Bunny on the ground gave me flashbacks.

She nodded. "I know. That's what I thought of immediately too. It's a definite trigger."

I took a deep breath and proceeded to update them. First, I briefly brought them up to speed about Mac's visit to my house the night before.

Adrian tilted his head. "Okay, now tell me what happened today when you got here. I know your observation skills outshine everyone else's."

"I don't know about that, but thanks. Bunny and Mac bickered while they were on live TV. He accused her by name as the person who stole his cabbage. Then he thought his cabbage was in another guy's plot. So odd. For starters, let me say that only an idiot would say that on live TV, and then murder the person he fought with. And Mac is definitely not an idiot."

Ashley shook her head. "So weird. Do you think he'd been drinking?"

"No. I didn't smell alcohol on his breath, and he was normal when I talked to him right before they started filming. I think he just doesn't do well when he feels wronged."

Ashley crossed her arms. "Who does?"

"True." I looked at Adrian. "I know he comes off as a grumpy and silly old man, but he's actually usually really nice and super smart. This cabbage thing just got under his skin."

Adrian nodded. "What did you do after the TV interview was over?"

"Let's see. I chatted with Melinda for a bit about the segment. She told me about how they'd edit it down to a shorter segment for the other news shows. I spoke briefly to a guy who I think was a PI—he reminded me of Jake a bit. And then . . ."

I suddenly remembered Bunny wanting to talk to me.

Adrian looked up from his notepad, pen poised. "What?"

"Then Bunny called out to me that she needed to talk to me about something important. I totally forgot about that."

Adrian raised his thick black eyebrows. "About what? What was important?"

"I don't know because I told her I'd talk to her later." I wailed, unable to hold in my emotions. "Why didn't I just go and talk to her when she wanted me to? Maybe she'd be alive right now if I did."

Ashley wrapped her arms around me. "Come on. How were you supposed to know someone was about to kill her?"

I sniffed. "What if that was what she wanted to talk about?"

Ashley leaned back to look me in the eye. "If it was, she would have insisted on telling you right then and there."

I wiped tears from my face. "Maybe."

Adrian cleared his throat. "Then what did you do?"

"I wanted to thank Melinda properly. I started out to the parking lot and then Mac grabbed me."

Adrian paused his notetaking. "He grabbed you?"

"Figuratively speaking. Not actually. He wanted *a word* with me. But I told him, as I'd told Bunny, that I'd get back to him after I talked to Melinda."

"So you talked to Melinda . . ."

I ran my fingers through my ponytail. "Yes. I thanked her and we were chatting and then Joey Hernandez, our property manager, came running out to the parking lot and said something awful had happened, and that Bunny was dead."

"He said she was dead? Like he knew for sure?"

I nodded. "Yes. He said she was unresponsive. Then we followed him back to the community garden. Oh, wait. No, Joey left and then Philip came running over and said Bunny had been hurt."

"His words?"

"Yep. He said he thought she'd been attacked."

Adrian told us they'd probably remove the CSI tape by the late afternoon. Ashley and Adrian held each other's gaze for several seconds before Ashley joined me as I walked back to my car. We came upon Joey and a masked maintenance man holding a trash bag. They were talking about straightening up the premises.

I stopped in my tracks. "Sorry to interrupt, but the police won't probably leave until the late afternoon. For now, nothing should be touched or disturbed. Leave everything as it is." I pointed to the maintenance man's trash bag. "Even though it might look like trash to us, it might be a clue for the police."

Adrian's voice boomed from behind me. "She's exactly right. In fact, I'll take that bag of trash. Thanks."

Joey was shifting his weight back and forth as if he were dancing a jig. "My bad, Officer. I'm the one who instructed him to clean out all the trash bins without thinking. Sorry."

Adrian held up the trash bag to the maintenance man. "Is this the only trash bag you've started?"

Joey dipped his head, but his eyes focused nervously on the maintenance man, who mumbled a faint "yes."

Adrian straightened up. "Good. Wait until we're out of here before you do any more cleaning up."

Adrian patted Ashley's shoulder as if he was going to leave, but he lingered in the background writing in his notebook.

Joey fidgeted with his jacket lapel and turned to me. "I was just trying to get a head start so we can hit the ground running once it's no longer a crime scene."

"I know. Don't worry about it. You're trying hard, and you just started here, so don't beat yourself up. Let's just make sure the police are totally done with their investigation before we start doing anything else."

Joey gave me a little salute. "Will do."

The maintenance man had picked up a rake and started to clear olive leaves that had fallen on the patio. Ashley nudged me and looked in his direction.

I held up my hand. "If you could just hold off on any raking, too, for now, please, until the police are gone."

The maintenance man nodded.

"Thank you." I turned to Joey. "Just remember—"

"To wait until the police are gone. Will do." Joey blushed, glancing at Adrian.

Adrian stopped writing and sauntered back to us and rested his hand on Ashley's shoulder. Ashley melted as she gazed at Adrian as if he were a cute little puppy. They stared into each other's eyes as if they wanted to linger a bit longer. I took my cue and walked out to the parking lot thinking that although Joey had already made a few mistakes, I was glad that he had recognized them and felt remorse. He clearly wanted to do a good job.

Several cop cars, a fire truck, and two smaller SSFD EMS vehicles were parked in the lot. Two masked and uniformed EMTs walked out and went to their truck. They were with Tate, the firefighter who was one of the inaugural gardeners. I stared at the trio and another blip flashed in my brain, as if there was something familiar about them, but again, the moment of potential insight was fleeting.

A silver Mercedes drove into the parking lot. Mac's wife, Kaley McGregor, a lithe blonde and former lingerie model who looked as if she were in her twenties but was probably closer to forty, jumped out as soon as she parked and jogged over to me. She was dressed in designer activewear, as if ready for a yoga class.

For a moment I felt disoriented. I could have sworn I'd seen Kaley talking to Mac in the community garden earlier.

"Hi, Tory, so glad I ran into you. Mac just called and shared the awful news."

Now she was acting like she hadn't been there. Maybe she'd left and come back?

"I know. Just horrible. Bunny was such a vibrant person, it's hard to believe she's gone."

Kaley's even-featured face had a blank look for a nanosecond, as if she didn't understand a word I was saying. "Oh, yes, of course. Bunny. Horrible. But Mac just called me about having to go down to the police station sometime today. The cops said they need him there for further questioning. What does that mean?

Mac said the circumstantial evidence, some note sent to Bunny and their fight on TV, makes him their prime suspect right now."

I reeled from her revelation. Mac was clearly a person of interest in my mind, one step shy of suspect, but I sure didn't consider him the prime suspect.

Kaley adjusted the strap on her tank top. "I know he thinks highly of you. He says he feels like he's being set up and you're someone he trusts. Could you help Mac clear his name before it ruins his chance to win the mayoral race?"

I thought the possibility of losing the mayoral race was the least of his worries right now.

"Any help you can give. Please. We both know about your reputation for crime-solving."

I winced. "That's one way of putting it, I guess."

Ashley patted my arm.

I jumped. "You scared me. Creeping up on me like that."

"No creeping involved, sis." Ashley laughed and turned to Kaley. "Tory's too modest. She hasn't chosen to be a sleuth, but unfortunate circumstances in the past have forced her to become one, to protect herself and other innocent people. I'm sure Tory will put her thinking cap on and see what she comes up with. Also, if you're looking for legal counsel—"

Kaley nodded. "That was my next question. Do you have any attorney recommendations?"

I threw my arm around Ashley and patted her shoulder. "Ashley is one of the best lawyers in Santa Sofia."

Ashley bowed her head. "Thanks, Tory." She gave Kaley her business card. "I'd be happy to represent Mac if you want. He comes highly recommended from Tory."

Kaley squinted to read Ashley's business card.

I dug in my handbag and found my business card and handed it to Kaley. "Call me if you need anything."

Kaley's phone rang and she looked at the screen. "It's Mac."

When she took the call, her expression shattered. "What? Right now?" She started to cry.

I exchanged glances with Ashley. "What's wrong?"

"Mac said they're taking him to the station right now. They're leaving from the community garden street exit, near his plot. They found a glove they think might be Bunny's in Mac's plot under a tarp."

"So? He found that in his plot last night when his cabbage went missing. He told me about it. He thought it was evidence that Bunny was the culprit."

Kaley pouted. "Not to the police. Mac said the police told him it's not unusual for killers to take an item that belonged to the victim. Like a trophy. They think it's another piece of evidence implicating him."

Or was it evidence of a plant? And that Mac was indeed being set up.

CHAPTER 4

Ashley left the Jacaranda Gardens parking lot in her black BMW first, with me closely behind. When I exited the condo driveway and rounded the corner, I encountered a small group of protestors with signs that read *Save the Environment Now*.

The next minute Ashley called me. "Did you see all the protestors?"

"Yep. Hard to miss."

Ashley turned onto Olive Branch Road. "Did you see what their signs said? That the condo and garden should never have been approved?"

I checked for cross traffic before I followed Ashley. "Yep. They're the same group, STEN, short for Save the Environment Now, that Bunny was involved with and that had objected to the condo project when it was initially proposed. Honestly, I thought we'd made peace with them after we doubled the size of the community garden, as they'd requested."

Ashley's red brake lights lit up as she halted at a stop sign. "How'd they get here so quick? I'd have thought it'd take time to organize a protest, no? It just hits wrong."

I stopped behind her. "I know. That's exactly what I was thinking. Like they were tipped off. Even with news traveling fast, that's still a quick turnaround."

Ashley pulled away from the stop sign and continued along Olive Branch Road. "Also, I've been thinking, what happens to the *Sentinel* now? Will Bunny's husband be taking over?"

It was past noon and the sun had burnt off all the clouds and was beating down on the vineyards and olive groves we passed. I turned my air conditioner to a lower temperature.

I checked both ways for traffic. "Good question. You're thinking about motive. I honestly don't know. I'm assuming there's a second in command who can take over in the short term for sure. I know Bunny has adult children. I don't know anything about them though, whether they're in line to succeed her in the family business or what."

Another call was coming in. The ID read *Caroline Brewer*. Caroline Brewer was the founder of a local animal rescue named Pom Pom Rescue, where I'd gotten my Pomeranian, Iris, four years ago.

"Ash, let me take this call, it's a potential client I spoke to the other day."

Caroline enunciated each word in her soft voice. "Tory, I was wondering if today's a good time for you to come over and take a look at our yards."

I hesitated at first, my racing heart rate and a million conflicting thoughts and emotions about Bunny's death making me on edge. But work would be a good distraction.

"Yes. Later this afternoon would be good for me. Does that work for you?"

"Yes. It does. See you then."

By the time I got back to my office it was twelve thirty. I turned on Manzanita Street and pulled into the Benning Brothers parking lot. My phone chimed.

Jake's deep voice was comforting to hear. "Hey, where are you? Still at Jacaranda Gardens?"

"Actually, I just got back to the office. Where are you?"

"At a stoplight. Just got off the freeway. Hungry?"

"Yes, I could really go for some comfort food after this morning. And by comfort food, I mean a lobster roll and some strong coffee."

Jake chuckled. "Sadie's Seafood it is, then."

"Why don't you come here, and we can go together."

"Okay. I'll probably be there in ten."

I parked and waited in my car rocking out to "Wolfgang" by Stray Kids until it was over. Visualizing them performing it on a recent South Korean competition show was a great escape, if only for a few minutes.

During the pandemic, Jake and I had kept in touch, but this would be the first time we'd be seeing each other in person in nearly sixteen months. Now that more of us were vaccinated, the future was finally starting to look brighter again.

I was getting out of my car when Jake drove up in his white Tesla.

He jumped out and ran toward me. By the time I'd closed my door, he'd reached me.

We embraced and shared a quick kiss, his five o'clock shadow tickling my cheek.

I tousled his brown hair. "Your hair's longer. I like it. Looks good."

"Thanks. Love yours. It's so long." He tugged lightly on my fashion ponytail and then brushed the side of my face as he let go of it.

A fleeting sizzle went through me. "It was even longer. Philip trimmed it a bit today for my TV appearance."

He beamed at me, gripping my upper arms. "Well, it looks gorgeous. You look gorgeous."

"Thanks. You look good too."

He blushed and dropped his hands after a few seconds. I was pretty sure I was blushing, too, because my face felt flushed. Why were we both acting so awkwardly?

A half hour later, I pushed away from the outdoor table on the sunny Santa Sofia pier. "I feel better now. Thanks for being so agreeable about where to eat. I just needed comfort food."

"Of course. I love Sadie's too. Now, fill me in on Bunny's death."

I took a swig of my coffee. "I'll start with last night, to give you context." I told Jake about Mac's late-night visit.

Jake leaned closer, elbows on the table. "You should have called me, although admittedly, I wouldn't be much good when someone's pounding on your door since I live twelve miles away." He gazed into my eyes with his baby blues and then looked away.

And there was that awkward vibe again. I felt like I was getting mixed messages. Something was up with Jake.

"To be honest, I was half asleep and, foolishly, wouldn't have been able to call anyone since I inadvertently let my phone die."

"That doesn't sound like you."

"I know. But since I've become obsessed with the Stray Kids, I've been using my phone more for music and videos, which I never did as much before."

Jake studied me with an amused glint in his blue eyes.

I sat up straighter. "What? They bring me joy. Blame Ashley. She's the one who turned me on to them."

He laughed slightly. "That's one of the things I like about you—you're unpredictable. I'd never figured you for a K-pop fan girl."

I twisted in my seat and smirked. "Yep. That's me. Full of surprises. And for the record, their fans are called Stays."

He chuckled. "I stand corrected. So, what happened the next morning when you got to Jacaranda Gardens?"

I described my interactions with Mac and Bunny, and then the on-air fight between them.

Jake let out a low whistle. "Wow. That's all I can say. Just wow."

"I know. I was mortified. Then Mac, of course, had to end with a threat by saying 'this isn't over.'"

Jake rested his hands on the table. "No! He didn't."

"Oh yes he did. And to top it off, Bunny's husband, Peter Yusem, claims that Mac left the same message on a note tied to a rock with a rubber band on their doorstep last night."

Jake tilted his head. "For real?"

I nodded. "That's what he claims. Apparently, it was unsigned, but what are the odds the exact same message isn't from Mac?"

"What did Adrian say?"

"At first, according to Mac's wife Kaley, he told Mac to meet him at the station for further questioning. But once they found a woman's glove in Mac's plot, they took him in."

Jake sipped his coffee. "So they arrested him?"

I exhaled loudly. "I don't know for sure. It was unclear. She was upset."

"Okay, I'll give Adrian a call and see what's up. Maybe the four of us can grab dinner together tonight."

After a year of intermittent lockdowns, all of us were excited about being able to see each other again in person. To me it felt like we were living a scene from *Sleeping Beauty*, where everyone wakes up from a long sleep. But unlike that scene, where the whole kingdom resumes their lives as if nothing had happened, I felt like Jake and I were back to square one again, almost as if we'd never dated at all. It felt awkward to simply pick up where we'd left off. We'd all had a lot of time to reevaluate our lives. I wondered if Jake felt the same way. Maybe that was part of the vibe I was picking up from him.

I adjusted my sunglasses. "Sounds good. I'll check with Ashley. Sorry how Bunny's murder has monopolized our first visit back to Sadie's. You said you had something important to tell me?"

Jake stared at me intently, then bowed his head. When he raised it again and our gazes met, he looked almost wistful. Or was it smitten? A fine line. I had no idea which.

I leaned my elbows on the table. "Is everything okay?"

He checked his watch. "Yeah. No. It can wait. I know you probably need to get back to work and I promised a PI based here in Santa Sofia I'd consult on one of his cases. We're supposed to meet in twenty minutes, so do you mind if we leave now?"

"No. Not at all. Yeah, I should get back to the office too."

We drove back to Benning Brothers, chatting about how Iris and Otis were now thoroughly spoiled by me being home so much during the lockdown.

He touched my arm lightly. "Do you have a preference where we eat tonight?"

"Not really. I've already gotten my lobster roll fix, thanks. Your choice."

"Great. I'll see if Adrian and Ashley have any preferences."

We hugged and then he rushed off to his car. Was there a different vibe or was I self-sabotaging myself? Was my fear of commitment in play, torpedoing my attempt at a serious relationship again? Thanks to Zoom, I'd been able to keep meeting with my psychologist, Ellen. But frankly, foremost on my mind during the last year had been my fear that we were all going to die. My love life had been a lower priority.

Once I got settled behind my desk in my office and started to respond to all the phone messages and emails that had piled up, I pushed Bunny's murder and Jake out of my mind and proceeded to catch up.

Just then, Danielle Murphy's number showed up on my caller ID.

"Tory! Looks like we have a deal."

"Yay! That's great. I'm so excited I won't have to worry about renting it anymore. Who's the tenant?"

Danielle gasped with exhilaration. "The client is a big celebrity who wants a low profile."

I straightened up in my chair. "You're kidding! Who is it?"

She sighed. "I can't reveal his name right now."

"Why not?"

"He doesn't want his identity revealed until the contract is signed. He loved the house. I just left them. I'll prepare the contract and call you when it's ready to be signed."

I tapped my phone as images of me popping over to the house to drop off a housewarming basket for someone like Brad Pitt flooded my brain. "No, wait! Let me guess! I love a good mystery! It's Brad Pitt, isn't it?" I sighed as I imagined Brad Pitt asking me to stay for a drink and possibly dinner.

Danielle laughed. "Guess away. I'm sworn to secrecy. I can't let you know until it's final, but there's a clause that you're protected if he pulls out of the lease early, so don't worry, trust me, I've done deals like this before. It's all agent to agent and the whole rental amount for the year will be placed in escrow."

"Sounds super. But please give me a hint at least."

She exhaled loudly. "Okay. He's a heartthrob actor looking for a change of scenery after a highly publicized, messy divorce. Who's willing to pay top dollar for a secluded retreat like your father's house."

I gasped. "So it is Brad Pitt."

Danielle chuckled. "I'll give you one more hint—it's not Brad Pitt."

I took that as an attempt to throw me off the scent. For now. I was keeping him in my rotation of possibilities. Oo-la. Who could it be if it wasn't Brad Pitt? I'd have to go online and check the *Daily Mail* or *People* magazine to see if I could figure out who it might be.

I leaned back in my chair. "When did this heartthrob get divorced?"

Danielle laughed lightly. "That's all you're getting. More than I should have revealed already."

Another caller appeared on my phone's screen. It was Kaley McGregor, Mac's wife.

"Hey, Danielle, I have another call. Fingers crossed the deal goes through. Please keep me posted."

I picked up Kaley's call.

"Tory! Thank God I got a hold of you. They've officially arrested Mac. I'm so glad you've agreed to help us. I don't know who else I'd have turned to. Your reputation for solving murders makes me hopeful you can solve this one. I just called Ashley and left a message. I also called the Hotel Santa Sofia legal department, but they haven't gotten back to me. But I think they'll be more focused on protecting the company than Mac, to be honest."

A few things she said registered, all screaming for attention. But my mind stuck on the part about me having a reputation for solving murders, one I reluctantly had to acknowledge, although it had been gained at a high personal cost, to put it mildly. My therapist could attest to that if there were any doubts.

"Kaley, let me try to get a hold of Ashley. I'll have her call you."

Kaley thanked me and I texted Ashley.

Now with Mac arrested I knew the clock had started to tick. There was a small window of opportunity to help convince the police that he was not the correct suspect, assuming he wasn't, which I believed in my gut to be true. He was volatile, but not an imbecile willing to risk all he'd worked for and accomplished. They'd hold him for up to forty-eight hours and then decide whether they felt they had enough evidence to charge him. Since I'd been officially asked to be involved and Ashley most likely would be representing him, I had to get a jump on figuring out who really killed Bunny. The best way I knew how to do that was to return to the scene of the crime.

CHAPTER 5

When I pulled into the Jacaranda Gardens parking lot, two police cars were still there, along with a CSI van.

No one was in the lobby. I decided to pay another visit to Brockett to see if she'd heard of anything new in the last few hours. The door to the security office was open.

I knocked softly on the doorjamb. "Hi, Barb. I see the cops are still here."

Brockett looked up from her computer. "Tor-nado! Yep. A-Ram left about an hour ago. He said CSI will be here for at least another hour, taking photos and scouring the property for clues."

"About that. What was your take on everything? Did you watch the newscast while it was being filmed?"

"Didn't watch it. I was on duty here in front. Heard about Mac McGregor saying on air that their dispute wasn't over." She clicked her teeth. "I assume that's one of the reasons A-Ram took him in."

"Wait. Mac was arrested here? His wife made it seem like he wasn't arrested until they got him to the station."

She shook her head. "Nuh-uh. Not after they found a spade with blood on it in his plot. They arrested him here."

"They did?" I took an unsteady step closer. "Was that the murder weapon? A spade?"

"Appears that way."

"Wow." My heart started to pound harder.

I was stunned. Kaley had only mentioned that the cops had found a glove in Mac's plot, not the murder weapon. This did not look good for Mac at all.

I took a step backward. "Okay. Thanks, Barb. Where's Joey? Have you seen him, or did he go home?"

She rolled her chair away from her desk. "Haven't seen him."

"Okay. Thanks. I'll look for him out back."

I hoped Joey hadn't jumped ship before he had officially started working at Jacaranda Gardens. He must be feeling a bit shell-shocked after all the commotion. When I reached the garden plot, the CSI team was busy collecting soil samples and taking photos.

A male voice I recognized called out to me, "Hi, Tory."

I turned to see Ernie Gomez, a SSPD sergeant with whom I'd also attended middle school.

He sauntered over to me. "I was wondering whether or not I'd run into you here."

"How's it going, Ernie?"

"Good. Any day is good when you solve a crime. We found the murder weapon already."

"So I heard. What makes you so sure it's the murder weapon?"

"It's a garden spade with blood on it, barely hidden under a tarp in a plot belonging to Mac McGregor, the guy who fought with Bunny on TV minutes before she was murdered. He must have hastily shoved it under there not knowing what else to do. Clearly a crime of passion. I saw the fight on TV earlier today myself."

Under the tarp? Where they found the glove? I thought that odd. If Mac was indeed the killer, why would he pick such a poor and self-incriminating hiding spot? And for two pieces of evidence against him? A smart person like Mac wouldn't make a rookie move like that. My mind went to all the stories where killers dismembered their victims and distributed body parts all over town. There was no such effort to hide these clues.

I rested a hand on my hip. "Yeah, that interview was a disaster."

Ernie's voice got softer. "I thought you were good though."

I studied Ernie's buglike eyes for hints of mocking and found none.

"Yeah, I thought you were great the way you explained the community garden. Made me want to grow my own veggies too."

I squinted at him. Still no sign of being made fun of. In the past, Ernie had usually behaved like a toad, but it appeared he was finally beginning to mature. Part of that, of course, was that I helped save his sorry butt from being blown away. Glad he recognized he owed me one.

He shifted his weight. "How's Ashley? It's been a hard year not seeing anyone."

"She's good. So, what else have you guys found out? Other than a spade you assume is the murder weapon?"

"It's a pretty safe assumption, given there was blood on it."

I crossed my arms. "How can you be certain it's Bunny's blood though?"

Ernie blinked twice. "It's at the lab now. Also being tested for prints. Mac admitted it was his spade already."

"He did? Well, of course, his prints would be all over it then, right?"

I was betting the cops weren't convinced Mac was necessarily the culprit either.

"We're nearly done with the crime scene. We can't let you in the garden until we're done."

He'd read my mind.

"Okay. I'm going to hang out for a while. Look around the other areas and see where our new manager is."

"You mean Joey?"

"Yeah. You know him?"

"He introduced himself earlier. Nice guy. Trying to be helpful but clearly really upset. I told him to go home and rest if he wasn't on duty anymore."

"Sounds like good advice. Thanks, Ernie."

I decided to do a perimeter check of the property. I walked back to the parking lot and looped around the circular drive to the other side of the condominium. A late-model silver Mercedes with an environmental "Protect our Coast and Ocean" license plate painted with a large whale tail and personalized with "Big

Mac" was parked at that end. It obviously was Mac's car. He must have had to leave it here when he'd been driven to the station in a squad car. I circled his car, peering inside. What I saw stopped me in my tracks. On the floor in the backseat was a gardening glove. Like the one Mac had shown me last night. But this one looked like there was blood on it.

I tried the back door, and it was open. I was in. Farther than I should be if I'd stopped to think before touching the door handle. Shoot! I was so mad at myself. Had I learned nothing after reading all of my favorite author Sue Grafton's Kinsey Milhone novels? You never want to leave prints. Since the damage had already been done, I bent down to inspect the glove. Yep. Sure looked like blood. But this glove looked like a man's glove by the size of it, compared with the one Mac had shown me last night. Great. I took a picture of the glove. Why I didn't think of that before I'd opened the car door, I didn't know. But what was done was done.

I walked over to a concrete bench on the side of the condo complex, sat down, and called Ashley. She didn't pick up so I left her a message, asking her what we should do. I shot her the photo in a text and asked her to call me. Then I resumed my inspection of the perimeter.

My tour of the grounds took me around the east end of the condo, past the pool, and then beyond the condo courtyard to the side street that bordered the community garden, where a row of pretty oleander hedges grew. Something white caught my eye in the hedge. It looked like a tall paper cup. Why would someone stick it in the hedge like that? A litterbug would just drop it on the ground, I would think. The CSI team probably hadn't gotten this far out yet. I took a photo with my phone to remind myself to ask Adrian about it later. Maybe it would have prints. As I rounded the other side of the property, Ashley called.

She breathed heavily. "Have you told the police about the glove yet?"

"No, not yet. I was waiting for you to advise me."

"Anything unique about it?"

"It looked like a men's size. I did something stupid though. I checked to see if the car was locked and it wasn't, so I opened the door to get a better look at the glove. I'm sorry, I know that was dumb. But it took me by surprise, and I just reacted. Is that breaking and entering or evidence tampering?" My voice wobbled.

"Neither. In California it could be viewed as auto burglary."

I gulped hard. "Oh."

"But since the car wasn't locked and your intent wasn't to steal the car or anything in it, I think I'd be able to argue that any auto burglary charges be dismissed if you were charged. But since you're Mac's friend, and he's my client, you don't have to worry about anyone pressing charges."

I let out a huge sigh. "Okay, thanks for letting me know. I'm so sorry. From now on I promise to think twice before I do anything that can even be construed as illegal in any way."

Ashley sighed heavily. "Yes, please do."

"Again, I'm so sorry."

"Okay, look, I just got off the phone with Kaley. Let me call her back so I make sure I catch her and ask her for a car key. That way we can legitimately touch the car with her permission. And I guess we'll be seeing each other for dinner tonight at the Hotel Santa Sofia."

"Oh, is that where? Which restaurant? El Colibri or the Mar Vista?"

"Not sure. Adrian said we're meeting at Burbujita's first for drinks, so my guess is El Colibri because they share a patio."

"What time?"

"Around five-ish."

After I hung up, I ran into Ernie again. He said they'd probably not take down the crime scene tape for another forty-five minutes or so. I checked my phone. I had a message from Caroline Brewer asking me what time I planned on stopping by Pom Pom Rescue. I inhaled sharply. Given all the drama, I'd totally forgotten we'd agreed to meet. I texted back that I was on my way.

Pom Pom Rescue, the only Santa Sofia rescue organization devoted exclusively to rescuing Pomeranians, was not only where I'd gotten Iris, but they also had one of my favorite Instagram accounts. Following the before and after photographs of the ragtag bunch of little Poms they plucked from the clutches of death on their journeys to their forever homes always warmed my heart.

Their rescue organization was located in an outlying industrial section of Santa Sofia, housed in a small, light green stucco bungalow that looked like a pastel candy mint, especially because the neighboring buildings on each side, a car repair shop and a window blind store, were white and pink, respectively. I pulled in between an Infinity and an old Volkswagen, the last narrow spot left in the three-space parking area in front of their building.

As soon as I cracked open my door and squeezed out of my car I was met with a ruckus of barking and shrill yelps coming from within the building that sounded just like Iris to the power of twenty. Yep, I had definitely arrived at PommieVille.

The two sad-looking walled courtyards in front of the building that bordered each side of the short center walkway leading to the front door were barren save for a few potted plants that had seen better days and scattered water bowls and dog toys. In my mind, I was already envisioning changes that could make the space more functional and have a more attractive curb appeal.

The front counter was manned by a woman who looked to be in her early thirties who smiled at me as soon as I walked in. She had long black hair highlighted with a couple of silver streaks. Both her arms had tattoo sleeves, primarily dominated by wolves on one arm and roses on the other.

"Hi, I'm Tory Benning. Here to meet with Caroline Brewer."

Her smile broadened as she snapped to attention. She shot up from her chair. "Hi. I'm Jules. I'll tell Caroline you're here."

Behind the counter a couple of white Poms stood watch, eager to lick my hand when I leaned over to pet them. The upper portion of the wall behind the reception area was all windows, allowing me to view the back room. Jules opened the door to the adjoining room, where two rows of stacked crates lined the far wall, and padded out of view down a hallway. Only four of the eight crates appeared to be occupied by Pomeranians from what I could tell from my angle.

Several Poms that had been running loose in the back room now ran back and forth through the opened door to the front counter and barked at me.

"Hi, guys. How are you doing today?"

The little dogs continued to bark but I could tell by their twinkling eyes and wagging tails they knew I was a lover of their tribe.

A couple minutes later, Jules came back followed by a petite woman wearing a dusty rose tunic, black leggings, and white athletic shoes that looked brand new. Her graying blonde hair was pulled up into a messy bun and fastened with a bear claw clip.

She extended her hand. "Hi, I'm Caroline. You must be Tory. So happy to meet you. Thanks for accommodating my schedule on such short notice."

"No problem."

"I'm sure you saw the sad state of affairs in our front courtyard and parking area. We need plants and flowers to beautify the place. Come and I'll show you our backyard. It needs work too."

I followed her down the hallway. We passed two other rooms much like the one I'd already seen, filled with crates and Poms. The backyard was even more forlorn than the front area, with dried weeds growing between the cracks in the old cement patio. An elderly female worker wearing a Pom Pom Rescue T-shirt and jeans was monitoring two tiny Poms. As we entered, the smaller one that looked like a little red fox scampered over to me as if I were her long-lost owner.

"Hi, there! How are you, little one? What's your name?"

Caroline smiled. "That's Ruby, one of our newest rescues."

I crouched down and the dog scrambled halfway up me and licked me right on my mouth. I burst out laughing, and that encouraged the dog to lunge again and plant another dog kiss. "Hi, Ruby. Aren't you the little charmer? A bit forward, but you're so cute you can get away with anything, I bet."

Caroline laughed. "Or at least try."

"How is it such a cute little munchkin hasn't been adopted?"

"Jules just picked her up from the shelter yesterday."

I petted Ruby. "The shelter? How did someone as cute as you wind up in a shelter?"

Ruby started to cough and couldn't stop.

Caroline shrugged. "Apparently, her owner died and the family couldn't take care of her. More like they just didn't want to, if you ask me. I have stories you won't believe. Also, she's on a course of antibiotics now for a cold or kennel cough as a precaution just in case she might have picked something up at the shelter, although these tiny Poms are prone to collapsed tracheas, so it might be that since she's a senior."

"How old is she?"

The dog settled on my lap as I remained crouched down and nuzzled her tiny body into mine. I was in love.

Caroline chuckled. "Best guess, around seven or eight."

"You are just too cute." I turned to Caroline. "I have a cream sable Pommie named Iris that I got from your rescue, actually, about three or four years ago. I have a black cat, too, Otis, a stray, but he's pretty chill with dogs. With Iris, at least. But man, this little one has captured my heart already."

"Well, fill out an application online and you'll be at the top of the list since we haven't posted any pictures of her yet on our website."

"I'm so tempted. But what if my dog and cat don't get along with her."

"We make a commitment to our pets. You can always return her. Trust me. She'll easily have a hundred apps once we post her pictures. We won't have any problem placing her."

"Okay. I'll fill one out when I get home tonight."

"Great! Now, about this backyard. Any ideas for how to make it more inviting?"

"Actually, I have several ideas. Just let me take some photographs right now. I can get a proposal out to you sometime tomorrow." I set Ruby down.

I found my phone in my purse and took several pictures of the backyard and of Ruby.

"Bye, bye, Ruby." I waved to her as the rescue employee scooped her up in her arms and Ruby continued to cough.

Caroline walked me out to the front.

"I wouldn't want my dog or cat to catch a cold or kennel cough."

"Nor would we. We won't release her until our vet gives her a clean bill of health."

I sighed. "Good. Okay, I'll take a few more photos and get to work on this proposal ASAP."

"Great. Thanks, Tory. So nice meeting you."

"Same."

After I finished taking photographs I hopped in my car and drove back to the office. In the parking lot I took out my phone and looked at the pics of Ruby I'd taken. I texted Ashley. *What do you think? A new sister for Iris and Otis?*

Back at my desk, I pulled up our boilerplate proposal and started to customize it for Pom Pom Rescue. An hour flew by and I was pleased with my progress. I sent the proposal to Caroline and then took another look at Ruby on my phone and saw it was already five fifteen. Gosh, no time for an application now. It'd have to wait till after dinner.

CHAPTER 6

I decided to take the most scenic route from my office to the Hotel Santa Sofia, following Santa Sofia's two main drags—the Avenue through town and the Promenade along the coast. The Avenue was where most of the commercial enterprises could be found. Originating in the surrounding foothills, the Avenue cut through the center of the upscale boutique-lined downtown, past the gourmet eateries and fancy galleries, and dead-ended at the beach. There, it intersected with the Promenade, the coast road where the Hotel Santa Sofia and its adjacent Beach Resort were located along the stretch that housed a few smaller boutique hotels. A bicycle lane ran parallel to the Promenade.

I turned onto the Promenade. The dazzling setting sun was still visible, its vivid purple, pink, red, and orange colors reflected on the ocean and the incoming cloud layer that was descending upon the coast again. As I barreled along, I passed cyclists and the last of the food trucks packing up for the day.

The Hotel Santa Sofia was a five-star luxury resort located on the coast at the southern tip of town. A hangout for affluent locals, it had put Santa Sofia on the map as a destination for the rich and famous internationally.

Every time I pulled into the long drive leading to the hotel, a wave of mixed emotions overwhelmed me. It was the venue for my marriage almost three years ago to my late husband, Milo Spinelli, an architect and my best friend. It'd been my workplace a couple of years before that when I redesigned the resort's gardens and created the Secret Maze and the Hidden Garden. It'd been a crime scene. And it was the venue for our last Benning Brothers holiday party.

The Spanish-styled main building and bungalows of the hotel resort were set on a sprawling twenty-five-acre site with lush gardens and lawns. In addition to its white stucco façades and red-tiled roofs, the property was peppered with colorful accent tiles, carved wood trim, wrought iron, and numerous fountains and courtyards.

I parked my car and took a narrow path up a slight slope to the main walkway to the lobby. The walkway led me past one of the pools, a courtyard, and a fountain with a cupid holding a fish. Benning Brothers Nursery had supplied the flowers, shrubs, and trees for the resort's landscaping renovation. I'd tried to specify native, drought-tolerant blooms as much as possible. I noted with pride the growth progress of the pink bougainvillea vines trailing up one side of an arched portico.

My heels clattered on the tile lobby floor of the main building. My gaze traveled to the high-vaulted churchlike ceiling as my ears picked up on the soft, steady rhythm of music emanating from the lounge. The lobby was flanked on one side by a casual restaurant, El Colibri, that shared a brick patio overlooking the Pacific Ocean with Burbujita's, a cocktail lounge, where we were meeting up tonight. At the other end of the lobby was another restaurant, the pricey Mar Vista, that specialized in seafood and its legendary Sunday brunch buffet, popular with both locals and out-of-towners. The Mar Vista featured an ocean-facing veranda that stretched across the front of the hotel.

Hotel employees wearing dark green blazers with the iconic Hotel Santa Sofia hummingbird insignia on the pocket manned the main entrance and front desk.

When I turned in the direction of Burbujita's I had a direct view of the ocean through the lounge and out the patio. I paused in the doorway. It took a second for my vision to adjust to the contrast of the bright sunset's glare and the darker lounge. My gaze found Ashley, who was waving at me. Her white jumpsuit popped in the dimmed light. I hurried over to join her and Jake. Adrian was nowhere in sight.

Jake, dressed in charcoal jeans and a white shirt, stood up and gave me a hug. "There she is. Finally. I was ready to send out a search party for you. Thanks for texting and letting us know you'd be late. I was worried."

"I texted Ashley."

"Oh, did you?" Ashley scrolled through her messages. "Sorry. I was running late and didn't have time to check my phone. There it is! You needed to finish a proposal . . . Hold up! What is this photo you sent me of heaven on earth? Sweetest little puppy angel ever! You're getting another dog?"

"Maybe. Probably. Yes. I'm definitely smitten. And I think Iris might like a little Pommie companion."

Jake leaned over Ashley's shoulder. "Adorable. So that's my competition, huh? I could never measure up to that level of cute."

We all laughed. It seemed like Ashley laughed because she thought Jake was funny, Jake laughed out of awkwardness when he realized what he'd said, and I laughed out of sheer anxiety. Competition? Measure up? That sounded like relationship and commitment talk to me. Help.

"Jake, when the waitress comes could you please order me a glass of the house Chardonnay? Thanks. I'm going to the restroom."

Ashley grabbed her purse. "I'll come with."

We made our way through the lounge to the restroom off the lobby.

I linked arms with Ashley. "So, where's Adrian?"

"He called me while I was driving over here. He's going to try to be here by six at the latest."

I opened the door to the restroom's mirrored foyer. I leaned against one of the two marble counters with double sinks and liquid soap dispensers with the hotel's hummingbird insignia on them. "Can you believe what Jake just said?"

"You mean about the dog being his competition?"

"Yes! Freaked me out. What did you make of that?"

"I don't know. Probably just said it without thinking. Plus, he was on his second glass of wine when I got here."

"Hmm. Okay. Maybe it didn't mean anything then. I'm just anxious because he said he wanted to talk to me about something important. I hope he doesn't want to get exclusive. I really like him a lot, but especially after being isolated in lockdown, I realize I don't mind being alone . . . and by being alone I mean with my besties Iris and Otis."

"So you don't want a relationship with Jake anymore?"

"Anymore? I don't know if I ever did. Honestly, I don't know what I want is the more accurate statement." I chuckled.

Ashley placed her hands on my arms, leaned back, and smiled slightly. "Hey, a lot of people feel conflicted about commitment but repress those feelings and then wind up divorced or unhappy. I know I do a bit because if I focused too much on the risk Adrian faces every day as a cop, I'd drive myself crazy. And after what you went through with losing Milo, it's totally understandable why you, of all people, might feel hesitant to commit and face the potential prospect of devastating loss again. Props to you for being mindful and reflective."

I hugged her. "Thanks, Ash, for not judging me. Heck, I can even act like a silly teenager and dish on cute guys and K-pop idols with you without fear of judgment."

Ashley pecked me on the cheek. "Hello! It's called bonding! I feel the same about you. That's what real friends do. Reveal their true selves, without fear of being judged."

I squeezed her shoulder.

"You do you, girl. That's all any of us can do. Jake's a good guy. I'm sure he'd understand."

"Yeah."

But in actuality, I wasn't so sure.

We navigated our way through the maze of tables in the dark lounge. When we got back to our table, near one end of the long bar with backlit display shelves, my wine was waiting for me.

I took a sip. "Okay, since Adrian isn't here, this is our opportunity to talk about Bunny's murder before he gets here and starts with his warnings to not interfere."

Ashley clinked her wineglass against mine. "Good thinking. I bet if we even mention Bunny he'll put his official kibosh on it, like he always does."

Jake smiled. "He's such a ruthless killjoy. Throwing his weight around like it's his job to solve the case."

Ashley and I met Jake's sarcasm with silence.

Jake's smile disappeared. "But, seriously, he does it because he cares about you guys, and he doesn't want to see you get hurt." He took a swig of wine. "As a private investigator myself, I get it."

Ashley nodded at Jake. "I know. From a lawyer's standpoint I get it too. He likes to play by the rules, so the prosecutor's case is airtight. He doesn't want us to inadvertently damage the case against his suspect."

I rolled my eyes. "Assuming he has the correct suspect in his sights. I know Adrian means well because he's a sweetheart, but because he must play by the rules, he's somewhat constrained. Anyway, let's look at possible suspects besides Mac."

Jake touched my arm. "Actually, why don't we start with Mac first. He has motive."

I swirled the wine around in my glass before taking a sip. "True. He's her rival in the mayoral race. Eliminating her would mean he would win."

Ashley cocked her head. "Or would he? If he gets caught, then no one wins."

Jake leaned in. "Drastic way to win an election. Who was favored in the race?"

I set my glass down on a cocktail napkin decorated with silver bubbles. "Hard to say. They both had strong support. Bunny by local activists and Mac by business and developers. I'd guess they were neck and neck. That's why Mac was so upset when he thought she stole his cabbage. He figured it would have to be something like criminal activity to besmirch his character since he was popular and had influential friends."

Jake fidgeted with the gold hobnail glass candleholder on the table. "But if they were neck and neck, it would seem to me that something silly like an alleged stolen cabbage wouldn't really matter that much in the scheme of things."

Ashley plopped back in her low leather barrel chair. "Alleged stolen cabbage is right. Do we know whether his cabbage really was stolen? What if Mac had made up that whole story to make Bunny look bad?"

I took another sip of wine. "Yeah, I thought of that too. But, man, that's a pretty ridiculous scheme that could so easily backfire and make him look crazy or petty."

Jake drummed his fingers on the table. "Okay, so back to motive. Did Mac have any other motive than the race?"

We all were silent for a few minutes.

I snapped my finger on my glass, wracking my brain for other possibilities. "I'm coming up empty."

Jake leaned back in his chair. "Okay, so then the only motive we can think of for Mac killing Bunny is he wanted to eliminate his opponent in the mayor race."

Ashley nudged my arm. "I have to agree with Tory. Mac doesn't look like the killer to me. He has too much at stake in terms of reputation. He's smarter than that. Killing your opponent to win is like those stories you read about men murdering their wives. Dude. Just get a divorce if you're so unhappy."

I thought about recent news stories I'd read.

"But often it's not a failed marriage that's the real motive. It usually has an underlying financial motive behind it all. At least in the cases I've read about."

Ashley nodded. "True."

Jake tilted his wineglass. "Yes, and I think we can all agree that killing Bunny, especially after their public argument on TV, could have just as easily hurt him."

Ashley hunched over. "Yeah. Weak motive. Too obvious. No guarantee he'd win the race after that."

Jack held up his forefinger. "Unless . . ."

I turned to him. "Unless what?"

"He has a temper problem. It looks like it was a crime of passion. People who can't control their anger get themselves into trouble all the time. They keep people like me in business because they don't think of the consequences of their behavior in the heat of the moment."

Ashley nodded. "They keep me in business too. The only thing that bothers me about that is even though it seems like a crime of passion, there was nothing immediately preceding her attack that anyone saw or heard, as far as I know, was there, Tory?"

I chuckled. "You mean other than their heated spat on live TV? None that I know of. No shouting, no screams. So weird. You'd think a crime of passion would occur in the moment. Not one that took place ten minutes earlier on TV. That suggests premeditation to me."

And then I remembered.

"Wait a minute. I do recall hearing raised voices after I left the community garden. But I was preoccupied and didn't think much of it. I'd totally forgotten about it."

"What do you mean? Someone was fighting?"

"Maybe. I don't know. All I remember thinking was *not again*."

Jake pushed away from the table. "Okay. You might have heard Bunny fighting with the person who killed her."

I felt dizzy and slightly faint. "If I'd gone to see who was fighting maybe I could have prevented Bunny's death."

Ashley lightly grasped my wrist. "Or been killed yourself. You can't second-guess these things. Surely someone else must have heard what you heard, no?"

"Most of the people dispersed after Melinda finished. A lot of them were at the coffee bar on the patio."

Ashley took a sip of wine. "Okay. Whatever. Adrian will be here soon. Next."

I inhaled and exhaled a deep breath. "Isn't it usually the spouse? What do you think about Peter Yusem, Bunny's husband?"

Ashley tapped her glass. "I know he's a Hollywood director. But I don't know anything else about him."

I pushed my glass toward the center of the table. "Bunny once mentioned he commutes back and forth between Santa Sofia and Los Angeles. So he's not around a lot. He and Bunny have been married for about ten years now, I think."

Jake hit me with a steady gaze. "Anything to suggest they were having problems? Do they have kids?"

"All I remember is that they'd both been married before, and I know Bunny has adult children. I don't know about Peter."

Jake ran his hand through his hair. "Do her children live here?"

I pulled my glass back toward me. "I think so. She never talked about them much."

Jake held my gaze. "Hmm. I wonder why."

I made a mental note to google them when I got home.

Jake leaned his elbows on the table. "What about people she worked with?"

I cocked my head. "At the *Sentinel*? Or do you mean her campaign people?"

"Both. Disgruntled employees often let their resentment build and then—boom." Jake opened both his fists to simulate an explosion. "Also, isn't she active in several groups dedicated to saving the environment and stopping unnecessary development and displacement of people and wildlife?"

I sipped my wine. "Uh-huh. We should look into the group that was protesting so soon after her death."

Ashley gazed out at the ocean. "But why would they protest if they were responsible for her death? That doesn't make sense to me."

I held my wineglass on my lap. "No, but maybe someone in the group didn't like her."

Jake flicked my ponytail. "Not liking someone doesn't mean you kill them."

I dipped my head and set my wine down. "Obviously. I'm just brainstorming. Okay, to summarize, these are the suspects we have to research to see if any of them had a motive: Bunny's husband, Peter Yusem, her children, her *Sentinel* and campaign employees, and fellow activists. Am I leaving anyone out?"

A deep voice boomed behind me. "Mac. You're leaving the main suspect out. The one with motive, means, and opportunity." Adrian, wearing black pants and a dark gray shirt, pulled up a chair between Jake and Ashley.

I wondered how much he'd heard.

"Let me remind all three of you right now"—he patted Ashley's hand—"this is an official police matter. We have the probable weapon. We have a probable motive. And we have evidence of the suspect actually threatening her on TV. Coupled with a note making the exact same threat left on the victim's doorstep last night, what part isn't incriminating to you?"

I stared at Adrian, who was seated directly across from me. "I know Mac personally and I don't think he's capable of murdering someone."

He tapped the glass candleholder. "Well, like it or not, the circumstantial evidence is all there."

I tilted my head. "So has he been charged?"

Adrian held up his hand to get the server's attention. "No—"

"Phew. That's good."

"—not yet."

I rested both hands on the table. "You're not even considering any other suspects?"

Adrian ordered a beer. "I didn't say that. You know the drill. We like to make sure we have all our ducks in a row before we charge anyone. Helps the prosecutor." He grabbed Ashley's hand. "Ashley can confirm that."

Ashley had her googly-eyed face on right now, likely due to a combo of swooning over Adrian and her empty wineglass.

I sighed. "Okay, one last question though. Was the leaked editorial real?"

As the words left my mouth, I realized it had been a mistake to mention it to Adrian. A big mistake.

Adrian turned to me. "What leaked editorial?"

I smiled weakly. "Didn't I mention it to you earlier? I must have forgotten."

"What editorial, Tory?" Adrian's eyes narrowed under his thick black eyebrows as he held me in his gaze.

I assumed Mac must have forgotten to mention it to Adrian

too. Whether accidentally or on purpose, I didn't know. After a few seconds I decided it was best to come clean. Trying to cover it up now would probably make it worse.

I played with the cocktail napkin under my wineglass. "Mac told me that he got an anonymous text that told him Bunny had written an editorial excoriating Mac, the Hotel Santa Sofia Corporation . . ."

The server set Adrian's beer on the table.

Adrian immediately took a swig of his beer. "Go on."

I glanced at him. "And . . . me."

He put down his glass. "What?"

I leaned back in my seat. "Right? For the heinous crime of replacing a run-down parcel of land and its derelict strip mall with a stunning condo complex and beautiful grounds with an adjacent community garden."

Adrian took another sip of beer. "But I thought she was on board with all of that. Wasn't she one of the founding community gardeners?"

"Yes! That's exactly why I figured it was a fake editorial . . . if it even existed. Mac said the anonymous texter said Bunny's goal was to take us all down and ruin our reputations because we were going against her environmental and anti-gentrification values or something."

Jake finished off another glass of wine. "Well, that's actually good news and bad news."

I pressed my lips together. "What do you mean?"

"Good news because maybe Bunny had an enemy who was making up a story about her trying to start drama."

"And the bad news?"

"If it's a real editorial that was leaked, that opens up another motive—revenge. And another suspect. And, Tory, that would be you."

I waved my forefinger. "None of that, Jake. You're starting to sound like Ernie. Or should I say old Ernie. New Ernie has been a good guy lately. He's been so nice to me. I can tell he's so grateful for me helping to save his life." I tipped my wineglass to get the last sip.

Ashley settled her gaze on Adrian. "I know. He loves me now for the same reason."

Adrian snickered. "Stop it. I know what you two are doing. Don't try to change the subject."

The server informed us our table was ready and we relocated to the El Colibri dining room. I ordered the shrimp taco dinner, like Ashley. Jake and Adrian went for the three-enchilada combo dinner. We also agreed to a pitcher of margaritas the server suggested.

After we ordered we were all silent. The server brought the pitcher and poured us each a glass. Ashley and I sipped our drinks and stole glances at Adrian. After what felt like ages, Adrian looked at me and shook his head.

I raised my eyebrows. "What?"

Adrian rested a hand on the table. "Have you learned nothing in the last year and a half about insinuating yourself into an active investigation?"

Ashley was in mid-swig of her margarita. She slammed her glass down and puckered her lips. "Wait a minute. As if Tory ever had any choice in the matter? *Insinuate* implies she intentionally chose to be involved. That couldn't be further from reality. Am I right, Tory?"

I nodded.

Jake smiled. "Adrian, have *you* forgotten Tory has been involved in recent cases because innocent people were being accused of crimes they didn't commit, including Tory herself? As a side note, have you not learned to not chastise Tory in the presence of her best friend and ace attorney, Ashley?"

Ashley fist bumped Jake. "Thanks, boo." She turned to Adrian. "Yes, not only Tory's best friend and ace attorney, but also, I'd venture to say, the woman with whom you've expressed an interest in pursuing a romantic relationship. Let me point out, sir, you are skating on very, very, very thin ice."

Adrian smiled at Ashley's alcohol-infused rebuke.

I reached out and patted Jake and Ashley simultaneously.

"Thanks for having my back, guys. Appreciate it. I feel loved."

At this, Jake's face turned a deep red.

Adrian held up his hands as if shielding his head and upper body from physical assault. He turned to Ashley. "Duly noted, Counselor."

I cleared my throat. "Adrian, if you can refrain from scolding me for a minute, I'd like to calmly present to you why I feel compelled to be involved at this point. First, I was minding my own business, fast asleep last night, when Mac involved me by pounding on my door because he couldn't wait to tell me Bunny's alleged wrongdoing with the cabbage and the leaked editorial and that my professional reputation might be at stake as a result.

"Second, I was an eyewitness to the fight between the murder victim and your supposed prime suspect. Mac was angry but never acted violent then, nor has he ever been violent in all the years I've known him.

"Third, I know how quickly a rush to judgment can result in implicating the wrong person. I've had the misfortune of experiencing that firsthand, and let me tell you, it's super scary being viewed as a murder suspect. I don't want a repeat of that. Since rumor has it there's a leaked editorial written by Bunny portraying me in a negative light, that gives me a motive, whether or not it's a hoax. So I think I have a perfectly legit reason to find out who the real perpetrator is, not only to protect myself from incrimination, but to make sure the real killer doesn't hurt me or anyone else."

Adrian wiped his hands on a napkin. "Look, Tory, sorry if I came off overbearing. You're free to google as much as you want. Frankly, if it wasn't for you, those previous cases might not have been solved as quickly or come to a fitting conclusion."

"Aw, thanks, Adrian." Now I felt I must be the one with a deep red face.

"But that being said—"

"There's always a 'but,'" Ashley chided.

"Never a good sign," Jake said under his breath.

"That being said, I can't have you talking to my witnesses,

messing up evidence and the like." His gaze drilled through me as if he had laser beams coming out of his eyes.

I gulped hard, dreading having to tell Adrian how I'd found the glove in Mac's car. My face was on fire. Was I trying to win the reddest face of the day competition?

Ashley grimaced. "I told him you found the glove in Mac's car, Tory."

I glanced nervously at Adrian. "Phew. I was totally convinced you must be a mind reader."

Adrian sighed. "Don't get me wrong. I'm very grateful for your past help. I just don't want you getting hurt, first and foremost. And I don't want you to inadvertently tamper with evidence that would in some way hurt the prosecutor's chance of a proper conviction."

At the end of the evening, Ashley told Adrian she needed to get home and prepare for an upcoming case. We all walked out to the lobby together. We had all parked in the same lot, so we took the main outdoor path to the smaller path I'd taken earlier. Ashley left first.

Adrian turned as he got to his car. "See you back at the house, Jake."

"You're staying with Adrian?"

Jake nodded.

Jake and I hadn't been alone at night after a dinner date for a whole year. It was strange to be at this point of an evening and to feel awkward. It was as if all the memories of the romantic dinners we'd shared when we'd end up going back to my place had been erased. We hugged.

"Text me when you get home to let me know you got home safely."

He lingered, as if he wanted to say more. I couldn't handle any more drama. A murder in a garden I designed was quite enough excitement for one day, thank you very much.

I skipped to my car. "I will. You drive safely too."

CHAPTER 7

Tuesday morning, after having a restless night, I got up earlier than usual, tended to the animals, showered, and dressed. My head was overwhelmed with thoughts about possible murder suspects and my mixed emotions regarding Jake. I sat at my kitchen counter drinking my second cup of coffee as the caffeine slowly kicked in.

When I checked my emails, I saw one from Pom Pom Rescue. Thinking it was in response to my proposal, I paused before opening it, bracing myself in case it was a pass. A lot of elements factored into the decision to hire a landscape architect, especially for small businesses or nonprofits that didn't have the budgets of larger organizations for an expenditure that some regarded as an extra, not a necessity. Of course, I begged to differ. The return-on-investment benefits for a well-designed outdoor space were numerous. Research had documented the therapeutic effects of gardens and parks on a wide range of both physical and mental health variables. In addition to the advantages of a pleasing aesthetic and the connection to nature, a well-designed outdoor space could also provide a wide range of emotional and social benefits, from sanctuaries conducive to solitary reflection to areas that fostered social interaction. And any realtor could tell you the importance of good landscaping to curb appeal.

I opened the email. It wasn't from Caroline Brewer, as I'd expected. It was from Jules, the employee I'd briefly spoken to at the desk. She said that two other parties, one a friend of Caroline's and the other a VIP donor, had both expressed a strong interest in Ruby since yesterday. Jules thought that Iris and Ruby would become fast friends and that Ruby also, surprisingly, loved cats. If I was interested, she needed an application turned in today. Their hours were two to six. I didn't hesitate about wanting to apply and jumped on their website to submit my application. But after spending twenty frustrating minutes online trying to fill out their form to no avail, I gave up and printed the application. After I filled it out, I emailed Jules that I'd drop it off in person later in the afternoon.

Once I got to the office, time flew by.

Jake texted me saying he'd just come back from breakfast with Adrian. *Are you free for lunch? I have a meeting scheduled for ten that should be over by noon. We still need to talk.*

Ugh. Did we? I agreed reluctantly, hoping I wouldn't hurt his feelings if I told him that I didn't think I was ready for a committed relationship. Yet.

About an hour later Kaley called to give me an update on Mac. "Thank God, they're going to release him this morning thanks to Ashley's intervention. The prosecutor declined to file charges, at least for the moment. Mac's been instructed not to leave town since he's a person of interest."

I figured Mac's release reflected the fruits of Ashley's morning court date.

I scrolled through my emails and there was another one from Pom Pom Rescue, this time from Caroline. She'd loved my proposal and it was a go. She wanted me to start as soon as I could. I told her I could come over today to take some measurements when I dropped off my application for Ruby.

I pushed back in my chair and gazed out the windows of my corner office. To celebrate getting a new client, I took a break and googled Peter Yusem. He had two children of his own who appeared to live back East.

I sat staring at my computer for a few minutes and decided to order some flowers for Peter. I called our nursery manager, Matt Ortega, and asked him to deliver our special premium arrangement of succulents and lilies to Peter at his home and another one to the *Sentinel* offices.

Then I debated whether I should give Peter a call to express my condolences. We'd gotten off to a rocky start at the community garden. I decided to give it a try anyway. He probably wouldn't even remember my name. I called the *Sentinel* to ask the best way to reach him. The woman who answered the phone gave me his number. She said he'd told her he'd be there later in the afternoon to meet with the staff and she'd tell him I called. I decided to drop by the *Sentinel* then.

I busied myself by reviewing my project list and checking the due dates for various projects. When the phone rang and the caller identified himself as Peter Yusem, I was surprised that he'd gotten back to me so quickly, especially given that his wife had just been murdered.

"I'm returning your call."

"Thank you. I'm so sorry for your loss. I didn't know Bunny that well, but I've enjoyed reading her editorials so much over the years I felt like I knew her through her writing. If you don't mind, I had a few questions for you."

He didn't respond. After about ten seconds I realized he was waiting for me to continue.

"Did Bunny have any enemies you know of?"

"You mean besides her rival, Mac McGregor? None that I know of. Everyone liked Bunny."

I cleared my throat. "Mac has an intense personality and doesn't tolerate frustration well."

Peter sighed. "Up until very recently, that's what I thought too. But then he threatened her twice."

"Twice?"

"Yes, leaving a threatening note on our doorstep and then live on TV."

I swiveled in my chair. "What was the threat?"

"He said 'this isn't over.'"

"Like he'd said on air. I don't know if I'd call that a threat exactly. More a warning?"

"I'm not going to argue semantics." He sounded annoyed.

"Who found the note at your house?"

"I did. I was on my way out after I'd watched Bunny on TV."

"So Bunny left before you in the morning?"

"Yes."

"But she didn't see the note?"

There was a long pause before he answered. "Huh. I never thought of that. I guess she didn't. Although I don't see how she could have missed it. It was in the center of our front doorstep."

"You're sure she left out the front door?"

"Yes."

"Bunny has two adult children, is that correct?"

"That's right."

"You didn't have any children together?"

"No. I have two college-aged kids from another marriage, but they both live on the East Coast."

"What about Bunny's kids?"

"Scarlett and Stone live here in Santa Sofia."

"Did they get along well with Bunny?"

"We barely saw them. Stone is always between gigs, as he quaintly puts it. Scarlett does what she needs to do to survive. Currently working as a server at some barbeque joint on the outskirts of town. Bunny was worn out trying to get along with both of them. When I met her, they'd already moved out. Look, I need to return a lot of calls."

After I got off the phone, I jumped on my computer and googled Bunny's kids. I found an address for Stone Hare. It appeared to be an apartment in a modest neighborhood. I didn't find anything to do with his employment. Scarlett Hare was twenty-seven. I learned she lived in Gilton, a small working-class neighborhood abutting northeast Santa Sofia, but I couldn't find a home address for her.

I strolled out of my office to see if my uncle Bob or aunt Veronica were around. Since my father died and I took over as president of Benning Brothers, my aunt and uncle only worked there part-time. They'd previously retired but agreed to lend their expertise for as long as I needed them. Since the pandemic, they now mostly worked from their home office.

No one was around except for our assistant, Raquel, and receptionist, Claudette. I grabbed a cup of coffee from the hallway alcove and padded back to my desk. I was just getting comfy making a list of what dimensions I wanted to measure at the rescue when Ashley called.

"Just wanted to give you a heads-up. I'm here with Mac now and he's finishing up a final round of questioning at the station and will be free to go soon, probably around lunchtime."

"Yes. Kaley called and told me he probably wasn't going to be charged. That's great."

"Don't get excited. As it stands now, he's still their prime suspect. I think they want to talk to more witnesses and follow up any leads before they make a move. But as of now, he's it. So if I were you, I'd speed up my sleuthing before they have a chance to charge him."

"Thanks for the tip. And can you—"

"I'll text you when he leaves."

"Thanks, Ash! You're the best."

I thought for a minute and texted Jake. *How about having a picnic lunch instead of going to a restaurant?*

He texted back about a minute later. *That's what I love about you, your sense of spontaneity.*

His mention of the *L* word threw me. I immediately texted him back without thinking. *Slow down, cowboy. You're confusing my pragmatism with spontaneity. My intent was to stake out, not make out.*

Why was it I was always so much more bold, clever, and flirty in my texts? Compared with my nonsensical stuttering and awkward silences in person. But when he didn't respond right away, I got nervous. I hoped I hadn't offended him.

I attempted a clarification. *Anyway, I want to follow Mac to see where he goes after he's released.*

Jake responded right away. *Ah, now I get it. Say no more. Do you want me to pick up sandwiches?*

Would you? That would be great and so sweet of you. Thanks.

I debated whether to add a heart emoji. What the heck. I

added the heart and sent my text.

A few minutes later he texted again. *Question.*

Yes?

What do you expect Mac to do?

I don't know. I'm hoping he just goes home and stays there. But I'm trying to brace myself in case he meets with someone that looks like a shady hit man. Or jumps on the freeway and tries to make a run for it. Or goes to the airport, books a flight to the Caymans, and skips town.

He texted back. *Got it.* He added three laughing emojis.

An overreaction in my opinion.

I pictured him with his sly smile and that deep sexy chuckle of his that I'd fallen in love with. Wait a minute. Ugh. Why did everything have to be so messy and complicated?

Around noon Jake texted me that he was in our parking lot. I met him as he was opening his car door.

"Would you mind driving? That way Adrian or Ernie won't spot me as easily."

"You want me to take the rap for you?" He chuckled.

"No. That's not why."

It's not like we were Bonnie and Clyde. If pressed, I preferred Nick and Nora.

"Adrian knows my car. It was parked in his driveway last night." Jake smiled.

"Yeah, I know. But just in case. Mac doesn't know your car. He knows mine."

He deadpanned, but his eyes were twinkling with amusement. "Fine. Just don't eat all the sandwiches while I'm driving."

"Oh my God, Jake. That happened one time." I mock pouted.

He was referring to one of our pre-pandemic outings at Sadie's Seafood Café, when we'd ordered a massive shrimp boil platter to share. I'd pumped him with questions, and he answered them at length, and meanwhile, I ate most of the shrimp.

Jake guffawed. "I can still see your huge, towering mound of shells and my tiny little pile."

I struggled to keep a straight face. "Towering's a bit of an overstatement."

"Not at all. I wish I'd taken a picture for proof."

I laughed. "No proof, it never happened."

"All I'm saying is I'm not falling for that one again." He winked.

We got into his white Tesla. The bag of sandwiches was on the passenger seat. I grabbed it in glee.

"You got subs from Bayshore Deli? I love you!"

Our gazes met.

"Er, I mean, I love you for picking Bayshore. One of my faves."

"I remember you telling me that."

I was positive my face was bright red. I pulled down the mirror visor, pretending to check my hair. Yep. Bright red. I lowered my head and buckled my seat belt.

I poked around in the brown paper bag filled with goodies. "What kind did you get? Oh, my goodness. You got my favorite sea salt chips too."

"Turkey and provolone. With the works."

When I glanced over at him, his eyes were creased with seeming delight as he put on his seat belt.

I gave him a thumbs-up sign. "Good job."

He chuckled and put the car in reverse. "Thanks. Glad it met with your approval, knowing how much you love food."

Wait.

"You noticed I've gained weight?"

With no gyms open and me doing my duty by supporting local restaurants, my pants had definitely gotten tighter.

He drove to the parking lot exit. "You have? No. You look great. Perfect actually. I was just referring to your strong opinion, frequently voiced, about Santa Sofia restaurants."

"Oh. I've already lost half of what I gained anyway. Only five more pounds to go."

"Like I said, you look great." He held my gaze.

"Could you please turn up the A/C?" I started to fan myself with a napkin.

He turned up the A/C fan and lowered the temperature. "So

where to? SSPD?"

"Correct."

Soon we were outside the SSPD, looking for a parking space.

"Try to find a spot near the door so we don't miss him coming out."

We found a good space on a side street adjacent to the visitor parking lot and visitor entrance. We parked and ate our sandwiches while keeping our eyes on the door.

Between bites I told Jake about my phone conversation with Peter Yusem.

"When I asked Peter about Bunny's kids it sounded like Bunny and her kids weren't particularly close and didn't get along that well."

"Did he give a reason why that was?"

"Not really. I tried to pry more out of him but all I got was that the son seems to be perpetually unemployed, and he might be a musician because he referred to 'gigs.' And the daughter works at a barbeque joint. I didn't have time to google that."

Jake reached in the bag for a napkin. "Hmm. How old is the son?"

I opened my chip bag. "Stone? The son's name is Stone. Kind of cool, especially if you're a musician. He didn't say. Assuming in his twenties since his sister Scarlett is twenty-seven and Bunny and Peter are late fifties-ish."

Jake wiped his hands. "Any mention about whether or not Bunny supported her kids financially?"

I ate a chip. "No. But I'm definitely going to explore that in terms of motive. See who benefited financially from her death."

Jake popped a chip into his mouth. "Probably Peter. Unless they had a prenup. Is the son single?"

I dabbed my mouth with a napkin. "I have no idea. I didn't ask. But Peter did mention where the daughter worked, not by name, but how many barbeque joints can there be just outside town? I'll google for deets."

Jake looked at me with apparent admiration. "Good. We can go there next."

Now it was my turn to look at him in awe. "Nick and Nora are on it!"

We talked about how good the Bayshore Deli sandwiches were and sat in silence munching away. I was finishing the first half of my sandwich when Ashley texted me that Mac had been released. The next minute, Mac emerged from the station with Kaley. They walked briskly to a silver Mercedes, got in, and sped away with Mac driving. Jake pulled out silently and we followed them. They drove directly to their home in Sycamore Canyon.

We pulled over on the side of the road.

I nibbled on a chip. "Okay. What now. He's being a good boy and staying home. Do we need to watch him further? Or should we go see if we can find Bunny's daughter to talk to her?"

Jake took a bite of his sandwich. "Let's finish lunch and wait here for a little while. If there's no immediate activity, I think it's safe to assume he's not a flight risk. I'd think if he was thinking of taking off, he'd do it sooner rather than later to get a head start before the authorities discovered he's gone."

"Good point and plan." I enjoyed the rest of my sandwich and started to shove my wrappings in a bag.

Jake grabbed my wrist. "Look."

The silver Mercedes emerged from the driveway, driven by Mac. No Kaley. Jake and I exchanged startled gazes. Jake started the car.

He let a car pass and then followed Mac up the hill. "Strange he's heading up the hill toward Sequoia Highway instead of the freeway. Maybe he's going to hide out in the hills?"

I packed up the rest of the lunch refuse. "That seems odd."

We followed Mac along the curves and bends of Sycamore Drive and then he turned onto a road that led directly to the mountains. We climbed higher into a heavily wooded area until it dead-ended at Sequoia Highway. We turned onto the highway and drove for about two miles and then Mac took a left down a narrow twisty road. We followed. Jake glanced in the rearview mirror.

"What?"

"A car that was behind us just pulled over and made a U-turn when we turned in. I'm checking to see if they're following us."

"We're being followed?" I twisted around in my seat.

The problem with curvy roads was you couldn't see that far behind you.

I craned my neck. "From what I can see no one is behind us."

Jake kept his eyes on the road. "Good."

After driving for a few minutes more, the road split into two. At the juncture a wooden arrow was nailed to a tree and underneath it a sign said *To Gaviota Grove.*

We pulled over to the shoulder of the road.

Jake turned to me. "What do you want to do?"

I checked to see if anyone was behind us. "You know what Gaviota Grove is, don't you?"

"Yeah, some hideaway spa or retreat place or something like that?"

"More like one of the last vestiges of shameless, elite, institutionalized misogyny. It's a secretive men's club that basically makes you sign something that says you die if you divulge any info about the club or its elite members."

He gulped. "For real? Sounds intense. I believe everything you said except the die part. You're joking, right?"

"Might be exaggerating *un peu*. But honestly, it's so secretive I wouldn't doubt it."

Jake's gaze roamed around at the woods surrounding us. "A perfect place for Mac to feel safe from prying eyes, in other words."

"Yes, exactly."

Jake turned to check out the road behind us. "What should we do?"

"Let's see how far we can get before we get stopped."

We drove down the road until we came upon another sign that said *Private Road.*

Jake turned to me. "What do you want to do?"

"There's another arrow under the sign pointing down the private road. Let's keep following the arrows."

As we continued, the road narrowed and was only wide enough for one car going one way. We rounded a bend and came to a large clearing with a graveled circular drive that surrounded a small grassy island. The clearing was the only spot in the dense forest to have found any sun. At the far end of the clearing was the entrance to Gaviota Grove, marked by a green-awning-covered bridge that spanned a small creek. The bridge led to a cluster of low buildings. Saplings on both sides of the creek swayed in the gentle breeze. There were two red-vested valets hanging out at the bridge and two scampering around the two cars ahead of us that were in the process of parking, exchanging tickets for key fobs. In front of Mac's silver Mercedes was a charcoal gray Porsche. Mac got out of his car and a valet drove it farther down a road, where I assumed there was a parking lot. Mac had his back to us and chatted to the other arrival, a tall guy in a baseball cap who got out of the Porsche. We were ignored as we circled and pulled over in the direction we'd just come from.

A large navy Bentley glided by us headed toward the entrance. A man jumped out and hailed Mac. They elbow bumped, a vestige of the pandemic.

I sucked in air with an audible lilt.

"Now what?" Jake turned to me.

I clutched his arm. "Oh my God!"

"What? What's wrong?"

"Is that who I think it is?" I started breathing more quickly.

"What?"

"I think that's Heath Grant."

"The actor?"

"Yes!"

Unlike starstruck me, unmoved Jake started to scroll through his phone. "I'm googling to see if I can find anything about Gaviota Grove online."

"Doubt it. It's kind of a secret society. That's the point."

"Oh, wait. There's a Wikipedia entry." Jake studied his phone for a few seconds. "An elite club of big hitters basically. All male, and I'm guessing not all that diverse. Members include former presidents, governors, artists, writers, musicians, university leaders, heads of major corporations, and philanthropists. It's referred to as a campground, but it sounds more like glamping to me, with all the luxury spa touches like gourmet meals, wine, and high-thread-count linens." Jake looked at me. "But you're right. No specific details other than confirming it's a secret club with secret membership. Oh, wait, it does say that supposedly there's a Hollywood contingent."

"Hmm. That explains Heath Grant. Oh. I just remembered Peter Yusem is a director and producer. Wonder if he's a member?"

"We'll never know according to Wikipedia. It's highly protective of its members' identities."

Mac and Heath Grant crossed the walkway to the campgrounds. One of the valets walked over to another valet and they both looked in our direction.

Jake started the engine. "I think that's our cue to leave."

We retraced our tracks back to Sequoia Highway.

I dusted some crumbs off my pants. "Mac didn't have an overnight bag, so I assume he just went there to hang."

"Agree. Doesn't look like he's a flight risk."

"Probably because he's innocent."

Jake studied my face. "You really believe he's innocent?"

"I do."

"Why?"

"Because he's a smart man and I don't think anything he's told us is a lie. It can all be verified. I saw the cabbage before it was stolen. I saw where it had been cut from its stalk. He mentioned anonymous texts. I'm sure he wouldn't have said that if it wasn't true. I bet Adrian asked to see them and he showed him. I bet you anything that's why they're not arresting him."

Jake nodded. "You're probably not wrong about that."

"Then there's the TV fight. Why would he fight on air and then murder her?"

"Passion?"

I shook my head. "Over a cabbage? Leaving a note with the

same threat the night before? No. If you ask me—"

"Which I literally am doing . . ." Jake winked at me.

"Mac is being framed."

CHAPTER 8

We drove back to Benning Brothers without talking much. I was deep in thought about Bunny and wondering who might benefit most from her death.

Jake adjusted the rearview mirror. "There it is again."

"What?"

"The same car that followed us up to Gaviota Grove."

"No!" I turned around and saw a silver car about three car lengths behind us. "What should we do?"

"Drive to the police station." Jake smirked. "My basic PI, go-to response."

The car continued to follow us from a distance. As we got closer to town more cars got between us. By the time we'd reached the police station there was no sign of the car.

I kept turning my head to make sure they were gone. "That was weird. I wonder who would be following us?"

Jake raised an eyebrow. "Do you have a secret admirer?"

I felt my face heat up. "How do you know they're following me, Jake? Maybe they're following you. We're in your car. You're the PI with all the shady contacts. And no, I don't have a secret admirer. And anyway, following someone is stalking behavior, not secret admirer behavior."

"Someone's a little intense today." Under his breath he said, "And doth protest too much."

I gave Jake the side-eye, my lips pursed. Jake tried to stifle a smile, but his eyes were twinkling, seemingly amused by my reaction. We waited another couple of minutes to make sure the car didn't come back and then drove over to the Benning Brothers parking lot.

I jumped out of the car. "Thanks for the murder mystery lunch adventure. Take care. And let me know if you get followed again."

"You do the same, Miss Marple. See you later."

Back at the office I checked my emails. Nothing new. I called Ashley to tell her about spotting Heath Grant.

She picked up right away. "Get out! I loved his last movie. Where did you see him again?"

I explained how Jake and I had followed Mac to see if he was going to leave town, which took us on our adventure to Gaviota Grove.

There was silence on the other end.

"What's the matter?"

"Didn't you hear Adrian tell you to stay out of trouble?"

"I did and I am. You were the one who told me when Mac was going to leave the police station. I thought you wanted me to follow him. Besides, I was with Jake. He plays by the rules."

"Uh-huh."

After a pause I cleared my throat. "We were careful. Mac didn't see us. And anyway, I don't think he'd hurt a fly, let alone murder Bunny."

Another pause. And then I heard a few sniffs.

"Ashley, are you crying?"

More sniffs.

"Why are you crying?"

"Because I don't want you to get hurt." She tried to stifle a sob but was unsuccessful.

I wished I was there in person to give her a big hug.

"Aw, Ashley. I'm always careful."

"I know you think you are. But bad stuff happens. I keep on thinking of last year . . ."

I had a flashback to two Christmases ago, when Ashley had been inadvertently involved in tracking down a killer. We'd all been traumatized to some degree. Especially afterward, when we realized that had one part of a showdown gone south, none of us might've been around to tell the story. And then to make matters worse, the pandemic lockdown happened. So much for catharsis.

"I'm so sorry, Ash. I didn't mean to be a PTSD trigger for you. I had no idea you were still struggling. You seemed okay last night."

But we'd all had wine and margaritas.

"Yeah. You're usually really good at guessing when I'm sad. But that's because we normally see each other a lot in person. But this last year . . ." She cried again.

"Hey, Ash. Want to do FaceTime?"

She agreed and we hung up and I called her on FaceTime.

"That's better. Now I can see your lovely face."

Ashley smiled.

"Just know you're not alone. The pandemic has taken a toll on us all. I need to up my steps and cut my calories. Little did we know that the nineteen in Covid-19 referred to the number of pounds we were likely to gain during lockdown."

Ashley laughed.

"There she is. Laughing at my corny, clichéd jokes. But seriously, Ash. I'm so sorry I didn't pick up on you not being over it yet."

"Why do you think I became obsessed with K-pop and Stray Kids all of a sudden?"

"I don't know. Because Hyunjin from the Stray Kids is hot?"

She sighed. "So hot. I mean that 'Play With Fire' dance video."

"I know. Smoking hot. I almost had to throw water on my computer."

Ashley guffawed.

She took a deep breath. "Beyond their brilliant talent and their humanity, they were a great escape. I'm sorry, but they're cheaper than daily therapy and less dangerous than drugs and alcohol."

"But no less addictive."

We both laughed.

Hoping to build on the lighter mood, I filled her in about renting my father's house.

"Oo. I wonder who it is? Promise you'll tell me as soon as you find out."

I chuckled. "I will."

"Glad Danielle was able to help. I told you she was a good realtor. Also, I've been meaning to tell you, after last year's incident, I now have so much more empathy for you, losing both your dad and your husband practically at the same time. You are one strong cookie."

A rush of emotion flooded my whole being.

My voice cracked. "Thanks, Ashley. That means a lot to me. I would never have weathered that storm without your friendship, that's for sure. You are such a good friend. Thank you."

"You're welcome. And likewise. So anyway, finish your story. You followed Mac to Gaviota Grove."

I wiped my cheek. "Yes. He seemed relaxed and jovial as if he didn't have a care in the world."

"And that's why you think he's innocent?"

"Yes. His current demeanor coupled with all my past interactions with him over the years are part of my reason. Then there's the note echoing what he said on TV. That smacks of being too much on the nose. Same with the bloodied glove left in his car. He's not a careless person. I don't think he had a strong enough motive. Sure, he might have had differences with Bunny, but they were silly and shallow. Not a motive for murder. I truly believe he's innocent and being framed by the actual murderer."

"Well, that makes one of us, at least."

I held the phone closer to my face. "What do you mean?"

"I met with Kaley at the station while Mac was waiting to be interrogated in a different room. She corroborated the animosity between Bunny and Mac."

I tilted my chin slightly. "She did?"

Ashley nodded. "Yep. And she said Mac wanted to win the race at any cost."

I leaned closer to my phone. "No. She really said that?"

Ashley stressed her enunciation. "Those were her exact words."

"Wow."

Ashley twisted her lips to the side. "But the weird thing was that then she made a point of insisting to me he was innocent."

I rested my head in my hand. "Talk about sending mixed messages."

"Yep."

After we finished our FaceTime call, I worked on some new proposals, but my thoughts kept returning to what Ashley had told me about Kaley. I needed to hear it directly from Kaley herself. I gave her a call, and she agreed to meet me for a drink later.

I stretched, walked around the office, and made myself a cup of tea and then settled back at my desk. I checked emails. There was one from Pom Pom Rescue. It was Jules letting me know she needed my application to officially be turned in ASAP. She said Caroline agreed that I was the best fit for Ruby, and she'd told her friend that Ruby had already been adopted. But they couldn't get a hold of the VIP donor after he'd left them a voicemail saying he was stopping by to turn in his application later this afternoon.

I got a sudden rush of energy. I made sure I had the application in my handbag and trotted out to my car. I headed over to Pom Pom Rescue as if I were on an urgent mission that I couldn't fail, making me realize how attached I already was to little Ruby. Their parking lot was empty. I scrambled out of my car and bounded into the building clutching my application. Jules was there with a couple looking at another dog.

Her face lit up when she saw me. "I'm so glad to see you."

I smiled. "Here's my application."

"Good. You're officially the first one. Ruby is yours."

I had a slight startle reflex. "She is?"

"Yep. I already did some research. Love your Instagram account with Iris and Otis. Plus, I'm friends with your vet, who you mentioned on one of your posts. She gave you a glowing recommendation."

I liked her style. An amateur sleuth after my own heart. "Wow. She did? That's great."

"Also, like I said, Caroline agrees you're the best fit for Ruby.

So she discouraged her friend. But the VIP donor isn't used to taking no for an answer."

Suddenly, her expression changed, and her gaze shifted to the left and behind me. I turned around and my jaw dropped open. It was Heath Grant. He was even better-looking up closer.

He smiled at both of us the way celebrities do when they know they've been recognized, a self-confident smile from having adoring fan encounters, but with an underlying wariness in their eyes, in case it's a whack-a-doodle fan. "I'm here to fill out an application for Ruby."

My knees buckled slightly at the realization that Heath Grant was the VIP donor. Suddenly my antenna went up and I was ready to defend Ruby if I needed to.

Jules slumped her shoulders and did a little curtsy. "Aw, I'm sorry. Ruby's already been adopted. We found her a perfect home with an experienced Pom owner who has another Pom. But we have many other Poms for you to choose from."

"Any that look like Ruby? She was so cute and tiny."

"Why don't you go out to our backyard and I'll have someone bring out our available dogs for you to meet."

"Thanks, but no. I'll come back another time. I really liked Ruby. But I will return." He flashed me a smile before he left.

As soon as he left, Jules grabbed my arm and steered me to a little room. "Wait here. I'll go get Ruby."

"Wait. What about her kennel cough? I don't want my Pom or cat to get it."

"Our vet did an X-ray. It's not kennel cough. It's a mild trachea collapse. If it gets worse, she can be put on a cough suppressant. But she's been great today. It was probably exacerbated by the stress of the last couple of days here and at the shelter."

"Okay. Actually, Jules, can I come back later this afternoon on my way home from work? Like in an hour or so. I still have to do some stuff and want her homecoming to go as smoothly as possible."

"Sure. That's fine. Just sign these papers and she's yours."

After I signed everything, paid the fee, and Ruby was officially adopted, I jogged back to my car. Heath Grant looked to be on a phone call because he was talking and no one else was in his Bentley. By the time I'd buckled my seat belt, he'd pulled out of the parking lot. I wondered if he was going to meet up with Mac again. I decided to follow him.

CHAPTER 9

I was so glad we'd taken Jake's car to Gaviota Grove. It made me feel a little less conspicuous as I followed Heath Grant into the hills. I wondered if he would be heading back to Gaviota Grove. But instead of heading straight toward Sequoia Highway, he turned into the affluent Sycamore Canyon area, one of Santa Sofia's most rustic neighborhoods noted for its tall, arching California sycamore (*Platanus racemosa*) trees that lined many of its hilly streets.

Up and down the curvy roads we went. Most of the Sycamore Canyon homes were set back from the street. The large downslope lots were valued for the privacy the thick woods provided the homes nestled in them. Many of the large upslope lots had spectacular ocean views. As we got deeper into Sycamore Canyon, I pulled over to let a couple of cars get ahead of me, so I wasn't too obvious. I was very familiar with the labyrinth of roads in the area since we were getting closer to my late father's house. In fact, if we kept on Sycamore Drive, we'd be passing my father's house any minute.

When Heath Grant pulled into my father's driveway I pumped the brake rapidly, not knowing whether to stop or continue following him. What was going on? I needed to know. I followed him up the drive, planning to find out why he was trespassing. My mind was trying to reconcile all I knew about Heath Grant beyond what I'd viewed in his films or read about him in the tabloids. He was definitely male perfection on-screen, but what an odd man in real life. Belonging to an elite and dated men's club, wanting to adopt a tiny pom, and now trespassing. I pulled up right beside him.

I was out of my car before he was out of his. I ran over to him as he climbed out.

He looked around nervously as if I were a crazy fan stalking him. "Hi. Can I help you?"

I stood about a foot away. "What are you doing here?"

He raised his eyebrows. "Me? You're asking me what I'm doing here? I just rented the place. I'm in the process of moving in soon. May I ask who you are?"

After a couple of seconds, I figured it out, and closed my mouth. I cleared my throat. "I'm your new landlord."

And that was how I met the new mystery tenant for my father's house.

"Oh." It took a moment for him to process. "I'm sorry, I didn't catch your name."

I held out my hand. "Tory Benning. No need for you to tell me who you are, I already know."

Smooth, Tory, really smooth.

"This was my late father's house."

He squeezed my hand firmly. "Heath Grant. Honored to be able to rent your beautiful house. This whole area is so special. So peaceful. I love the calm vibe. Exactly what I need in my life right now." He cocked his head slightly. "Hey, you look familiar. Have we met before?"

Oh, God. He remembered me from Gaviota Grove. Still in his grip, my hand got sweaty.

He released my hand and snapped his fingers. "Got it. I remember now. You were at the dog rescue place."

Phew.

I sighed. "Um, that's right." I subtly wiped my hands on my pant legs. "I'm so glad you like the house. My realtor told me she had an interested party. I've been waiting to hear from her."

He smiled. "Have you checked your messages recently? I was there when she tried to call you about an hour ago."

"What?" I dug around in my handbag for my phone and checked my messages. "Yep. Three missed calls from Danielle."

"She was trying to arrange a time for you to sign the lease. I signed it right after I saw the house earlier this afternoon."

My phone rang. It was Danielle.

"Speak of the devil." I walked a few steps away. "Yes, I know. I'm actually at the house right now. And so is Heath Grant." I turned and Heath Grant was staring at me in a way that made my heart flutter.

"He's there now? He's so nice and so is his realtor. So professional. He has great references and financials. Can you stop by now and sign the lease?"

I told Danielle I would be on my way.

"Well, you just got the seal of approval from my realtor. And she's a tough crowd."

"Good."

I glanced at the time on my phone. It was nearly three. I whipped out a business card. "Danielle Murphy, my realtor, will handle most things to do with the house. But if you can't reach her, please don't hesitate to call me for whatever you need."

For whatever you need. I did a mental face slap.

He took my card and read it. "Interesting. A landscape architect. Great line of work to be in for this part of the world. Great weather, lush plants. I actually know a developer up here, a former actor in his youth, who prides himself on properties with lush landscape. Maybe you know him, Mac McGregor."

I nearly fainted. "Yes, I'm the landscape designer for the Hotel Santa Sofia. Mac was instrumental in getting me hired."

"You don't say. Love that place. The grounds are phenomenal. I'm in awe of your talent."

By the hot flashes I was experiencing, I was sure I'd turned beet red. "Thanks."

"Do you happen to have another business card and a pen?"

Was he going to promote me now?

"Yes, I do." I pulled out another business card and handed it to him.

I fumbled in my purse and finally found a pen.

He wrote on the card and handed both the card and pen back to me. "That's my cell phone number. I don't have business cards.

Give me a call and maybe you can come over for a drink and you can give me a custom tour of the house. I should be moved in by tomorrow night according to my assistant."

I was floating. Heath Grant gave me his phone number. How I ever made my way back to my car without tripping, I'll never know. Thank God. I felt his eyes on me. I couldn't wait to call Ashley. She answered on the third ring.

"Hi. I'm on my way to sign the lease for my father's house, then I have to pick up Ruby, but I couldn't wait to tell you who my new tenant is." I shrieked, "It's Heath Grant."

"Shut up."

I gave her a quick Heath Grant recap.

"Heath Grant asked you over for a drink? Unreal."

"I know. Can you believe it?"

"I can't. Are you sure he asked you over for a drink?"

I snickered. "Of course I'm sure."

But I quickly replayed our whole conversation in my mind to really make sure.

"Yes, he said to call him, and I could come over for a drink and give him a tour."

"A tour of what?"

We both burst out laughing.

"Of the house. He said a tour of the house." I chuckled. "Okay. I need to focus on driving because that encounter just literally took my breath away."

"Hold on. What are you doing for dinner?"

"No plans for dinner. Meeting Kaley for a drink at five. Jake said he'd call. But we didn't make plans."

"I was thinking takeout? I want to meet your new little Pommie."

"Yes. That sounds great."

Danielle's real estate agency was located on the Avenue. It was a cute little office with a window box of pink, white, and red impatiens and begonias lining the storefront. When I opened the squeaky door, its loud chimes alerted Danielle to my arrival.

Danielle sprung up from her desk. "Tory! Thanks for coming

by. I'm so happy we got you such a great tenant. He oohed and aahed the whole time I was there." She winked at me.

I signed all the copies of the lease. Danielle gave me my copy, and we were all set.

"Thank you. It's such a relief to get it rented. And I'm not going to lie, it's so cool to have a movie star renting it."

My next stop was Pom Pom Rescue.

When I entered, Jules was manning the front desk. She beamed at me like I'd won the lottery. I felt like I had.

I clapped my fists together. "I'm so excited."

Jules smiled broadly. "Here's Ruby's folder with all her paperwork. I'll go get her now."

"Great. But I need to take some additional measurements for the backyard and the front courtyard. Can I do that quickly first?"

"Yes. Of course."

I trotted to the backyard. I took my shiny silver E-Z Read measuring tape out of my handbag and pulled out the tape and zapped it back again, quickly jotting down the initial measurements as I went around the perimeter. I also took more photographs. Then I moved to the front courtyard and did the same.

Jules was working at the computer behind the counter when I came back inside. "All done?"

"I am. For now. I can't wait to see little Ruby again."

"I'll go get her."

A few minutes later Jules came from a back room carrying Ruby. She looked even cuter and tinier than I remembered. With her sharp, pointy snout, she resembled a little red fox. Jules handed her over. Ruby looked content and nuzzled into the crook of my arm like she belonged there. She made eye contact that didn't quit and gazed at me as if to say *What took you so long?*

"She's such a little nugget. I can't believe she was at a shelter. What was her backstory again?"

"The shelter said her owner died. The family couldn't keep her."

"So strange. She's so little you'd think the family would try to keep her."

She handed me the folder. "Here's her information about her vaccinations and her medical exam."

Jules gave me a towel for my car and told me to let her know how Ruby adjusted. As soon as I placed Ruby on the towel in the passenger seat, she started to do a cute little paddling movement with her front paws like a happy dance.

I buckled my seat belt and backed out of the parking space. Ruby continued to paddle all the way home. I checked the time on the dashboard. My meetup with Kaley was in about an hour. My plan was to make sure Ruby had a proper introduction to Iris and Otis. While I was away meeting with Kaley, I'd separate Ruby in a different room so she could decompress in peace and Iris and Otis could have the run of the house as usual.

I pulled into my driveway on Mariposa Drive. "We're home!"

Ruby sat up and looked around. I retrieved my house keys from my handbag, slung my handbag over my shoulder, and gathered Ruby in my arms. Iris was a lightweight, weighing in at around eight pounds. But Ruby was a flyweight, in comparison, at only five pounds. Once again, Ruby snuggled up to me as if we'd been together for a long time. I was sure she had been well loved in her prior situation. She didn't tremble and trusted me without reservation. As I walked up my front path Iris barked her greeting from inside the house.

Boy, was she in for a surprise.

I unlocked the door and stepped inside. Iris immediately homed in on Ruby and took a few steps back while keeping her gaze riveted on Ruby. I bent down and Iris came rushing up, her tail wagging fast with excitement. The dogs sniffed each other, and I put Ruby on the ground. Iris lunged to sniff Ruby, and jerked repeatedly into the play posture, with her arms stretched out in front and her rear end up in the air. Ruby had a twinkle in her eyes.

"Okay. Calm down, Iris. We don't want Ruby to get overwhelmed. Who wants to go outside? Let's take a walk."

I scooped Ruby up and Iris followed me to the back door. Outside Iris did zoomies several times around Ruby, who stood and watched Iris. Iris seemed so excited to have a little pal. I hoped her infatuation would last. Ruby seemed equally enchanted with Iris. Jules said they were told Ruby was around nine. Iris was about six or seven, based on her estimated age when I got her. Once back inside I noticed Otis lurking by the front door.

I picked up Ruby and introduced her to Otis. In true feline fashion, Otis turned his back on her as if pretending she didn't exist and walked into another room. I got down on the floor and played with Iris and Ruby. After a while the novelty started to wear off for the two of them and they both settled down to rest.

"Okay, guys. I need to go meet someone now."

I gated a space near the back door for Ruby. I placed a dog bed, a water bowl, and a pee pad in the enclosed area. Ruby immediately curled up in the bed. It would be good for her to rest after her exciting last couple of days. Iris seemed to approve of the arrangement.

I freshened up and swept my hair into a ponytail, my go-to style now that my hair was so much longer. I checked the time on my phone. Kaley had picked Hotel Santa Sofia's lounge, Burbujita's, for drinks. At this rate they were going to consider me a regular. With luck and light traffic, I'd get there right on time.

When I opened my front door to leave, I noticed a car parked down the street. As soon as I started to walk down the path it sped away. It looked like a silver Mercedes. Coincidence, or was someone stalking me?

CHAPTER 10

I got in my car and immediately locked my doors, a move I normally do anyway, but this time it was in record time.

I texted Jake. *I think that same car that followed us from Gaviota Grove might have been stalking me at my house. As soon as I went to my car, they sped away.*

After waiting a couple of minutes for his response and receiving none, I started my car and drove to the hotel, monitoring my rearview mirror the whole time. I parked in the hotel's front lot and took the same pathway I'd taken when I'd met with Ashley, Jake, and Adrian the night before.

By the time I arrived at the entrance to Burbujita's it was five. Right on the dot. I peered into the darkened lounge. No Kaley. I strolled through the lounge, navigating the round tables and low bucket chairs to its outdoor patio. No Kaley there either. I turned around and was face-to-face with Kaley. I gasped audibly.

"Hi, Tory. Sorry, didn't mean to startle you."

"Oh my goodness. No problem."

Suspecting I'd been followed twice in as many days had taken its toll and made me jumpier than normal.

"It's just that I didn't expect to see you right next to me after searching for you inside and outdoors." I chuckled. "Where'd you come from?"

Kaley McGregor exuded an aura of understated elegance, whether dressed for yoga or drinks. Her shoulder-length blonde hair was pulled back in a low ponytail and she was wearing trim black pants, a crisp white linen shirt she wore fashionably half tucked in, diamond stud earrings, and black espadrille wedge sandals.

"I just walked in from the lobby." She laughed lightly.

We found a table outside with a great view of the beach and ocean. A server took our order for two glasses of Chardonnay.

"Thanks for agreeing to meet with me. How are you? How's Mac doing?"

She slung her black leather Coach shoulder bag on the back of her patio chair. "Mac is doing well. Everything seems to just roll off of him. Me? I'm a bundle of nerves."

For someone claiming to be a bundle of nerves, I was amazed how well put together she was. Perfect makeup and hair. French tip mani-pedi. Matching accessories. When I was upset, I was a hot mess, too anxious to think of my hair, and lucky if I wore shoes that matched, let alone anything else.

"I guess I'm feeling anxious for both of us. I can't bear the thought of him having to go to jail."

"I'll do everything I can to see that he doesn't."

"Thanks for believing in him. You're about the only one who does."

"And you."

Kaley threw her head back slightly and let out a laugh that contained no joy. "Two supporters." She shook her head. "But it's his own fault, frankly."

The server delivered our glasses of Chardonnay to the table.

I sat back up straighter. "Why do you say that?"

"Because of his stupid temper. Obsessing on the gardening competition like it was the make-or-break component in the mayoral race. Giving Bunny a harder time than was warranted. He's his own worst enemy."

After you. She was throwing her own husband under the bus. Why?

I sipped my wine. "But you still believe he's innocent, right? I hope you're not keeping any secrets from me. If I'm going to spend my time and energy fighting for him, I've got to be sure you, of all people, believe he didn't kill Bunny."

Her gaze roamed the room, the ceiling, and focused on a point out at sea so intensely that I turned to see if there was something intriguing out there I'd missed. Our gazes met.

"Kaley! You do believe Mac is innocent, don't you?"

She exhaled loudly. "Of course he's innocent, Tory. How can you even doubt it?"

I was about to remind her I wasn't the one hesitating but decided to try to be more compassionate and kinder. I remembered being a suspect myself in the past. It played havoc with my nerves, too, and with those to whom I was close.

She smoothed a stray hair away from her face. "He always seemed to have a chip on his shoulder when it came to Bunny. Maybe because she was a successful female."

This take on Bunny and Mac's friendship was different than described by Peter. From what Peter had told me on the phone, Bunny and Mac had had an uneventful relationship up until the cabbage incident.

She took a sip of wine. "I don't know. I just hope he doesn't do something stupid now to make things worse."

I hoped she hadn't conveyed this "with friends like these who needs enemies" impression to Adrian when she'd spoken to him, but I feared she had. Surely, she knew this ambivalence about Mac would only hurt his case.

This back-and-forth continued while we finished our wine, and twenty minutes later we walked out to the lobby together. She'd valet parked. I strolled back to my car trying to reconcile what she'd said about Mac and Bunny with Peter's version. Either they'd always been at odds or it was only recently. They couldn't both be true.

Ashley texted me. *How about I pick up our usual salad order from Tender Greens?*

I texted her right back. *You're a doll! Thanks! Just what I need, some salmon. Maybe it will help my brain figure out some stuff.*

She sent me back a laughing emoji.

I drove out of the lot past the valet parking area. Kaley was just getting into her car. Like Mac, she drove a silver Mercedes.

Driving home, my head was in turmoil. Was it possible that Mac was guilty, and he and Kaley were playing me? Was that why

Adrian seemed to always be warning me off? Did he think that too? Or was Kaley trying to tell me that Mac alone was guilty? Maybe she felt obligated to put on some semblance of the good wife by enlisting my help. But the trouble was, in my gut, despite what Kaley had told me, I still felt Mac was incapable of murder based on my years-long friendship with him. I couldn't wait to hear Ashley's opinion about the whole thing.

When I got home, all was well. Iris greeted me at the door as usual, and when I went to check on Ruby, she sprang up from her bed to greet me at the gate. We went out to the backyard and then I scooped kibble into three dishes. Otis appeared when he heard the kitchen activity.

I was just giving them all a treat after they'd finished their dinner when there was a knock at the door that made me jump. Iris rushed to the front door. By the wagging of her tail, I knew it must be Ashley, and when I peeked out the peephole, I saw that it was.

As soon as I opened the door Iris started to jump on Ashley.

"Hi, Iris. How are you?"

"Iris is so happy to see Aunt Ashley."

"Where's the new—oh my God, there she is. Look at that little dumpling!" Ruby had followed me to the front door.

Ashley bent down to pet Ruby, who licked her hand.

"She likes you."

"Is it me or because I come bearing food?" Ashley chortled and handed me the take-out bag.

"Probably both, to be honest."

I set up the salads on the kitchen counter and we hopped on the barstools and dug in.

After we ate our salads, I scooped up Ruby and motioned Ashley into the living room.

We sat down on the leather couch and I lowered Ruby to the floor.

"What do you think about Lily as a new name for Ruby? She could keep Ruby as her middle name."

Ashley smirked. "I didn't know dogs had middle names."

"Show me the rule that says they can't. Besides, all the pedigree dogs have multiple names, like British royalty."

Ashley leaned down to Lily. "Okay, Miss Lily Ruby it is." She winked at me. "Keeping with the flower theme, like Iris. I like that."

"Thanks."

"Iris and Lily are so cute. Maybe I should get a dog."

I patted Ashley's arm. "Do it."

"I don't know how my cat Ginger would take to a dog."

"So far, so good with Otis."

Ashley picked up Lily. "I still don't know what to make of what Kaley said about Mac's temper and him resenting Bunny."

"That's been bothering me too. To my mind, the only reason for her saying that is to imply that Mac indeed had a motive to kill Bunny. That just doesn't jibe with her asking me to help him."

"What next?"

"I want to pay a visit to the *Sentinel*. Get a feel for how the staff felt about Bunny. Whether they knew of any enemies she might have had. I also want to see what Bunny's kids are like."

Ashley stiffened and her face clouded over. "Uh-oh. All of that sounds like it's dangerously close to what Adrian warned you not to do."

I threw my arm around her. "Ash, I heard what you said on the phone earlier today. I'll be careful. I always am. When that car followed us, we drove straight to the police station." I winced as soon as the words were out of my mouth.

"Wait. What? Someone followed you? When?"

"When I was with Jake. I thought maybe it was Jake who was being followed because he's a PI and involved in criminal investigations. But then when they were parked outside . . ."

"It happened more than once?" Ashley got up and paced around my living room. She put her hands on her hips. "Have you told Adrian?"

I lowered my head. "Not yet."

"Please do. And sooner rather than later, or I will."

"Okay, okay. I will tomorrow."

"No. Do it now. Was it the same car both times? What kind of car was it?"

"A silver Mercedes. I think. Not positive. Both times I only saw it from afar."

Ashley sat down. "I don't like this. Getting a really bad vibe right now."

"They didn't try to run us off the road or anything."

Sadly, I'd had that happen to me in the past.

She exhaled loudly. "That's supposed to make me feel better? Honestly, Tory. Sometimes I don't know about you. Listen. A killer is on the loose. No matter who it is, even if it's Mac, they might be starting to feel cornered and get desperate."

She left off the "and strike again" part but I knew that's what she was implying.

"Got it. Message received."

"Good."

I bit my lip. "Oh, one other thing."

"What?"

"Both Mac and Kaley drive a silver Mercedes."

CHAPTER 11

After Ashley left, I checked the *Sentinel* website to see who else besides Bunny ran the paper. We were lucky to still have a local print newspaper in Santa Sofia. Many small-town newspapers had been either bought out, closed down, or converted to a network of other small newspapers that read more like a realtor's sales update of the neighborhoods they represented than an actual newspaper.

There was a black banner at the top of the *Sentinel*'s website announcing Bunny's death and thanking everyone who'd sent thoughts and prayers and flowers. For people wanting to donate in Bunny's name, Save the Environment Now was one of the organizations listed. Below the banner was a photo of Bunny with her birthdate and date of death. The statement about her death was very brief. Bunny had been assaulted by an unknown assailant at the Jacaranda Gardens community garden. Police were investigating. It said it was a developing story.

When I pulled down a link Bunny was still listed as publisher and editor in chief. I skimmed the list of associate and assistant editors and the members of the editorial board. I didn't recognize any of the names.

I did some googling of all the *Sentinel* personnel listed on the site to see if anything came up that suggested they were at odds with Bunny. Nothing came up. And then I thought of Simon, my wedding photographer, who also freelanced for the *Sentinel*. He'd been at the community garden yesterday, but I'd never gotten a chance to speak to him. I'd make sure to give him a call tomorrow to see if he had any insights.

I took Iris and Lily outside for the last walk of the night. I decided to see if Lily would be okay gated by herself near the back door for her first night. I breathed a sigh of relief when she immediately climbed into her bed and curled up, ready to go to sleep. I retreated to my bedroom with Iris and soon, we were hunkered down in bed too. Otis had made himself scarce since I'd brought Lily home and had continued his standoff. As I reached over to shut off the lights, Otis appeared, lurking in the hallway, which I considered progress. I hoped we all would have a peaceful and uneventful first night with Lily in her new home.

• • •

I woke up Wednesday morning to a surprisingly quiet house. I tumbled out of bed earlier than usual to check on Lily. She greeted me with a wagging tail. She fell in with Iris, stepping with the same swagger, for a backyard constitutional as if it were her normal routine. All was going smoothly so far, considering it was the start of her first full day. I attributed her good house manners to her former owner and wondered what had happened and why the family hadn't wanted to keep her. They both galloped over to the back door when I opened it and then waddled in, side by side, like fuzzy miniature sheep. Otis rubbed against my legs as I distributed kibble in their bowls, while Iris and Lily's gazes bore into me. After I fed all the animals, I got ready for work.

Dressed in slim black pants and a fitted charcoal top with three-quarter-length sleeves, I padded back to the kitchen and poured myself a cup of coffee, having decided to make my calls from home so I could hang out with the animals a bit longer.

I called Simon and he said he was going to be at the *Sentinel* offices today around midmorning and that I could stop by then.

I put a call into my aunt Marian, the head librarian at the Santa Sofia Public Library. When Google failed to yield any information on someone, I always fell back on my aunt's extensive social network to ratchet my information gathering up a notch. I was hoping Simon would be able to provide me with basic knowledge about the *Sentinel* employees from the perspective of a fellow employee, whereas Aunt Marian would be good at digging up dirt. I guess it ran in the family.

Aunt Marian told me she was going in early to the library and to meet her there.

I let the Poms outside one more time before putting Lily back in the gated area. At this rate I felt that before too long I could try not gating her when I left for short periods of time and, hopefully, she'd be able to run free soon.

"I'll be back at lunchtime, Pommies. See you then."

On my way to see my aunt, I stopped by a Starbucks and picked up coffee for both of us and then headed to the library, located off the Avenue. When I'd reached the library parking lot, I texted her to let her know I was there. She told me she'd meet me at the main entrance to unlock the double glass doors to let me in.

"Tory! So good to see you." She threw her arms around me.

I handed her the coffee.

"Thanks so much, dear. So sweet of you."

I pecked her cheek. "How are you, Aunt Marian?"

"Glad to be back at the library. How are you doing? Come on back to the break room."

Aunt Marian led me through the small one-story library's tiled entryway, past the information desk, the glassed-in computer room, the children's library with whimsical wall murals of Winnie-the-Pooh and Piglet, and through the stacks to the staff lounge.

We sat down at a rectangular table, Aunt Marian at the head and me to her right.

"Now, what's all this about the *Sentinel* employees. What is it you want to know? And moreover, why? Don't tell me you have your detective hat on again, Tory. Haven't you done enough investigating to qualify for a PI license by now?" Her light blue eyes danced with merriment.

"Mac McGregor told me that he received an anonymous text the night before Bunny was killed. The text said Bunny had written a negative editorial about Mac and me and Jacaranda Gardens, saying the only way to stop development is to get rid of development advocates like me and Mac. Anyway, supposedly the editorial was leaked on Twitter and that's how the content was discovered."

Aunt Marian leaned in closer, her silver bun gleaming under the long fluorescent light fixture running down the center of the ceiling. "Who leaked it? Was he sure it was real? Maybe someone wrote a fake editorial pretending to be Bunny. Does he have any idea who texted him?"

"I had all those same questions and, unfortunately, don't have answers to any of them. I'm not even certain Mac didn't make the whole thing up, but I'm sure the police will be tracing his messages now that he's shared this story with them."

"Oh my. Mac's too smart to have made it up or orchestrated it. And too ethical, at least from all my experience interacting with him. Certainly not perfect. He does have his mood swings, but that's more about him being impulsive than being mean-spirited. Personally, I can't imagine him being violent, can you?"

"No. I can't. But the mood swings you mention make me nervous. Because that's all the police will need, I fear, to justify that it was a murder of passion."

Aunt Marian fiddled with her bun. "Oh, dear. I didn't think of that. But you're right."

"So that's why I'm interested in finding out more about other people who might've had a motive for killing Bunny. Like her employees at the *Sentinel*. Do you know any of them?"

"I have over the years. Let's look at their website and I'll tell you if I know any of the current ones."

It turned out Aunt Marian knew most of the editorial board members.

"If you like, Tory, I'll ask around to see if anything was up at the *Sentinel*. I've never heard any of these folks complain about the management of the *Sentinel* in terms of working conditions or fairness. In fact, Bunny was seen as a savoir since so many small-town papers have gone under and she had the means to keep it afloat."

"That was another question I had. Where did Bunny's wealth come from?"

"I know her family was wealthy. They helmed a conglomerate of newspapers that segued into online media and other related companies. Since she was an only child, she inherited it all. She could always be counted on as a donor for several local charities. She was a good person and I'll miss her." Her eyes teared up and a single tear dripped down her cheek.

"So sorry, Aunt Marian. In the midst of trying to find out who killed her, I forgot for a minute the grief that results when someone is murdered. You'd think I'd be more sensitive to that, but you know me, keeping active by trying to solve the murder and bring the killer to justice is my way of dealing with the shock of a sudden death, especially homicide."

She reached out and patted my hand. "Singing to the choir, Tory, dear. Everyone grieves in their own way."

She looked at me with tender eyes, the fine wrinkles around her eyes creased into a softened expression that struck me as both loving and wistful. I knew she was referring to her own grief over the death of my mother, her sister, who was killed in a car accident when I was only eight.

We drank our coffee and chatted about our relatives on my father's side, my uncle Bob and aunt Veronica, for about ten minutes.

She stood up and adjusted her marigold gauze scarf and smoothed out the boxy rust-colored tunic she wore over loose straight black pants, an outfit that had a designer Eileen Fisher vibe. "Do give Veronica and Bob big hugs from me, please. We should all try to get together soon."

"Yes. That would be fun. I'll talk to them and then let you know."

During the short drive to the *Sentinel* offices, I thought about questions I wanted to ask Simon. I parked in the lot adjacent to the one-story, flat-roofed, gray stucco building. I'd worn a comfy pair of medium-heeled booties that I appreciated as I walked across the parking lot. I opened the glass door to the lobby area. After I checked in with the receptionist and she told me Simon would be right out, I sank into a black leather armchair next to a glass coffee table with copies of the *Sentinel* on it.

The next minute one of the doors in the lobby opened and Simon bounded out. "Let's go into the small conference room. It's free for the next ten minutes and more private."

Simon Walker was a lanky guy, in his early forties, who was always chipper, a trait that came in handy in the wedding photography business he had, in addition to his freelance work for the *Sentinel*.

We seated ourselves at one end of a long oval table.

I played with my chain necklaces, which had gotten tangled. "I'll cut to the chase since we don't have much time. You worked for Bunny. Was she a good employer? Fair? Easy to work with?"

He nodded vigorously. "Yes, yes, and yes. She was the best."

"That jibes with the impression I had of her. I didn't know her that well myself, but what I knew I liked. So based on that, I'm presuming the rest of the *Sentinel* staff felt the same way?"

Simon scratched his chin and emitted a light laugh. "If you're looking for a motive, which I assume you're doing by coming here, you're going to have to look elsewhere. Bunny was opinionated and demanding, but also self-effacing, and had a great sense of humor she injected into even serious topics when she thought things were going too rough. These days the newspaper business is teetering on the brink and I think I can say with a fair amount of certainty that her employees were very grateful to her for providing them employment."

I nodded. "Do you know whether she had any kind of succession plan? Who's in charge now?"

He fiddled with the cuff of his checkered shirtsleeve. "Her husband, Peter, is in charge, for now."

"Do people like him?"

"Yes." He creased his eyes. "So far."

"How did he and Bunny get along? Any problems there?"

Simon pushed back in his chair and let out a long breath. "I see where you're headed with that line of questioning. Honestly, I really don't know. This is the first time I've even seen him at the *Sentinel*. I never heard any buzz from the other employees. But then, because I'm freelance, I'm not here much. And when I'm here it's mainly to discuss work, so Bunny's personal life never came up." He checked his phone. "Yep. Time's up. We're having a meeting here in five and I have to prepare. Sorry I couldn't be of more help."

"Thanks for your time, Simon. You've actually been very helpful."

Based on what Simon had said, I doubted that Bunny had any enemies at the *Sentinel*. So I was guessing I could eliminate workplace disgruntlement as a motive. As we walked out to the lobby, I froze momentarily as we passed an older man wearing stylish tinted eyeglasses who I recognized from our brief but frosty encounter at the community garden. Peter Yusem was focused on his phone. His tousled dark brown hair and trendy five o'clock shadow gave the impression of one of those hip Hollywood types in their fifties who looked and acted younger than their years.

Simon trotted by him, said, "Hello, Peter," and then disappeared into another room and shut the door.

I took a deep breath. "Excuse me."

Peter turned to look at me.

"Hi, sorry to bother you, but we met the other day at the community garden."

Peter's face registered recognition. "Um, hello."

"I'm sorry for your loss and so sorry to have met under stressful circumstances the other day. I was upset and I'm sure you were."

He held up his hand. "No need for apologies. I understand. I'm sorry to have been so rude myself."

He extended his hand and smiled. "Peter Yusem."

"I'm Tory Benning. We also spoke on the phone."

He threw his head back. "Yes. Okay, now I'm piecing it all together. Didn't remember we'd met and had that little kerfuffle at the community garden when you called me."

"Sorry I didn't mention that and connect the dots over the phone. I just wanted to say again that I'm so sorry for your loss. Bunny was a great person."

"Thank you. What brings you here? More questions, I take it?"

"Um, yes. But I also wanted to pay my respects to the staff. I'd interacted with some of them through our communications regarding the community garden and getting Bunny involved." Immediately I felt my face heat up.

I might as well have just said it's because of me and my community garden that your wife is dead. Had I never asked her to participate as an inaugural gardener she might still be alive.

Peter touched my arm. "That garden brought her a lot of joy. Thanks for including her."

"Oh, thanks for saying that . . . especially given the circumstances."

He pointed to the floral and succulent arrangement on the coffee table in the small lobby. "Now I'm making all the connections with your face. Thank you so much for these and the beautiful flowers you sent to my home."

I smiled. "Glad you like them."

"It's somewhat comforting knowing she died doing what she loved, especially because it's an organic garden. She was a great advocate for the environment."

"Totally."

I hoped the condo and the garden wouldn't be forever triggering for him, like it had been for me at first. The old, deserted mall that previously occupied the space came with baggage for me. Not only because of its proximity to a crime scene involving my late husband, but because it was where an attempted crime ended up being thwarted. But with the help of my psychologist, Ellen, I'd addressed that association before the condo had even been built. When we won the landscape bid for Jacaranda Gardens, she suggested I view it as a perfect opportunity to replace an old memory that had negative associations with a new one having positive ones.

I took a deep breath. "I hate to bother you with this right now, but I've been curious about a rumor I heard, and I wanted to ask you if you know anything about a supposed leaked editorial from the *Sentinel*."

Peter tilted his head. "What do you mean by 'leaked'?"

"I heard that a leaked *Sentinel* editorial was floating around the internet. Apparently, someone got a hold of a prepublication draft and posted a link to it on Twitter, though when I searched Twitter, I couldn't find any mention of it, and if I don't mind saying so, I consider myself a pretty good online researcher."

He raised his eyebrows. "You mean recently? I don't think I have . . . what was the editorial about . . . that might jog my memory."

"Allegedly, Bunny did a scathing takedown of Mac as a greedy and corrupt developer and . . . also she ranted about me and the Jacaranda Gardens community garden, saying it was a manipulative ploy to distract from the condo development, rather than for the benefit of the community."

His eye widened in what I interpreted as his consternation at even imagining such shenanigans from his late wife. "What? No. I certainly don't know about anything like that. And I can't imagine Bunny writing any attacks like that on individuals. She was a straight shooter. She would have contacted you for a comment beforehand too. She might criticize people's policies or behavior certainly, possibly with implications to their character, I suppose, but all her opinion pieces were based on facts, not innuendos."

"So you weren't aware of an editorial about Jacaranda Gardens? You think it was a fake editorial then?"

"Absolutely. Bunny would never write something like that."

"Not even about a rival? She wasn't angry enough with Mac to go after him in an editorial?" I paused. "Um, was all well in her life otherwise? Anything you can think of? Some dispute she had with anyone else? I'm trying to get at motive. Any disagreements over money or her campaign maybe? Or with her friends or family?"

Peter glanced at his feet before looking me in the eyes. "We had our ups and downs like everyone, but we were happily married, if that's what you're getting at. We'd had a rough patch this year because she got sick from Covid in January, before either of us had had a chance to get vaccinated. She started to lose her sense of smell so we both got tested. When we both tested positive, Bunny blamed me for infecting her because I was asymptomatic. Of course, it could have been the other way around, but she didn't accept that. She was really annoyed, and it definitely stressed our relationship. Her symptoms lingered and she had long-haul side effects, which didn't help matters."

"Oh, that's a tough situation. Sorry. I didn't mean to pry . . ."

I so did. But at least I got an answer to my question about their marriage. "Again, so sorry for your loss."

His expression softened. He seemed relieved. "Her kids are another story though. As I mentioned to you on the phone, I'm afraid they both caused Bunny a lot of grief in the past. One's a deadbeat and the other one not much better."

"Did she fight with them a lot?"

"Not lately that I know of. She hardly had any contact with them since I've known her. That is, until Bunny got Covid. After she recovered from that, she and Scarlett had gotten closer. Scarlett would bring her mother vitamins and smoothies from a health food place to build up her strength."

"And her son?"

He adjusted his glasses. "Like I said, none of them kept in touch with each other much."

"Do you have any idea who might have written a fake editorial and then leaked it?"

He shrugged. "None. No idea. I'll ask around and see if anyone knows anything about it. I'll let you know if I find out anything."

"Great. Oh, one last thing. What are your plans for the *Sentinel* now that Bunny's gone?"

The color drained from his face, as if he'd just seen Bunny's ghost. He spluttered and coughed before he spoke. "She was approached recently with an offer to buy her out by the franchise *Community Scoop*."

I double blinked. "I thought that was more like an advertising vehicle with kind of an open-source approach to news."

His color had switched to bright red. "That's one way to view it, I suppose. But online news is where it's at right now."

"You mean there wouldn't even be an actual print newspaper anymore?"

He pursed his lips. "Trend of the future, I'm afraid."

"Bunny wasn't actually going to sell the *Sentinel*, was she?"

Peter crossed his arms. "No. Dead set against it. But now it might be the right choice."

I pushed my slipping purse strap up my shoulder. "For who? Certainly not the reporters. Or for Santa Sofia."

He rubbed his stubbled chin. "Well, we'll see. I have to leave for Canada in a week to direct a film. I have to figure out what to do. I'm a busy person and can't be overseeing a newspaper in addition to all the other work I have." He made an exaggerated twist of his wrist to check the time. "Speaking of work, I have a lot to do."

"Thank you for your time!" I rummaged through my purse and found a business card. "Here's my number. If you think of anything else, please give me a call."

"Of course. Anything to help get to the root of who killed Bunny."

In the parking lot I ran into Simon again.

He motioned me over to his car as his gaze roved the lot. "I have to run to shoot some pics of a small brush fire, but I overheard a few of my colleagues chatting about something I think might interest you."

I rested a hand on my hip. "Oh, really. What were they talking about?"

Simon clasped his hands. "How Peter and Bunny were fighting all the time during the past year."

I nodded. "Because of the pandemic? Everyone was cranky and on edge."

He pointed at me. "Partially correct. But Bunny was mad because she accused Peter of being selfish and risking her health and her staff's health when everyone else was self-isolating and taking care to be socially distanced."

I cocked my head to the side. "What does that mean? Was he an anti-masker?"

"I don't know exactly. But I got a sense it was something more personal than that, if you know what I mean."

I tilted my head to the other side. "No, I don't know what you mean. An anti-vaxxer?"

Simon's gaze roamed the lot again. "Must I spell it out for you, Tory?"

I chuckled. "Apparently so. What are you saying?"

"It sounded to me that they were hinting that Peter was unfaithful. It's gossip, mind you. When I asked for details, they said nothing firm, so they didn't want to say any more."

Having an affair was bad enough. But during the pandemic? Peter sounded like a risk-taker who valued thrills over caution and safety.

"Wow. Thanks, Simon. If true, that's quite a revelation."

Especially in light of how Peter had just sworn to me they'd been happily married.

A police car entered the far end of the parking lot.

My heart started to beat faster.

"Okay, nice seeing you, Simon. I need to get back to the office. Thanks again." I jumped in my car and exited from the opposite end of the parking lot.

I hoped Adrian hadn't seen me.

CHAPTER 12

As I drove back to my office I reflected on my visit to the *Sentinel*. Depending on who I believed, Peter and Bunny either had a good marriage with its ups and downs or a rocky marriage because Peter was cheating. And according to Peter, Bunny and her kids were estranged. But if Peter was lying about being happily married, maybe he was also lying about Bunny's kids. That was the problem once you suspected someone of lying. Even on the occasions when they might be telling you the truth, you tended not to believe them because they'd lied to you before. The boy who cried wolf syndrome.

Perhaps Peter led a double life. He was nice to Bunny in public, but a cheater behind her back. Maybe Bunny knew he'd been cheating and had been okay with it up until the pandemic lockdown, when mingling with someone else not only betrayed her but also risked her health. I couldn't think of any better way of determining the truth than tracking down her kids to get their side of the story.

Simon called me as I pulled into the Benning Brothers parking lot.

"We both left so quickly I forgot to mention what the buzz on Bunny's kids was. The staffers said the kids occasionally stopped by the *Sentinel* office."

I parked in my usual spot. "Really? Peter said she hardly ever saw them."

"Peter was never at the *Sentinel*. He wouldn't have seen them anyway."

"Did they say how often or whether they seemed to get along?"

"They said the daughter visited her mother more than the brother. They gave me the impression it was pretty frequently, especially after Bunny had gotten over Covid. They said the daughter was a spoiled brat."

"Hmm. Maybe the possibility of losing her mother knocked some sense into her and made her appreciate her more. And what about the son?"

"They only recalled seeing him once or twice during the time they've worked there."

I unbuckled my seat belt. "Do they both live in Santa Sofia?"

"Yes. As far as I know."

I slung my purse over my shoulder. "Okay. Great. Thanks, Simon."

"I'll keep my ears and eyes open."

"Appreciate it." I got out of my car and locked it, and headed to my office.

As soon as I got to my desk, I jumped on my computer and tried to learn more about Scarlett Hare. I still couldn't find a home address for her. I did hit the jackpot with Scarlett's Facebook and Instagram accounts, however, with a treasure trove of selfies, including photos of her waitressing at a place called Wargo's River Ranch Barbeque Restaurant and Saloon, where country-western acts were featured on weekends. I got excited until I checked the dates of the photos and realized they were taken before the pandemic. Except for the last one. She'd posted a photo from the restaurant two days ago. Looked like Wargo's had reopened and was back in business. It opened for lunch at eleven thirty.

I called Ashley. "Whatcha doin'?"

"Okay. I know that fake folksy style. You always use it when you're trying to persuade me to do something you think I'll disapprove of. To play it down."

"Wow. You know me well."

"Never forget that."

I laughed. "Understood. Okay, I'll come clean. I want to try to track down Bunny's daughter Scarlett to see if she can shed any light on who would want Bunny dead."

"You mean to ask her about Bunny's marriage."

"Damn, you're good. Got me again. Yes. I found out she works at a bar in Gilton—"

"And you want me to accompany you there tonight. Tory, you know Adrian would be so mad if he knew you were poking your nose around where it doesn't belong."

"You're slipping. Yes, I want you to accompany me to the bar where she works. But no, not tonight. I might be a bold sleuth, but I'm not stupid. Anytime I come across a news story about a bar fracas it always seems to be in Gilton. It can get pretty sketchy there at night since it's a magnet for motorcycle gangs. Last thing I need is a belligerent drunken biker who's trying to hit on me."

"I second that."

"That's why I thought it would be safer if we venture there during the day. Like today. Like in a half hour or so."

"Did you not hear what I said about Adrian getting mad? Or are you just ignoring that part?"

"Choosing to ignore. What harm is there in just going for a bite to eat and some observation? Scarlett might not even be there. Maybe she only works nights. But it's worth a shot."

Ashley sighed heavily. "Okay. But I want to drive. I can only afford an hour and a half, tops. I'm preparing for a case. That way I can control the length of our adventure and keep it from turning into a stakeout."

"I don't mind driving."

"Tory. Take it or leave it. That's my final offer."

"Okay, okay. Jeez. You drive a hard bargain."

"Good. See you in ten."

I was waiting outside in the Benning Brothers parking lot when Ashley drove up in her black BMW.

I hopped in and appraised her outfit, a cream-colored blouse and tan pants cinched with a brown leather belt. "You look nice."

"Thanks, boo." She glanced at me and smiled. "So do you."

Ten minutes later Ashley and I were on the 101 Freeway

heading north. Gilton was a community very different from Santa Sofia, yet they also shared a lot of common qualities found in many of the cities in Santa Barbara County. Santa Sofia was home to an artsy community whose art galleries lent a sophisticated charm to the small-town atmosphere and was located on the coast. Gilton was located inland, home to mainly blue-collar workers, yet was also home to a Chumash Indian casino and a luxury dude ranch, hidden in the hills above the town. Santa Sofia had a glamorous aura, famous for the five-star Hotel Santa Sofia resort, a favorite getaway that attracted the rich and famous from Los Angeles. Gilton also drew the same crowd to its luxury dude ranch for more of a Wild West experience, replete with horseback riding and rodeos. And while Gilton held the distinction of having one of the highest overall crime rates in the county, my personal experience led me to believe Santa Sofia's recent death by homicide body count was quickly catching up.

As we breezed along, I observed the consequences of California's drought on the freeway landscape. The towering, drought-tolerant, blue gum eucalyptus trees (*Eucalyptus globulus*) seemed to be holding their own, but the grass was brown and dried out. I spotted a few Russian thistles (*Salsola tragus*), aka tumbleweeds, lurking on the shoulder, waiting to roll out in the path of oncoming cars with the next wind gust.

When we passed the exit for the casino, I knew we were getting close. We took the second of only two exits for Gilton, which led to a small downtown. We turned onto its two-laned main drag, passing an animal feed and supply store, a country general store whose display windows featured manikins in studded and bejeweled cowboy hats, western-styled clothing and boots, and a liquor store with a giant lottery sign in its window. At the end of the street was Wargo's River Ranch Barbeque Restaurant and Saloon. Wargo's was a throwback to the Wild West. Except instead of horses reined to a hitching post, there were pickup trucks and motorcycles in the dusty parking lot.

Ashley looked over at me with wide eyes but said nothing.

I knew what she was thinking.

I cleared my throat. "Look. If it looks unfriendly, we'll leave right away, okay? I'm sorry. I really didn't think it would look so stereotypically hostile."

"Seriously? Look at the playbill tacked to the hitching post. It says the Dupre Brothers are playing this weekend. There are eight of them."

"Nothing wrong with big families."

Although, admittedly, they had more of a *Sons of Anarchy* than a *Seven Brides for Seven Brothers* vibe. I studied the playbill, which pictured eight bearded, heavily tattooed and pierced men in denim overalls without shirts, all with long hair poking out of cowboy hats, ranging in age from about eighteen to forty. "Looks like they're only appearing this weekend. Since it's a weekday, maybe it will attract a different crowd."

"Right." She stretched out her response and rolled her eyes.

We climbed three wooden plank steps to the entrance. I breathed in deeply. "Wow! That's a barbeque aroma to die for."

Ashley gave me the side-eye. "Not literally, I hope. But agree. That smells absolutely delicious."

We entered through the louvered, swinging double doors that looked right out of a western movie set. When our eyes adjusted from the bright sun outdoors to the dark saloon inside, I was relieved to see two families with kids at round tables. The men eating at the bar looked benign enough, none of the motorcycle gang member stereotypes dressed in leather clothing with skull and crossbones insignias that I'd pictured in my head. They looked more like construction workers for the most part, which jibed with the pickups outside. Behind the bar was a female server. It was Scarlett Hare, who was easy to recognize from her Facebook pics with her shoulder-length red hair. Her off-the-shoulder blouse and short skirt showcased the freckles that covered her face and body.

"That's Bunny's daughter."

"Are you sure?"

"Positive."

We sidled up to the bar.

Scarlett looked at us and barely cracked a perfunctory smile. "What can I get you?"

My eyes scanned the blackboard menu over the bar. "What would you recommend?"

"Our house cheeseburger is our bestseller."

"Sounds good. And an iced tea please."

Ashley cleared her throat. "Make that two."

After we paid, we climbed up on the barstools and leaned on the slightly sticky bar. Scarlett dropped off our iced teas and scooted away before I could ask her anything. When she delivered our food a few minutes later, I knew it was now or never.

"I just wanted to say I'm sorry for your loss."

Her startled look rested on me. "Excuse me?"

"I knew your mother. Just wanted to express my condolences."

She stood up straighter and adjusted her top. "Thank you. How did you find me here?"

There were times in the past when I've stretched the truth a bit in order to obtain key information. Sometimes that worked. Especially if I'd rehearsed a bit and anticipated responses. Sometimes it backfired and nearly got me killed. I wanted to try and avoid that. Since this had been a seat-of-the-pants adventure, I surrendered to the realization that honesty was the best policy in this instance.

I took a deep breath, taking in the tantalizing aroma of my charbroiled burger. "Honestly, I was remembering Bunny and started to google her and came across your Facebook page in the process. I couldn't find your address to send flowers so decided this was the next best thing."

Sometimes the truth wasn't the best way to go either, if the way Ashley paused mid-chew to look at me with wide eyes was any indicator.

Scarlett cocked her head, as if sizing me up and trying to tell if I was legit. "Thank you."

I glanced at the melted cheese on my burger and my mouth watered. "What do you think happened? Do you know anything about what might have led to her murder?"

"The police are on the right track. Mac McGregor, her rival in the mayor race, obviously."

"But why?"

"Because my mother was beating him in the race for mayor."

Ashley took a bite of her burger and gave it a thumbs-up as she savored it.

I unfolded a paper napkin. "Oh. I thought they were about even."

Scarlett tapped her foot. "Even if they were, he wanted to win at any cost, apparently."

I sipped my iced tea. "Were you close to your mother?"

Scarlett sighed impatiently. "Why do you ask?"

I placed my glass back on the bar. "No real reason. Just curious."

Scarlett shifted her weight. "As a matter of fact, we were."

"When was the last time you saw her, if I may ask?"

"After she got Covid. We talked on the phone and did FaceTime."

"Yeah, I heard she was sick. Sorry. Did you ever visit her in person after she got better?"

Scarlett tapped her foot again. "No. It wasn't that bad. She was busy with her campaign, trying to make up for lost time. We planned to see each other soon though."

I fidgeted with my silverware. "And your brother? Did he contact your mom when she was sick too?"

"Stone? I haven't seen or spoken to him for a couple of years."

"You don't know whether he was in touch with your mother when she was sick?"

"Nope."

"Why is that?"

"Let's just say he and I had a falling out. I don't want to talk about it. It's in the past."

I glanced at Ashley, who'd nearly finished half her burger already. "You haven't reached out to each other since your mother's death?"

"No."

"Were you close to your stepfather?"

Scarlett tossed back her head slightly. "Peter? He wasn't my stepfather. He married my mother when I was eighteen."

"So no?"

Scarlett crossed her arms. "Not that it's any of your business, but no. It's hard to be close to someone who you know is cheating on your mother."

Ashley and I exchanged glances.

I sat up straighter. "What? Peter was cheating on your mother? Did your mother know?"

Scarlett surveyed the floor. "Doubt it. She was too busy with her precious paper and saving the world."

I lowered my voice a bit. "Does Peter know you know?"

"I don't know. I do know my dumb brother told Peter he knew about him having an affair with Mac's wife, Kaley."

I shot Ashley a look. This revelation made her pause mid-bite again.

I placed both my hands on the bar and pushed back in my seat. "Wait, slow down. Peter was having an affair with Kaley McGregor? And your brother confronted him? Wow. How did that go over? I'm guessing not well."

Scarlett patted her skirt. "You guessed correctly. I hadn't spoken to Stone for a while before that, and that move just validated my decision."

My phone pinged. I glanced at the screen. A text from Jake. It was about Bunny's preliminary autopsy results.

Ashley studied my face. "What?"

I lowered my voice as I read his text. "Jake said the initial autopsy has come in."

Ashley turned her back to Scarlett and leaned in. "And the results confirm blunt-force trauma. Am I right?"

I shook my head. I reread Jake's text as my heartbeat quickened. I put my hand to my mouth. "No. I can't believe it. Bunny was poisoned."

Ashley raised her voice. "Bunny was poisoned?"

"Louder, for the people at the back of the restaurant." I shook my head at Ashley. "So much for discretion."

Scarlett dropped her empty tray. "What? My mother was poisoned? How? With what?"

I looked at my phone's screen. "I have no idea. But good questions that the full autopsy, I'm sure, will answer."

"An autopsy will answer everything except who poisoned her." Ashley folded her arms.

"I'm sure it was Mac." Scarlett spoke quickly.

I shook my head. "Don't be so sure. I don't know what the police will make of this. This sheds a different light on her death. Until we find out more, it shakes everything up in terms of motive, opportunity and means."

Scarlett narrowed her brow and stared at me intently. "What do you mean?"

Ashley wiped her hands on a napkin. "Well, for one thing, it diminishes the crime of passion theory. Poison seems like it had to have been premeditated."

I rested my elbows on the bar. "I don't know when she was poisoned, but if it was earlier in the day, I don't think it could have been Mac because he was with me all morning."

Ashley drummed her fingers on her plate. "So someone poisoned her, and then someone hit her on the head, why? To make it look like a crime of passion?"

"That's my thinking. And to implicate Mac."

Scarlett was silent this whole time. A family of three sat down at a table next to the bar and Scarlett said she needed to take their order.

Once Scarlett was out of earshot, Ashley let out a whistle. "What do you make of Miss Scarlett."

I took another sip of iced tea. "I don't know. She's kind of hard to read."

"Agree."

"Not quite the spoiled brat I was expecting. She seems more disgruntled than spoiled to me."

Ashley wiped her hands on a napkin again. "You haven't

touched your food. We should leave soon. If you don't want it now, wrap it up and take it home with you, because it was delicious."

I wracked my brain for any other questions I might ask Scarlett before we left. My gaze rested on a familiar face across the room. It was the good-looking guy with the sardonic humor who I'd spoken to briefly at the community garden right after the disastrous TV interview. He was staring at me.

I spoke in a low voice. "Don't look now but a cute guy I met at Jacaranda Gardens is heading our way."

Ashley performed a subtle panoramic gaze of the restaurant. "Oh, he's super cute."

He walked over to us and looked at my plate. "Howdy. I see you ordered cheeseburgers. Good choice."

I gave my plate a nudge. "Oh, we just stopped by to talk to someone, not to eat."

"Speak for yourself. Hi, I'm Ashley." Ashley flipped her hand up in a modified wave.

The man smiled at Ashley. "Hi. I'm Luke." He turned to me. "And you're Tory Benning. I watched you film your TV interview at Jacaranda Gardens. You're here to see Scarlett?"

"Why, yes. Do you know her?"

"No, not really. But I know of her. She's Denny Wargo's girlfriend."

"Who's Denny Wargo? The namesake of Wargo's?" Ashley sat up straighter on the barstool.

"Correct. He's the shady owner of this joint."

Ashley twisted her mouth to the side. "Why shady?"

"He's a gambler. Gamblers often run up big debts to nasty people. Sometimes drives them to do bad things to get money to pay their debts."

I smiled slightly. "How do you know all this?"

"I was hired to investigate him."

He slid his card across the bar.

Ashley picked it up and read it, "Lucas Barrett, Private Investigator."

I leaned closer to Ashley to glance at his card. "You're a private detective. Here in Santa Sofia."

He nodded.

Ashley tapped his card. "Hired by whom?"

"Bunny Hare." He paused and looked at his feet. "She wanted me to follow her kids because she thought they were involved in some shady stuff."

I dipped a French fry into the ketchup on my plate. "Then she turns up dead. Were they up to something shady? I say this because based on my experience, often when a person hires a PI, their suspicions are correct. Either that or they project their own nefarious behavior onto others." I took a bite of the French fry.

Ashley nodded. "Agree. Or they use the PI for nefarious reasons. To get dirt."

I dabbed my mouth with a napkin. "Let me say that my friend Mac McGregor is a prime suspect in Bunny's murder, so if you're in any way involved in trying to incriminate him . . ."

Luke's brown eyes twinkled. "Good to know. For the record, I always view my role as an evidence gatherer. I'm interested in determining the truth, wherever it leads me. I don't have an agenda. At least in my professional life."

Ashley reached in her bag for a business card and handed it to him. "I'm representing Mac McGregor." She drilled her gaze into me and nodded.

"Oh, let me give you my card too. I'd appreciate it if you'd let me know if you find anything that could help prove Mac wasn't involved in Bunny's death."

He tilted his head down, and when he looked up again, he locked eyes with me. I felt like someone had just looked into my soul.

His phone rang and he checked the screen and moved away. "I need to take this."

Ashley kicked my leg and mouthed, "Hot."

He was only on the call for a few minutes. "I need to go. Hope to see you around."

Ashley looked at me and fanned herself with her napkin.

"Phew. It's getting hot in here."

I smiled. "What?"

"You know very well what. The chemistry, tension, whatever you want to call it, between you two?"

"You think?"

"I know."

I held my chin. "I'm still in shock about what Scarlett said. I wonder if Mac knows about Kaley and Peter?"

"I don't know about that." Ashley checked the time on her phone. "But I have to get back to work. Wrap up your burger."

I followed Ashley's suggestion and wrapped up my food. "Wait."

Ashley took a sip of tea through her straw and froze. "Are you thinking what I'm thinking?"

"That now two more people had a motive to kill Bunny—Peter and Kaley."

She gripped my arm. "Yes. Do you think one of them did it?"

"Maybe. Or maybe both of them were in cahoots?"

Ashley nodded. "And then tried to make Mac the patsy?"

"That way they get rid of both of their spouses. One dead. The other goes to jail."

Ashley tilted her head. "Fun theory. But I have one question."

"What's that?"

"Why not just get divorced?"

I came down to earth hard.

"You're right. Why risk going to jail themselves unless—"

Ashley made a sucking sound with her straw. "Peter stands to inherit big bucks with Bunny dead? Oh my God. I bet that's it."

"But what's Kaley's angle?"

Ashley slid off the barstool. "Maybe with Mac in prison she'd have more control of their money? I don't know."

"Yeah. Maybe"

Ashley raised her chin. "Ready to go?"

CHAPTER 13

On the ride back Ashley focused on the road while I enjoyed my cheeseburger and mulled over the autopsy results.

"Yup. Poisoning opens up a lot more possibilities for suspects." I paused, waiting for Ashley to chime in.

I glanced over at her. She was still intent on driving.

I scrunched up the wrapping from the cheeseburger. "But I'm afraid Mac is still in the mix."

I turned to see if perhaps her facial expression would give me a hint on her thinking. But her face gave away nothing, except her intense concentration on driving. Her gaze switched back and forth between the road straight ahead and the rearview mirror.

Exasperated by her lack of response, I let out an exaggerated sigh. "What do you think?"

She shot me a glance. There was fear in her eyes. "I think we're being followed. That's what I think."

"No! Really?" I checked her face for signs of joking. There were none.

I twisted around in my seat. Traffic was moderately heavy, as always after the lunch hour.

"There are a lot of cars behind us. Which one is following us?"

"The silver one."

My body tensed and I snuck another peek behind us. "Practically all the cars behind us look silver to me. Some are silvery gray, some silvery white, others silvery blue. Which one is following us?"

Ashley's chest heaved as she inhaled and exhaled deeply. "The silvery silver one."

I turned around longer this time to study the school of silver autos behind us and couldn't for the life of me distinguish one from another to get to silvery silver.

I sighed. "Can you count back and tell me which one? Maybe I'll be able to locate the one that's following us that way."

Ashley sighed loudly and kept her eyes on the rearview mirror for several seconds straight while she softly counted to herself. "I think it's the fourth car behind us."

I counted back. "I can't tell what kind of car it is or whether it's a male or female driver, can you?"

"Nope."

"How long has it been following us?"

"I noticed it about five minutes after we left Wargo's."

We were coming to an intersection just as the light turned to yellow. Ashley sped up like the car in front of us and made it through as it turned to red.

Ashley checked the mirror and let out a wild hoot. "Yay. They didn't make the light. I'm going to try and lose them for good now."

"Drive to the police station. That's what Jake did."

"Okay. Good idea."

We wove in and out of residential blocks.

I pivoted halfway in my seat. "No one seems to be behind us now. I think we've lost them."

Ashley pumped her arm. "Yes! No Payne, no gain." She turned to me and spoke slowly. "Like my last name, Payne. Like you can't hurt me if you can't catch me."

I laughed. "Oh, I got it. As in no pun, no fun."

We both giggled like the schoolgirls we were at heart.

She glanced at me. "No need to go to the police station now, right?"

"Right. No point now."

"I'll let Adrian know. I told him about the other times."

I made a note to be careful what I told Ashley, given her propensity to tell Adrian everything.

We pulled up to Benning Brothers.

"Thanks for driving. And good luck on your case prep."

"Thanks. What are you going to do now?"

"Run home and check on my menagerie and then go to the rescue place and take more measurements."

"Weren't you just there?"

"Yeah. But every time I've gone there, I've been too distracted, either by Lily or Heath Grant."

We both laughed.

The dogs were barking when I got to the front door. Iris was right at the door. Lily was still in the gated area near the back door. Based on her easy adjustment thus far, I had a hunch she'd be fine having the run of the house when I was gone, but it wouldn't hurt to keep her separated from Iris and Otis a little longer just to play it safe. Otis had made himself scarce, in protest I assumed, now that he was outnumbered by two female dogs. I took the Pommies outside, refreshed their water bowls, and placed Lily in the gated area again.

"I'll be back soon."

I hummed along to a Stray Kids song as I drove back to work, attempting a Korean line every now and then. Back at my desk I checked my emails. One from Jules at Pom Pom Rescue about picking up Lily's crate at the shelter. And another one from a principal at a local architectural firm. She asked if I was interested in joining their team for Santa Sofia's Natural History Museum's Arboretum and Botanical Garden. The original arboretum and botanical garden had been partially destroyed by a wildfire and then finished off by a huge mudslide. I responded with an enthusiastic "yes, please" and started to jot down some notes as ideas popped into my head.

I took a break to do another online search for Stone Hare. He had a Facebook account, but he hadn't posted anything for years. I went to the site I'd looked at before and wrote down the address listed for him. I clicked on maps. His address wasn't too far from my office. I decided to go and cruise by to check it out.

Ten minutes later, I was on Alameda Street, a bustling thoroughfare lined with tall skinny palm trees, aka Mexican fan palms (*Washingtonia robusta*), a couple blocks south and parallel to the Avenue in a mixed residential and commercial area. The address I'd found online for Stone Hare turned out to be a small apartment complex, with the tucked-under, front carport parking that made it vulnerable to collapse in an earthquake. I drove by slowly and then drove around the block again. There was a handyman in a gray coverall and a baseball cap sweeping the front entrance.

I decided to park.

I strolled up to the guy. "Hi there. Sorry to bother you, I was wondering whether you know Stone Hare. I think he lives in this building."

He lifted his head to reveal a red beard and freckles. "Who wants to know?"

"Oh. I'm an acquaintance of his mother who just passed away and I—"

"I'm Stone."

That I'd already guessed, given the likeness of his coloring to Scarlett's.

"What do you want?"

"My friend, Mac McGregor, is a person of interest in your mother's case, and I don't think he would hurt a fly, let alone a lovely person like your mother. I'm trying to help him by trying to find out who did."

"I don't know."

I took a step closer. "You have no idea? Did she have any enemies? Anyone she fought with lately?"

"Not that I know of but . . ."

"But what?

He paused and looked down, as if compiling information.

He lifted his head. "Except for the threats."

"She'd gotten threats? What kind of threats?"

He squinted. "I don't know. They were kind of vague. Notes wrapped around rocks. Like don't make trouble. And to back off."

Notes wrapped around rocks. Just like the one left at Bunny's house the night before she died. Peter hadn't mentioned anything about there being other notes.

"Recently?"

He adjusted his cap. "Yep. At least twice."

I put my hand to my chest. "Oh my goodness. Did she know who was threatening her?"

He rested on his broom. "She claimed she didn't know."

"You sound like you didn't believe her."

He pressed his lips inward. "I believed her. But she didn't believe me when I told her who I thought had sent them."

I shifted my weight. "Who did you think sent them?"

"Mac McGregor."

My stomach flipped. "Why did you think he'd sent them?"

"Because my mother was beating him in the race for mayor."

Just what Scarlett had said. They both believed Mac was guilty.

I exhaled hard. "When was the last time you saw your mother?"

Stone scratched his head. "I don't know. Maybe a month ago."

I rested a hand on my hip. "Were you on good terms?"

"Good enough. She wasn't thrilled with my employment status, or should I say my lack of full-time employment."

I nodded. "What about Peter?"

"What about him?"

I crossed my arms. "Do you get along with him?"

He lowered his eyes. "I guess. I don't have much contact with him. I never see him."

My phone pinged.

It was a text from Heath Grant. *Are you free to have a drink around five at the house? I'm absolutely in love with the place and would love to celebrate with the person who made it all possible.*

I felt flushed. I checked the time on my phone. Four thirty. My heart was beating out of my chest as I thought for a minute. What the heck. I texted him back and accepted his invitation.

Stone had moved to the rear of the building to continue his sweeping.

"I need to take off. Here's my card. Please contact me if you think of anything else, related to the threats, or whatever."

I started toward my car and remembered I'd forgotten to ask Stone the million-dollar question. I caught up with him again near the trash bins in the back of the building.

"Hey, one thing I forgot to ask you. How did your mother and Peter get along?"

His face turned dark red.

He sneered. "Let's just say he earned the name Peter the cheater."

I flinched slightly, taken aback by his mean tone. "Okay, then. Thanks."

I was tempted to press for more details, to see if he corroborated his sister's revelation about Kaley, but I chickened out. I'd learned to trust my gut long ago, and poking a hornet's nest rarely ended well.

I drove up the winding road to my father's house, excited as a schoolgirl who'd just gotten a love note from her crush. What was going on? What about Jake? Was I excited about Heath Grant to distract myself from really facing how I felt, or didn't feel, about Jake? I was so confused. As if Jake had been able to hear my thoughts, he called.

"What are you up to? I stopped by your office and you weren't there."

"Up to?" All of a sudden, my car felt uncomfortably warm. "Nothing much. Just left Pom Pom Rescue. I needed to get more specs."

The lie flowed from my lips more easily than I liked, but I felt justified. If I told him I'd spoken with both Scarlett and Stone, I was pretty sure he'd snitch on me to Adrian. Or at the very least, scold me.

"Oh, good. So, are you off for the day? Do you want to meet for a drink and finally take a minute to talk?"

"Um . . . I can't right now. I'm on my way to my father's house."

"Something wrong?"

"No. Not really." I turned down the A/C to the lowest temperature. "I don't know. I'm feeling confused. I guess we do need to talk."

"I meant something wrong at your dad's house. Like a dripping faucet."

Shoot. I should have kept my big mouth shut.

I cleared my throat. "Oh."

"I didn't realize there was something wrong between us."

"No. There's not. I didn't mean to give you that impression." I turned the fan way up.

"Then what's wrong?"

I giggled.

Or rather, I meant to giggle and it came out as a fake witch's cackle. "Nothing's wrong. I think the pandemic did a number on me and I'm just questioning everything. How about I give you a call after I leave my father's house and we can meet then?"

"Fine. You never told me what's going on with your father's house."

"Okay, I'm here. Talk soon."

I pulled into the driveway feeling guilty and flustered. At least I hadn't outright lied to Jake, so there was that. Okay, maybe I did. I really had to sort out my feelings before . . . before what, Tory, before you got involved with someone else? First it was that new PI, Luke what's-his-name, and now a famous actor.

I shook my head as if doing so would clear out the confusion.

Prior to the pandemic, I'd thought I had it all figured out. Then the pandemic hit and turned everything upside down. Were my feelings for Jake based on gratitude for his remarkable friendship or on love? Obviously, the jury was still out.

Heath Grant emerged from the front door and strolled over to my car. "Hey, landlord. Good to see you again." He flicked his longish brown hair out of his eyes.

Why was it that if any other guy wore the same basic gray T-shirt, shorts, and slides Heath was wearing, it wouldn't even register, but on his tall, lean frame with his washboard abs and broad shoulders they looked so incredibly hot? And why did a corny line like "Hey, landlord," which I'd normally categorize as cringe-worthy, seem so cute when uttered by him? Why, Tory? Because he's friggin' Heath Grant, probably the handsomest movie star alive, that's why.

My hands and whole body were sweaty. Mercifully, he didn't extend his hand.

"Hi. Same. Glad to hear you're liking the house."

"Loving it! It's so private and secluded. Just what I was looking for. And the interior is wonderful. The kitchen is great—I cook for a hobby, so I appreciate the chef-grade appliances. In fact, I'll be doing most of the cooking for a small dinner party I'm having this weekend. Would love if you could join us."

My knees nearly buckled. This cowboy seemed hot to trot. Slow your roll. But like the "Hey, landlord" corniness, showing early eagerness to get together from a hot guy hit differently.

"That sounds lovely. What night?"

"Friday."

"I'll have to get back to you if that's okay. I have a friend I promised to get together with this weekend, and I don't know which night it will be."

He smiled slightly. "No problem. Just text me when you find out."

Hmm. He could have said bring your friend. But he didn't. Did that mean he was fine if I wasn't able to make it? Did he really want me to attend or was it just a friendly gesture?

"Thanks. Sounds like fun."

His smile broadened. "Great. Now, how about that special landlord's tour."

We went around the house, focusing mainly on the new features of the bathrooms and kitchen, as well as the new intercom and sound system, solar panels, remote-operated shades, backup generator, and computerized home security system.

"I'm surprised your realtor didn't debrief you."

"Oh, she tried to. But she tends to be long-winded, and I didn't have the energy to go over it all and deal with the movers too. My assistant, who normally would have dealt with the brunt of moving details, had a family emergency, so instead of having a relaxing time getting together with old friends at Gaviota Grove, I ended up dealing with most of the move all by myself."

Like most normal people have to do.

Outside I showed him where to shut off the gas and water in case of an earthquake. "Also, this house has been retrofitted for earthquakes."

"Good to know."

"By the way, what's it like at Gaviota Grove? Seems a tad antiquated to have an exclusive men's club nowadays."

"Incredibly antiquated. That's what we have been meeting about recently. Opening up the membership. The terms of some of the outdated board members just expired and the remaining board members, like me and Mac McGregor, have all been pushing for more inclusiveness for years. So, we finally feel like we can bring the club up to the twenty-first century."

I sucked in air trying to suppress my excitement, not only because an old bastion of male elitism was coming down, but because Heath had brought up Mac organically.

"You mentioned you knew Mac the other day. Where do you know him from?" I followed Heath back inside to the kitchen.

"Wine?"

"Only half a glass, please."

He took a chilled open bottle from the fridge. "Red okay?"

I nodded.

"Mac's an old friend. We go way back. We met when we were both poor struggling actors many years ago." He handed me a half-filled wineglass.

"Mac was once an actor? That I didn't know."

"Yes. And a good one. Didn't get a break like me. But yeah, he was a pretty good actor."

I held my glass with both hands. "I assume you know Mac has been questioned extensively by the police in regard to Bunny Hare's murder?"

Heath leaned on the kitchen counter. "Yeah, he told me all about it. He's hanging in there."

"His wife, Kaley, asked me to help her prove Mac's innocence."

He raised his eyebrows. "Are you kidding?"

I blinked. "What do you mean? She's distraught he's under suspicion."

Again with the raised eyebrows. "That may well be. Although I suspect Kaley has her own agenda. But I have a feeling you already probably know that."

"You mean her affair with Peter, Bunny's husband?"

"Bingo."

"Mac knows about it?"

Heath sipped his wine. "He just recently found out. Apparently, it's been going on for a couple of years."

"Really? That long? And he just found out?"

He nodded. "Sometimes the spouse is the last to know."

I wondered if he was referring to his own divorce.

I took a small sip of wine. "How is he taking it?"

"He's been down the same road before."

"Haven't we all."

There was an awkward silence, when it seemed we both wondered where to go next as we tiptoed through relationship territory.

He swirled the wine in his glass and then gazed at me. "I've read about your late husband's murder. Seemed like a great guy. Sorry for your loss."

"The best." I felt my face heat up, realizing, once again, that Milo's murder had increased my online profile. "Yes, I've read about your recent divorce too. Sorry."

He nodded.

I took a deep breath. "You don't think Mac killed Bunny, do you?"

"No. Why would he? If Kaley asked for a divorce, he'd give it to her. This isn't his first rodeo."

I set my wineglass down on the counter. "Do you think Peter killed Bunny?"

"If he wanted out of their marriage, I'd assume he'd just get divorced."

"Unless there was some type of financial benefit to killing

her?" I drummed my wineglass.

"I know for a fact his production company just swung a big investment deal, so he's far from hurting financially."

"What's his reputation in Hollywood?"

"Good. He's an award-winning director."

I tipped my glass for a last sip, weighing Heath's reaction to Mac and Peter as possible suspects. "So you don't think either Mac or Peter is capable of murder?"

Heath chuckled. "That's not exactly what I said." The smile left his face. "If I've learned anything from the list of heroes and villains I've played it's that anyone's capable of murder, given the right set of circumstances. I just don't think either Mac or Peter had compelling reasons to murder Bunny."

The fleeting steeliness of his gaze for a moment convinced me that even he might be Bunny's murderer. But then, he was an award-winning actor.

"Okay, thanks for your insights. I need to get going."

Heath's face softened into a charming smile. "My pleasure. Let me know about Friday. Hope you can make it."

As soon as I was back in my car, I called Ashley.

"I'm so glad you answered, otherwise I would have burst. I have so much to tell you. I just had a drink with Heath Grant." I screamed the last part.

We both squealed.

"More on that in a minute but, first, let me tell you about what Peter Yusem told me."

I started to give her a blow-by-blow retelling of my time with Peter at the *Sentinel*.

"Hold on. This sounds like it's going to take some time and I'm famished. I have about a half hour more of work to wrap up before I call it a day. How about I order takeout, my treat, from that same barbeque place where we had lunch—if you wouldn't mind picking it up. I haven't stopped thinking about those cheeseburgers. They were to die for."

I chuckled. "Wargo's? The place I had to twist your arm to go to? Okay. That cheeseburger was good. Probably the best I've had in some time. Maybe this time we could try some of their barbequed ribs too."

"I like the way you think. Yes, definitely get some ribs too. Then we can meet at your place to catch up. I want to hear every detail about Heath Grant, Peter Yusem, and, of course, I want to play with Iris, Otis, and little Lily too."

"Sounds good. I need to pick up Lily's crate at the shelter anyway. It's in the same direction. The rescue emailed me and told me the people who'd turned in Lily to the shelter brought her in the crate and the shelter forgot to give it to the rescue when they picked her up. Let me know when our order will be ready for pickup."

I headed northwest on the Sequoia Highway. I loved that summer days stayed lighter longer because it seemed I could pack more into each day. The shelter was set to close in twenty minutes, so I called ahead to let them know I was on my way.

The Santa Sofia City Animal Shelter was up a dusty dirt road on a hill off the highway, hidden from view by a thicket of trees. When I reached the peak, I drove into a small parking lot surrounded by a chain-link fence. The shelter was a low-slung concrete building with fenced kennels on both sides. My immediate thoughts were about how much the whole ambience could be improved with proper landscaping. A few small changes, like succulent borders and planters, could work wonders on the aesthetic appeal of the shelter, drawing visitors to it rather than repelling them with its current "mid-century penitentiary" landscaping. I tucked it into my mental file as a possible pro bono project.

As I got out of my car and skipped toward the entrance, the doleful yelps and barks made me grateful Lily had been rescued so quickly. I wondered if the shelter might have any additional information about her.

As daunting and dour as the shelter seemed in its appearance, the opposite was true once I walked inside. The woman at the desk stood up and smiled as I approached. She was about five foot three and I'd guess about a hundred and fifty pounds. She had brassy blonde hair with inch-thick black roots pulled back in short pigtails and a snake tattoo on her neck. Her name tag said Kim Leyva.

"You here for the crate?"

"Yes."

"Let me get it for you. Follow me."

Most of the enclosures were empty.

"I read in the *Sentinel* that people are starting to return the dogs they adopted during the pandemic?"

"Yeah. A few. Not many here at this shelter, thank goodness."

"That's good."

She led me to an outside shed that had a lock on it.

She opened it, plucked up the crate, and handed it to me. "It's a good crate. That's why I called to remind the rescue about it. Thought whoever had adopted Ruby might like it."

"So nice of you. Yes. Thanks. By the way, her new name is Lily. Lily Ruby, actually. I'm a landscape architect and big fan of flowers. My other dog is Iris."

She cocked her head. "Huh. Lily. That works. Cute."

I set the crate down. "Thanks. What was her backstory? Was she at the shelter long? She's so tiny I can't imagine her thriving around a lot of bigger dogs."

"No. Not at all. She was surrendered about three or four days ago. She didn't even spend a night here. Jules from Pom Pom Rescue was here to pick up another dog, saw Ruby, and took her too."

"Oh, that's good. Why did someone surrender her? She acts as if she was treated well and loved."

Kim locked the shed. "She was. Apparently, her owner was deceased, and the family couldn't take her."

I picked up the crate. "Such a little bit of a girl. You'd think they would."

Kim nodded. "Yeah, well, we've seen it all here. Takes all kinds."

"And lucky for me because now she's mine."

We strolled back to the main desk, where a guy stood with his back to us.

I rested the crate on the floor. "Did she get named Ruby here at the shelter?"

"No. Because she was turned in by her owner's family, we knew her name."

"Oh. Does that happen very often? Where a family member turns in a dog?"

The guy turned around. It was the PI, Luke.

He smiled and bowed his head to acknowledge me. "More than you'd think. The owner dies, the family tries to handle the dog for a while, and it doesn't work out."

"Hi. Luke, right?"

"That's right. Good memory." He pointed at me like he was holding a gun. "Tory Benning. What are you doing here?"

"Picking up this crate for a dog I just adopted." I lifted the crate.

Kim pointed to her watch. "And I'm Kim, birth name Kimberly, if anyone wants to know."

We all chuckled.

Luke straightened up and edged toward the door. "Yeah. From what I've heard, a lot of families figure the dog will have a chance to get adopted into a good home." He turned to Kim, the shelter employee. "Am I right?"

Kim nodded and looked at her watch again.

I gasped slightly. "Oh, you're about to close. Thank you so much for the crate. Take care."

Kim walked us to the door and locked it as soon as Luke and I exited. We walked together a few yards away from the entrance.

I stopped. "So what are you doing here? Looking for a lost dog?"

He turned and looked at me with a steady gaze, his gorgeous sharp jawline and high cheekbones mesmerizing me.

I shook my head. "Oh, I'm so sorry. Didn't mean to be flippant. When did you lose it?"

He looked away and then turned to me again. "It's not my dog. It's a client's dog."

"A client?"

"Uh-huh." He gazed at me and smiled slightly, the smile extending up to his eyes.

I felt a tension between us. So, of course, I couldn't think of anything to say.

We walked to my car. There were only two other cars in the lot. One a dusty pickup truck I was guessing was Kim's. And a silver Mercedes I guessed was Luke's.

I pointed to the Mercedes. "That your car? Nice."

"Actually, it belonged to my parents before they got a newer model."

It looked pretty new to me.

"What a coincidence. I was followed recently by a silver Mercedes. It wasn't you, was it?"

His face changed drastically. Gone was the warmth, replaced by a troubled frown, but the intense stare was still there.

He licked his lips slightly. "Are you serious?"

In my mind I smacked myself on the side of the head. Now he probably hated me for accusing him of following me. I fell back on my default defense mechanism, denial, and ignored his comment.

I spoke quickly. "So, what's your case about? Someone stole your client's dog and then changed their mind and turned it in? Was it a French bulldog by any chance? I hear those are a popular target of thieves down in LA. I hope the dognapping ring hasn't moved to Santa Sofia."

He looked down and then locked eyes with me. I couldn't tell if he was offended or not. His brows were still furrowed.

Mercifully, my phone pinged. It was Ashley. Our food would be ready for pickup in about ten minutes. By the time I'd read her text and texted her back, Luke was getting into his car.

I waved. "Nice seeing you again, Luke."

He waved back but I felt like the damage had been done.

I put the crate in my backseat thinking I'd probably come off as a deranged nut. I buckled my seat belt. But what if it had been Luke who'd been following me? Maybe Luke was the deranged nut? Or maybe he was still working on Bunny's behalf and viewed me as Bunny's killer?

It was dusk by the time I reached Wargo's, aka happy hour. The parking lot was packed. I circled a couple of times and finally found someone pulling out of a space. I trotted into the restaurant to the bar register, where the chalkboard sign said *Pickups*. I looked around to see if Scarlett was working but didn't see her. I gave the server Ashley's name, and they went to retrieve the order.

As my eyes adjusted to the dimly lit lounge, I saw that the restaurant was almost full. And then my eyes nearly popped out of my head like a cartoon character's when they rested on a familiar face. It was Jake. At a table with three other people. With him were Adrian and two females. I turned around quickly. Was my eyesight okay? I slowly rotated with my hand up to cover my face and stole a peek. Yep, it was them alright, because he and Adrian were facing in my direction. I turned my back and leaned into the bar for support. What the heck was going on?

"Here's your order, ma'am. All paid for. Thank you."

I grabbed the food and hurried out of there with my back slightly turned to them, hoping they hadn't seen me, although from my stinging cheeks it felt like my face must have been bright red like a neon sign. I pivoted when I got to the door to check them out one more time. I didn't recognize either of the two women.

Coming into the restaurant through the swinging doors as I was leaving was Scarlett Hare. We practically bumped into each other.

She sighed loudly. "What? Are you stalking me now?"

I shook my head and held up the bag of food. "No. Just picking up dinner. Have a nice night."

CHAPTER 14

When I pulled into my driveway, Iris's barking filled my ears. Only hearing Iris, panic gripped me. I hoped that little Lily was okay. As soon as I opened the door, I saw that all was well. Lily was right next to Iris, wagging her tail.

"Lily! How did you get out? I thought I gated you."

I jogged to the end of the hallway. Sure enough, Lily had knocked down the gate. Otis lurked nearby, returning to the scene of the crime, as usual. When I ran back to close the door, where Iris and Lily were stationed waiting for my reaction, the beam of headlights lit up my driveway. In the dark the car looked silver, not black like Ashley's BMW.

Something snapped inside of me. I was done with being followed and being intimidated. I dropped the bag of food on the hallway table and grabbed the large lantern I kept underneath it, put the door on the latch, and walked back to the driveway. I shined the light on the car. I was right, it wasn't Ashley's car. A hand waved at me through the open driver's side window. It was Simon. He held his other hand up to prevent being blinded by the light I was shining at him.

I clicked off the lantern. "Simon. What brings you here?"

He got out of his car. "Hope it's not too rude to drop by like this. I had your address from your wedding account. But I was on my way home and thought why not just swing by and tell you in person."

I moved closer to his car. "Tell me what?"

He slammed his car door shut. "About the latest gossip."

"Oh, do tell."

Ashley pulled up and parked at the curb. She scurried up to

us. "Where's the food? I'm starving."

I chuckled. "Inside. The door's on the latch."

She went to the door and the dogs ran out.

Lily ran up to Simon and wagged her tail.

I smiled at her enthusiastic reception. "She likes you."

Simon's mouth hung open. "Ruby! What on earth are you doing here?"

"You know Ruby?"

He crouched down to pet her. "Of course I do. Why wouldn't I? Bunny used to bring her to the *Sentinel* offices all the time."

Now it was me who had to pick my jaw up from the ground. "Wait. Lily was Bunny's dog?"

He nodded. "Ruby, yes."

"I've renamed her. She's Lily Ruby now. How on earth did she wind up at the shelter then?"

He stood up. "You got her at the shelter?"

"I got her at a rescue organization who got her from the shelter. The shelter told me a representative of the family dropped Lily off because the family couldn't care for her. What about Peter? Why didn't he just keep her?"

Simon shook his head. "I have no idea."

"Another mystery. Just what we need." Ashley scooped up Iris. "Sorry. I take no responsibility for what I say when I'm hangry."

I pointed to the house. "Then go eat."

Ashley headed back to the house with Iris.

Simon blushed and looked embarrassed. "I didn't mean to interrupt your dinner, but I just had to tell you what one of the staff members told me."

I picked up Lily. "I'm all ears."

"Peter came in about a week ago and he and Bunny had a heated argument. Apparently, this happened almost every time Peter came to the *Sentinel* recently."

"About what?"

Simon rested against his car's hood. "Not positive, but I'm pretty sure it sounded like he wanted out of their marriage and

Bunny wouldn't consider a divorce."

"Really?"

Simon nodded.

I shifted my weight. "That's definitely not the impression he gave me. Quite the opposite, actually."

He stood up straighter. "Well, anyway, just wanted to let you know."

I stroked Lily under her chin. "You're sure about your source? Not just someone who wanted to stir up trouble or get attention?"

Simon pointed at me. "That's the thing. Two people told me something like this today. Separately. And both of them are people of good character in my mind."

I cocked my head to the side. "I don't suppose you can tell me who? I'd like to ask them some follow-up questions."

Simon shook his head as he climbed into his car. "I don't think that would be a good idea. They told me in confidence. I probably shouldn't have even told you, now that I think about it. But I knew you were concerned about Mac being falsely charged."

I exhaled. If Peter wanted out and Bunny wouldn't divorce him, he had a motive to kill Bunny. I waved goodbye to Simon as he backed down my driveway.

When I came back inside, Ashley was in the living room playing with Iris. I lowered Lily to the floor, and she skipped over to Iris and Ashley.

Ashley put Lily on her lap and Lily licked her face. "She's so tiny! And so cute. She seems happy. She's very affectionate."

I told Ashley everything Simon had told me.

Ashley nodded. "Yep. If Peter wanted out of his marriage and Bunny didn't want a divorce, looks like Peter might have taken it to the next extreme."

I scratched Iris's stomach. "Pretty much open-and-shut case to me. Nice touch Peter trying to pin it on Mac, his lover's husband."

Then I filled Ashley in on Lily's backstory I'd learned at the shelter.

Ashley petted Lily. "Since Simon just verified that Lily was Bunny's dog, and Bunny was Luke's client, and Luke said he was looking for a client's lost dog, then Luke must have been at the shelter tracking down Ruby. I wonder why? And if Bunny hired Luke to find Ruby, that means Ruby was placed at the shelter *before* Bunny was killed, not after."

"Hmm. We never got that far into it. When you texted me, he made his getaway. Did I mention he looked super hot? And has a jawline to die for, just like Hyunjin from the Stray Kids?"

"Sis, I noticed that when I first laid eyes on him at Wargo's. But I was distracted by that delicious cheeseburger. Speaking of which . . ."

We moved to the kitchen, where I quickly scooped kibble in bowls and set them down for the animals. Ashley had laid out our food and already eaten about a quarter of her cheeseburger. I hopped onto a barstool next to her. She munched on her cheeseburger and listened intently as I told her how I also had accused Luke of following me.

She nearly choked on her burger. "No! You didn't. What did he say then?"

"'Are you serious?' Totally ruined the tension that we were feeling. Or at least that I was feeling. He just frowned at me but kept the eye contact."

"Huh. So open to interpretation, in other words. That could mean he's insulted, annoyed, or maybe even concerned about you."

I took a bite of my cheeseburger. "Right? So hard to read. So naturally I started babbling incoherently about a dognapping ring in LA."

"As you do." Ashley grinned. "So smooth."

We laughed.

"Did Simon say anything else?"

I shook my head and put my burger down. "No. But I'm afraid I have a breaking news scoop to report that hits closer to home."

Ashley's eyes widened. She stopped chewing momentarily. "I don't like that look on your face. Something to do with Jake?"

I nodded. "And Adrian."

She put her cheeseburger down. "Now what?"

"I just saw them when I picked up the food. They were at the restaurant together. Sitting at a table with two girls."

Ashley stood up. "What the . . . he told me he was working tonight."

I crossed my arms. "Liar."

Ashley put her hands on her hips. "What were the girls like? Young? Pretty?"

I nodded. "Yup. But I didn't get a real good look at them. The girls' backs were facing me at first. That's how I spotted Jake and Adrian, because they faced the bar where I picked up the food."

"Oh." Ashley drew out the word. "Did they see you?"

"I don't think so. They seemed pretty engaged in conversation with the girls."

Ashley hopped back onto the stool with a clamor. "Gee. I've always told Adrian to be honest with me. That's super important to me."

"Me too. How can you trust someone after they lie to you?"

We stared at each other for a few seconds, shaking our heads.

"Hey, we need something to drown our sorrows. Wine?" I went to the fridge and grabbed an open bottle of wine.

"Definitely."

I put two wineglasses on the counter. "Oh, I've got more juicy news too."

"Go on."

"Heath Grant asked me to dinner this weekend." I poured the wine.

Ashley grabbed her wineglass and gave me a playful shove. "Get out! I need deets."

"He loves to cook, apparently, and he's having a dinner party this weekend and invited me. That's it. That's the whole story."

Ashley drooped over her wineglass. "Are you going to go?"

"I'm intrigued. I wanted to make sure Jake didn't want to have plans. But after seeing him on a double date with Adrian, screw that. I'm going. I wonder if any other movie stars will be there?"

Ashley tilted her glass. "How many people are invited? He just invited you? He didn't ask whether or not you were single?"

"He knows I'm a widow because he said he read about Milo's murder."

"Maybe he's your date." Ashley squealed.

"No. Wait. You think?" I took a swig of wine.

We finished eating our burgers, sampled some ribs, and had more wine. Next, we moved to the living room to watch a YouTube video of the Stray Kids playing a house party game based on secret assignments. To continue the mystery theme, we decided to watch a Hallmark mystery movie that opened as they usually did with a murder.

I grabbed Ashley's arm. "I hate the openings because you know some unsuspecting soul is going to get whacked."

Ashley laughed. "And the culprit always wears a hoodie, so you have no clue who it is."

No matter how much I tried to prepare myself, I always flinched when a scary stranger emerged from the shadows. I gripped Ashley's arm more tightly. Lily started to bark.

My gaze followed Lily as she ran toward the front door. "That's the first time she's barked. Such a shrill little bark from a tiny pipsqueak."

Ashley loosened her belt a notch. "She's going to be a good watch dog, like Iris."

As if on cue, Iris rushed after Lily barking, then they both returned and barked at me.

The next minute the sound of glass shattering made Ashley and me jump off the couch. Iris bolted in the direction of the noise.

I shrieked, "Iris! No. Stop. There might be broken glass. I don't want you to cut your feet."

For once, she obeyed me and let me scoop her up. Ashley grabbed Lily. Who knew where Otis was? After he'd eaten his dinner, he'd disappeared. We tiptoed toward the front door. Across the hall from the living room was a spare room I used as a home office. I turned on the light and my worst fears were confirmed. The front window had been shattered.

"Wow. Someone must have thrown something through your window." Ashley's gaze roamed the room and then she pointed. "Look! Is that a rock over there on the floor?"

I started toward it.

Ashley grabbed my wrist. "Wait. Let me get my phone and I'll take a photo. Be careful of the glass."

"I will."

Iris was alert but content to stay in my arms, probably sensing this was a big deal.

Ashley, still holding Lily, came back with her phone and took her pictures.

I repositioned Iris under my left arm and bent down and picked up the rock. A piece of paper was wrapped around it, attached with a rubber band.

I removed the rubber band and opened the folded paper. It was a note. It read "Stop snooping or else."

CHAPTER 15

"What the . . ." Ashley stomped up and down the hallway, in fight mode. "I wonder if whoever's been following you in the silver car did this?"

I covered my mouth. "It's like the one Peter Yusem said he got the night before Bunny was killed."

Ashley stopped her pacing. "Did they throw his through a window?"

"No. It was left on his doorstep. Supposedly. I never saw it."

Ashley bit her lip. "I'm sure Adrian would have the details."

"I'm calling him right now." I punched in Adrian's number, wondering if I'd hear a noisy bar and female voices when he answered.

"Tory! What's up?" Adrian answered right away, amid a quiet background.

I told him what happened.

"I'll be there as soon as I can. On my way. Are you okay?"

"We're all fine. Except for the rattled nerves."

"We? Is Ashley there? Tell her to be careful around the glass."

"Yep. She's here." I glanced at Ashley. "I'll tell her to be careful."

Ashley's eyes popped.

I hung up. "Adrian is coming over. I already feel better knowing he knows, especially given the similarity to the one left on Peter's doorstep."

Ashley twisted her mouth to the side. "But didn't Peter say that Mac left the rock?"

"Yeah, but—"

She held her chin. "And didn't Mac come over to your house

late the other night too?"

"Yes, but—"

She put her hands on her hips. "Why are you so adamantly defending Mac when all the clues point to him?"

I ran my hand through my hair. "For that very reason. I think the real killer is trying to frame him. He's a very bright man, despite his volatile temperament. Way too smart to leave clues at every turn. I just can't see him doing all these dumb things that clearly implicate him."

"Well, Tory, let me remind you, the man came over here because of a stupid cabbage."

"It wasn't just the cabbage. It was what it represented. Plus, he was mad about the supposed leaked editorial too. He was mad and afraid it would make him lose the election."

"But still. He has anger issues."

About ten minutes later a knock on the door made us both jump. Lily and Iris barked and wagged their tails in our arms.

"Tory, it's Adrian."

I peeked out the window to confirm it was in fact Adrian and not some demon imitator killer. When I opened the door, Jake was there too.

We all hugged, although Adrian and Jake were the huggers, and Ashley and I were the huggees. Ashley rolled her eyes at me when Adrian embraced her. Jake hovered behind Adrian and winked at me. I responded with a half smile.

I showed Adrian the note. "Does it look like the note Peter got?"

"What note?"

"The one with the rock he said he found on his doorstep."

"Oh. I haven't seen it yet. He hasn't brought it to the station yet like he promised."

Ashley spoke in a low voice. "If it ever existed at all. Sometimes things we think exist really don't."

I mouthed an "ouch" to Ashley, impressed with her quick double entendre. I wondered whether Adrian would pick up on her comments and realize she was also referring to their relationship.

Adrian cocked his head at Ashley. "What are you saying? Peter made it up?"

Jake threw his arm around my shoulder and gave me a squeeze. I stared straight ahead.

"Glad you're okay and nobody got hurt. I know you're scared right now, but we don't even know if the real killer did this. It might have been a stupid prank."

"I'm not scared now. I'm just glad none of us got hit by the rock. I was more concerned about the animals getting hurt by the glass. By the way, I haven't seen Otis. Hopefully, he's under my bed."

Adrian went outside and dragged in a huge piece of plywood. "I brought this and some tape. Jake, want to help me out here and board up her window? This should work for the short term."

"Thanks, Adrian. That's so sweet of you. I have a contact who does window repair. I'll call him right now." I grabbed my phone and left a message for the repairman.

Adrian and Jake spent about ten minutes boarding up the window. I heard a loud meow. Otis appeared to see what was going on.

My chest heaved in relief. "Otis! There you are. So glad you're okay."

He rubbed up against my leg and meowed when I scratched his head.

Adrian stood back to inspect his handiwork. "There. That should work for tonight. I agree with Jake, it might not be the killer who did this. But that being said, I'd feel a lot more comfortable if Jake and I stayed here tonight. He and I can camp out in the living room, and you girls can get some rest without worrying about someone breaking in."

Ashley and I exchanged gazes. She nodded almost imperceptibly. I had to agree. Despite feeling angry at these two and their cheating ways, I was touched by their gesture. I felt their warmth and caring. Someone had just resorted to violence to warn me off investigating Bunny's murder and these two were willing to serve as the first line of defense. I was almost moved to tears by their gesture. Plus, I was scared.

Jake studied my face.

Adrian inhaled and exhaled loudly. "We're not taking no for an answer."

I nodded. "Okay. Thank you. I'm too tired to argue."

Adrian smiled. "Good. And you're very welcome. I'll get on this bright and early tomorrow. I'll talk to Peter and Mac. Have to admit, not looking good for Mac right now."

I pressed my lips together. "Assuming Mac sent the notes. I still think he's being set up by someone. And my guess is Peter."

Adrian directed his gaze at me. "What makes you so sure it's Peter?"

"Let's just say I have my sources."

Adrian furrowed his forehead, making his thick eyebrows nearly touch. "Tory, I'm warning you. Again. Please stay out of this. Obviously, you haven't since it looks like you've attracted someone's attention enough for them to threaten you."

I felt my face heat and rolled my tongue over my teeth. "But it means I must be on the right track, no?"

Jake tackled me playfully, wrapping his arms around me and spinning me around. He whispered in my ear, "He's getting mad. Drop it."

Again, for some reason I felt almost moved to tears. Jake released me and I straightened out my clothes.

I brushed some dog hair off my pant leg. "What I meant to say is, since I can't imagine Mac ever hurting me, the suspect who makes the most sense to me is Peter. And you know what they always say, it's always the spouse."

Jake winked at me. Adrian nodded, apparently accepting my explanation.

Ashley and I gathered up the dogs and Otis followed us toward the bedrooms.

Once we were out of Jake and Adrian's sight, Ashley gently punched my arm. "That was what I call a good save. Adrian was on the verge of a big-time lecture."

"Yeah. Jake warned me when he tackled me."

"Uh-huh. Wonder what's going on with these two. I'm getting a lot of mixed messages."

"Yeah. Me too."

I put Lily's crate in my room, left the door open, and set out a pee pad in the bathroom and hoped for the best. Ashley took Otis into the guest room. Iris kept watch at the end of my bed. Lily fell asleep quickly; it had been an eventful first full day in her new forever home.

• • •

I woke up around seven on Thursday to a phone notification. I had two messages. One was from Luke Barrett. He wanted to know if I had time for coffee this morning. That was a bold move. I guess he wasn't that put off by me accusing him of following me after all. He must have known I was kidding. Unless it was an intervention and he wanted to warn me off making false accusations.

The second message was from Caroline at Pom Pom Rescue. She sent me a pic of a hedge she liked. I liked when clients sent me pics, it helped me get a better idea of what they wanted. It was an oleander (*Nerium oleander*). She liked its long feathery leaves, red flowers, and drought tolerance. She wondered whether I knew of some other shrub that looked similar since she knew that it wasn't a great choice for a rescue, because every part of the oleander plant was extremely poisonous for dogs, as well as humans.

And then I froze. I remembered the pink oleander hedge that bordered the property line at Jacaranda Gardens, separating the street and public landscaping from the condo's private property. I made a mental note to google oleander and read more about its poisonous properties. I wondered if it could possibly be implicated in Bunny's death. Could someone have plucked some oleander and slipped it to Bunny somehow? But I seemed to remember reading it was bitter-tasting, something that didn't always deter dogs, but surely a human would pick up on it. I'd have to double-check later.

As I threw on some sweatpants and a T-shirt, I heard a noise coming from the other end of the house. For an instant I panicked but then remembered Jake and Adrian had spent the night. Lily was sitting in her crate staring at me and Iris was dancing around waiting to go outside.

"Okay. Who wants to take a walk?"

When I emerged from my room the aroma of coffee, toast, and bacon and eggs flooded my senses.

I padded to the kitchen.

Jake and Adrian were plating four breakfasts.

Adrian smiled. "Good morning."

"Hi, guys! I need to take the dogs out."

I walked to the back door but both dogs lingered in the kitchen. Bacon was Iris's downfall and apparently Lily's too.

"Come on. Walk first. Eat second."

They scampered outside.

"Hurry back. We'll have breakfast waiting," Jake called as we left.

I wondered if the two of them were overcompensating with the boyfriend material behavior out of guilt for cheating on Ashley and me last night. Maybe *cheating* was putting it too strongly, speaking for me and Jake at least, since we weren't in an exclusive relationship. It seemed like we were assuming we'd been in one, but we'd never really discussed it. So why was I so upset? After all, we'd only dated for about two months before the pandemic hit.

Ashley came out to join me and the dogs, already out of the PJs I'd lent her last night and back into yesterday's outfit, looking like a slightly more disheveled version of herself from the previous night. "Did you see what's going on in your kitchen? Are they auditioning for *The Bachelor* or something?"

I chuckled. "My thoughts exactly. Why are they being so nice?"

Jakes's deep voice answered, "I was under the impression we

were always nice."

Ashley headed back to the house and motioned to the dogs. "Come on, girls. Who wants some bacon?"

Iris slammed into my leg in her rush to follow Ashley. Lily followed suit.

Jake rubbed my shoulder. "Still on edge from last night?"

"What part of last night would you be referring to? The rock crashing through my window or seeing the guy I've been dating with another woman?"

He dropped his hand. "What are you talking about?"

"I saw you last night with Adrian and the two girls."

He blushed but didn't say anything. But that said it all for me. I marched back inside.

Jake grabbed my arm. "Tory. Wait. I can explain."

My cheeks were wet. Where were these tears coming from? And why? I turned to leave.

"Can I at least give you an explanation? It's not what it seems."

I sniffled. "Fine. I'm listening. But make it quick. I have a breakfast date."

He took a step back. "Someone doesn't waste any time."

I brushed my cheeks. "That's right. Life is short. I don't have time for games."

"Who's playing games? Not me."

I crossed my arms. "Well, what would you call sneaking around with other girls? Especially when Adrian told Ashley that he was working."

"Ashley knows?"

I glared at him. "You're darn right she knows." I stormed inside.

Jake followed me. Back in the kitchen, Ashley was feeding bacon to the dogs.

I pointed to them and chuckled. "They'll be your friends for life now."

Jake smiled and picked up a strip and offered it to me. "Bacon?"

Ashley stifled a laugh.

Jake glanced at Ashley and smiled at me. "Oh, come on. That was a little bit funny, no?"

I poured myself a cup of coffee. "No."

Adrian had parceled out scrambled eggs to four plates. He'd placed a slice of sourdough toast on each plate. He was in the process of distributing bacon strips when his phone rang.

He looked at the screen. "Sorry. I need to take this."

His face grew grave, and his thick eyebrows nearly met in a deep furrow. "When? How long ago? Okay, I'm on my way."

Adrian hung up and grimaced.

Ashley had a resigned smirk on her face. "Saved by the bell once again, huh? Don't tell me. You gotta go."

Adrian nodded. "Stone Hare has been shot."

CHAPTER 16

I gripped my coffee mug with both hands. "Oh, no. Is he okay?"

Adrian compressed his lips. "Don't know."

Ashley stepped closer to me. "Where was he shot?"

Adrian's gaze shifted to Ashley. "At the beach."

I crossed my arms. "The beach?"

Adrian nodded. "Yep. And the suspect is at large."

My stomach somersaulted. "Who would want to shoot Stone?"

Ashley entwined her arm with mine. "And why?"

"That's what I'm going to try to find out." Adrian wiped his hands on a napkin. "Okay, I need to get to the hospital to check on his condition. See if he's able to answer any questions."

Ashley rushed over to one of my kitchen cabinets and rummaged through my shelves. She pulled out two paper plates and slid Adrian's and Jake's breakfasts onto them.

She grabbed napkins and forks and handed them to each of them along with their breakfasts. "Here. Take it to go."

Adrian tilted his head back slightly. "No. I'm good."

Jake accepted his. "Thank you."

Ashley pressed her lips into a smile. "I'm not taking no for an answer."

Adrian leaned toward Ashley, kissed her cheek, and took the food. "Thanks."

We watched them walk down the hall to the front door.

Then Adrian spun around. "This is a PSA for both of you. Back off in your investigating. This has now become even more risky. The killer is probably getting desperate and will resort to desperate measures. I don't want either of you being the next victim. Do you both understand? I'm serious."

Ashley and I both nodded and responded with muted "okays."

After Adrian and Jake left, I turned to Ashley. "With Stone shot, there goes one of my suspects. I don't like it. Last night, someone throws a rock through my window, warning me to stop snooping into Bunny's murder. Today, someone shoots her son."

Ashley pulled her lips into a thin line as she pondered my words. "You think the same person who threw the rock also shot Stone?"

"It would be too much of a coincidence not to be." I clicked my tongue. "But I intend to find out who it was either way."

"Tory. You heard what Adrian told us."

"I heard. I understood what he said. But I'm not going to stand by passively and let all the circumstantial evidence keep piling up around Mac."

"Well, at least Mac doesn't have a motive for shooting Stone, does he? So that should go in his favor."

"Hopefully, you're right."

We walked back into the kitchen.

Ashley grabbed a plate of bacon and eggs and popped onto a stool. "What are you going to do today?"

"I'm going to try to see Scarlett. To let her know Stone's been shot."

"I thought you said they were estranged."

"They are. But, come on, he's her brother. Wouldn't you want to know if it was your brother?"

"I guess. But I don't have a brother."

I rolled my eyes. "You know what I mean. Do you want to come with?"

She checked the time on her phone. "Why don't you just call her? The restaurant won't be open yet. Unless you know where she lives."

I stopped in my tracks. "You're right. But I don't have her number. Let me google again to see if I can find it."

I poured myself a cup of coffee and brought a plate of bacon and eggs to the counter next to my laptop.

I did yet another search for Scarlett's name and an article with a Bunny interview popped up. "Hmm. Interesting."

"What?"

"This article says Bunny didn't believe in leaving a lot of money to her kids. She thought it would take away their motivation to make something of themselves."

Ashley cut her toast in half. "Doesn't look like that worked out too well. The daughter is a waitress with poor taste in men and the son is barely employed."

I ate a couple of bites of egg. "I know. No wonder there was no love lost among them. But on the upside, at least that eliminates them as suspects. No financial gain. No motive."

"True. I wonder who the beneficiary of Bunny's will was then? Peter?"

"Probably."

Ashley gasped slightly. "Maybe you've been right all along. Maybe when Bunny wouldn't agree to a divorce, Peter decided to knock her off."

I shook my head. "Had she never watched a true crime show? They're filled with husbands doing that."

Ashley twisted her mouth to one side. "Didn't Peter give you the impression they were happily married?"

I sipped my coffee. "Yes. But all the rumors say otherwise."

"Could both things be true? Like maybe Bunny wanting to stay married, despite Peter having an affair? Or Peter having a lover but still wanting to stay married too."

I scrolled down on my computer. "Sounds very French, very European. Turning a blind eye. But yes, possibly."

Ashley took a sip of her coffee. "Did you find Scarlett's number?"

"Not yet." I opened a link. "Found it."

I called Scarlett and left a message for her to call me back.

Ashley ate a small piece of toast. "What are you going to ask Scarlett when you talk to her?"

"For more details about Peter's reaction when Stone told him he knew he was cheating on Bunny. She said it didn't go over well, but never elaborated."

Ashley broke off a bit of bacon and popped it into her mouth. "Like whether Peter was mildly annoyed or ready to kill him?"

"Exactly."

I clicked my tongue. "The only person I know of who might want Stone out of the picture is Peter. Scarlett told us Stone confronted Peter about the affair. Maybe Stone figured out more. Maybe he figured out that Peter also killed Bunny."

Ashley shuddered. "Do you think Stone threatened to go to the police? You think Peter shot Stone because he was trying to silence him?"

I pushed some eggs and bacon on my fork. "I don't know. Can you think of anyone other than Peter who would want to shoot Stone?"

"Not really." Ashley tapped her cup. "Hey. Maybe Stone was blackmailing Peter about the affair. And threatened to tell Bunny unless Peter paid up."

I munched on some toast. "But then Bunny was killed."

Ashley sipped her coffee. "So then Stone suspected that Peter killed Bunny? And upped the ante? That's when Peter decided to kill Stone—but botched it."

I nodded. "Makes sense to me."

Ashley dabbed her mouth with a napkin. "Makes a lot more sense than thinking Mac killed Bunny over a cabbage."

"That's for sure."

Ashley's phone buzzed.

She viewed the screen. "It's a text from Adrian."

She read it and lifted her head. "He just wanted to give us a quick update. Adrian says Stone is going to be okay. He only has a graze wound in the leg."

I sighed. "Thank goodness. At least whoever shot him was a bad shot. Did Stone see who shot him? Any other details?"

"That's all Adrian said." Ashley shrugged her shoulders.

My phone rang. It was Jake.

"It's Jake. I'm not going to answer it."

"Still mad at him?"

"Yes. Mad and confused."

My phone pinged. "Now he's texting me."

I read Jake's text. *Adrian left out an important detail. Stone described his shooter. His description matches Mac's.*

My shoulders slumped. I read the text to Ashley.

"What? Oh, no. I can't believe that."

"Neither can I."

"For God's sake, text Jake back or call him for more details."

I called Jake. "Just read your text. How did Stone describe his assailant exactly?"

"An older man. Tall. In a hoodie."

"How can he tell if the guy was older if he wore a hoodie?"

"Assuming he saw him face-to-face."

"Ugh. Let me call Mac and see where he was this morning. Thanks for the heads-up."

I filled in Ashley on what Jake had told me.

She tapped the counter. "Call Mac to see if he has an alibi."

I called Mac's house and Kaley answered. "Why do you want to know where Mac was this morning? What's wrong?"

"There's been an incident. Actually, it would be helpful to know where both of you were since then we can eliminate both of you as suspects."

"Suspects? For what?"

"Bunny's son was shot."

"Oh, no. Is he dead?"

"No, thank goodness. Don't take this the wrong way, but since Mac is still a suspect in Bunny's murder, it would be helpful to know where he was. And where you were."

Several seconds went by before Kaley responded. "I was at home as usual at that hour. Oh, wait. No. I was at my yoga class. Or coming home from yoga. What time did you say it happened exactly?"

I paused. "I didn't. But Adrian got the call around eight this morning, so I'm assuming not too long before that."

"Then I was at yoga. My class starts at seven thirty."

"Where is your class located?"

"My instructor runs classes out of her home. Near the Avenue."

"And does Mac take yoga classes with you?"

She laughed. "Mac? Hardly. His idea of exercise involves swinging a golf club on the golf course. With a golf cart."

The idea of Mac swinging anything that could be considered a potential weapon didn't do anything to assuage any nagging doubts I might have about his innocence at the moment.

"So he was at the golf course this morning?"

"I don't know for sure, but most likely. His car wasn't there when I left for yoga."

I exhaled loudly. "Okay. Thanks. That's good. Both of you basically have alibis then since you were with other people."

She hesitated. "I guess we do. Thanks, Tory. You've been a great source of comfort with your support. We both appreciate it."

After I hung up, I turned to Ashley. "Okay. Looks like Mac and Kaley probably have alibis, thank goodness. Kaley was at a yoga class and Mac was at the golf course. I'll have to check them out, of course, but I have my coffee date with Luke in thirty minutes."

"Hold up, Missy. What's this about a coffee date with Luke? When did that happen? I must have blinked."

I laughed. "Didn't I tell you?"

"You know very well you didn't tell me."

"He messaged me this morning."

"What did he say? Maybe he wants to serve you with a restraining order since you falsely accused him of following you. Or was it him actually following you?"

"Oh, stop." I giggled. "Crazy, huh? And I still have to get back to Heath Grant about Friday night."

"Aren't we Miss Popular all of a sudden."

"All of a sudden. Thanks, friend?"

"Okay, since you won't be here, I should stay and guard your dogs. I'm uneasy with that broken window, despite it being boarded up. Give me the number of the window guy. I'll call him again and I can wait for him here. Auntie Ashley would love a playdate with Lily, Iris, and Otis. After having you around twenty-four-seven during the pandemic, it will be nice for them to have someone home during the day again."

"Aw, thanks, Ash. That would be great. By the way, I'd planned to spend more time working from home. But that was before the rock incident. And before Stone got shot."

"Before you thought your rock and Stone were related."

We held each other's gaze for a moment before we both burst out laughing.

Ashley doubled up, shaking with laughter. "Truly, I did not hear that until the words left my mouth."

I tried to catch my breath. "I needed a good laugh." I wiped away my tears. "Ah, anyway, in answer to your question, I don't know for sure if my rock and Stone are related . . ."

We both stifled our giggles.

"But like I said before, seems too much of a coincidence not to be. My gut tells me they are related."

I took one more swig of coffee and trotted back to my room. I showered and threw on a pair of black pants and a black top.

Back in the kitchen, I patted Ashley's shoulder. "I'll check back with you after coffee. If the window isn't fixed by then, I'll come back and relieve you."

"Sounds good. Thanks."

"I'm the one who should be thanking you."

As I drove over to the Starbucks that Luke had suggested, my mind was flooded with thoughts of poor Stone. Here I had him pegged as a possible murder suspect and he turned out to be the next victim.

Solid sleuthing, Tory.

I pulled into the Starbucks lot and found a spot. My phone rang. I dug in my purse to get it, annoyed when I saw the notification said *Scam Likely*. A tapping on my window made me jump. It was Luke. I got out of the car.

Luke was wearing a white T-shirt under a black sports coat and jeans. "Hi. So sorry. I didn't mean to scare you."

I leaned against the side of my car and put my hand on my chest. "That's okay. The last twenty-four hours have been harrowing."

He rested his arm on the roof of my car. "Oh, no. Are you okay?"

"Yeah, I'm hanging in there. Just more jumpy than usual after last night. Someone threw a rock through my window at my house. Wrapped around the rock was a note basically telling me to back off."

"What? Did you see who did it? Are you sure you're okay?" His penetrating gaze gave me a once-over.

My first interpretation was that he was assessing me for injuries. The alternative interpretation I preferred was that he was checking me out. I slumped further against the car and nearly slid off the front hood while trying to retain a modicum of cool.

Focus, Tory.

I straightened up. "Did you hear that Bunny's son, Stone, was shot?"

"Wait, what? No, I hadn't. When? Is he okay?"

"I don't have any details. Except that he was conscious and the description he gave of the shooter was an older white man."

Luke whistled. "Wow. That sounds like a match for Mac McGregor."

"I know. That was what I thought right away too."

Oh, my goodness. We were so similar in our thinking.

I had butterflies in my stomach and felt like I was floating on air as we walked into Starbucks. We put in our orders and found a table in a corner away from other people.

"Thanks for agreeing to meet me. I've been thinking about you."

My face heated up.

Calm down, girl.

"I was curious about your interest in tracking down Bunny's killer. As a PI I have to be curious about everyone involved in any of my cases. And I came across all the press about your late husband's murder and the Christmas tree lot murder and now

I think I understand more where you're coming from and why you're so interested in helping Mac."

I felt sweaty all over, thinking my face must be glistening.

"So that being said . . ." Luke took a deep breath.

There it was.

"I have some information you might want to know. Now even more so, with Stone shot. I know you're not a licensed PI but, since a killer is loose, we have to all work together and pull out all the stops to catch them."

I sat back in my wooden chair with my hands crossed on my lap. I hadn't expected what I deemed was his invitation for me to join the Santa Sofia branch of the Justice League, but I was listening and here for it.

"I have information about your new dog that you might find helpful."

"Lily? That she was Bunny's dog? I already know that."

He raised his eyebrows. "Impressive."

I chuckled. "Never underestimate me."

He smiled slightly. "Noted. Not that I ever intended to."

Was he flirting with me? Or not? Also, his dimples.

The barista called our names. Or at least I think he did. Luke's gaze had almost made me forget mine.

Luke stood up. "Let me get them."

"No, let me."

His gaze caught mine. "I insist."

"Okay, thanks."

A few minutes later Luke returned with our coffee.

Luke took a sip of his coffee and drummed the table. "I have something else to tell you that you might not know."

I folded my arms and rested my chin in my hand. "Go on."

"I thought of something and I circled back to the shelter after we left yesterday and caught Kim on her way out. I asked her to describe the person who had dropped off the dog."

"Didn't she say it was an assistant?"

"Yeah. That's when I remembered. Because Bunny's assistant was on maternity leave. So, it wouldn't have been her."

"Okay. If it wasn't Bunny's assistant, who was it? Why would that matter?"

"Because of the timing."

"What do you mean?"

Luke leaned in. "According to Kim at the shelter, the dog was turned in the day before Bunny was killed, suggesting that her murder wasn't an act of passion, but planned and premeditated, which steers suspicion away from Mac . . . and onto Peter."

I played with the heat sleeve on my cup. "I already presumed it was premeditated, given the initial autopsy report that said Bunny was poisoned."

"Yes, I remember your friend Ashley's announcement at Wargo's." His eyes twinkled.

I smiled. "Was she really that loud?"

Luke covered his mouth and laughed lightly before gazing at me intently. "But did you know that it was Peter who brought the dog to the shelter?"

I leaned in and slapped the table. "What? How do you know?"

"Kim said it was a male."

"Did she ID him from a photo?"

He dropped his head. "No. She said it was really busy that day so she couldn't remember."

"So in other words, we don't know for sure it was Peter."

He shook his head. "But it would have to have been Peter, because who else would have had access to the dog?"

I raised my forefinger. "But wait, wouldn't Bunny have noticed that Lily wasn't there? I certainly would know if my dog Iris wasn't there when I returned home. In fact, just thinking about it gets me borderline hysterical."

"My understanding is that Ruby went to doggie day care on some days and sometimes had sleepovers there. And with Bunny's assistant on maternity leave and knowing the TV news team would be at the community garden, maybe Bunny had booked Lily for an overnight to make the next morning less hectic."

I nodded. "I guess that sounds plausible."

Luke dipped his head.

When he looked up, his gaze was loaded with the tension I'd felt at Wargo's. "The problem is Kim can't really remember. She said it was a guy in a baseball cap and sweats, and she didn't take a good look at him."

I sipped my coffee, trying to regain my composure and remember what the heck we were talking about after practically melting from his stare.

Luke tapped the table. "Plus, he was wearing a mask, so hard to ID."

I took a deep breath. "But even if Kim can't ID Peter, that's still good for Mac, because it suggests another possible suspect. Someone who had access to Bunny's dog who might have premeditated Bunny's murder."

Luke nodded. "Agree."

"So that's good not only for Mac, the Hotel Santa Sofia corporation, Jacaranda Gardens, and the community garden, but also for yours truly . . ." I pointed to myself. "Now we have to find out who might have benefited from Bunny's death."

"And from Stone's death, had the murder attempt been successful. Assuming the same person was responsible for both crimes."

I stroked my chin. "I'd initially thought Peter might have killed Bunny for her money, but then I found out he was fine financially. So why else would he have killed Bunny?"

"Because Bunny wouldn't give him a divorce?"

"That's been one of my theories. Ashley and I were just talking about it this morning."

Luke steepled his hands. "What I learned in the time she'd been my client was that she was opinionated and stubborn. Maybe she felt a strong need to save their marriage. I know she felt that way about her kids. When I found some dirt on Scarlett's boyfriend about his ill-gained money, Bunny didn't want to disown Scarlett. She wanted to redeem her."

"Hmm. That would explain her rationale. Ashley and I were trying to figure that out. But I don't think Scarlett saw Bunny that way. Nothing definite, but the way she spoke about both her mother and her brother was cold and detached."

Luke swigged his coffee. "Anyway, the big question is who benefits from both Bunny's and Stone's deaths?"

I tilted my head. "Assuming money is the motive for both their deaths."

"True. But it often is." He winked. "I'm working on trying to find out Bunny's and Peter's beneficiaries from their wills."

"That would be great to find out and might prove very enlightening. Do you know whether Peter has any kids?"

"He has two. But they live on the East Coast and go to Ivy League schools."

I nodded and thought for a few seconds. "Who else would be motivated by money?"

He tapped his cup. "Her kids, her employees, her campaign staff, her environmental groups?"

I finished the last of my coffee. "What about other motives? Like jealousy or revenge?"

"Don't know about revenge. But jealousy, on the other hand . . ."

Our gazes met. His knowing look was easy to read.

I sucked in air. "No. You don't actually think Kaley killed Bunny, and when Stone figured it out, she tried to kill him too?"

Luke got up to leave. "Can't say it hasn't crossed my mind. Love can make you do crazy things."

I stood up, not breaking our gaze. I felt like he was staring into my soul again.

A shiver went up my spine. I didn't know if it was from Luke's sexy stare or the realization that Kaley might be a killer who'd been playing me all along.

CHAPTER 17

Back at the office I tried to distract myself from my growing doubts about Kaley that were bubbling in my inner mind by responding to some client emails. I'd sent Caroline some suggestions for possible hedge alternatives for oleander, and she'd okayed my favorite choice, toyon (*Heteromeles arbutifolia*), commonly known as the Christmas berry or California's holly, whose berries could only be poisonous in extremely large quantities. I started to think about additional plant materials for Pom Pom Rescue's makeover.

Philip texted me. *FYI I just did Melinda Yang's hair and she told me she's doing a follow-up story on Bunny's murder at Jacaranda Gardens in an hour.*

I texted him back. *Thanks for the tip, boo. Hope to see you soon.*

I called the manager's office at Jacaranda Gardens. Joey picked up on the third ring.

"Joey! I'm so glad I caught you. I didn't know whether you'd be there."

"Today is my first official day."

"Great! I just found out Melinda Yang is on her way to Jacaranda Gardens again to film another segment."

"Thanks for the heads-up. Because of the protest?"

"What protest?"

"There are some anti-development protestors here. They started to gather on the street behind the community garden around fifteen minutes ago."

"Hmm. I don't know anything about that. I assumed it was about Bunny. But since Bunny was anti-development, maybe they're protesting her murder?"

"I don't know."

"I'll be there in about twenty minutes. Hold the fort till I arrive."

I gathered my handbag, phone, and a bottle of water, and jumped in my car. As I drove up to Jacaranda Gardens, Ashley called.

"I've got some updates for you."

"Cool. I was just going to call you. I'll be home as soon as I can, but right now I'm headed up to Jacaranda Gardens. Philip texted me that Melinda Yang is coming back to do an update."

"No worries. Lily and I are bonding, and Iris and Otis are loving Auntie showering them with attention."

I chuckled. "Yay! Thanks so much for being there, Ash."

"No problem. Okay, I won't keep you, but let me bring you up to speed. First, your home office has a new window."

"Great! Thanks, Ash."

She cleared her throat. "You're very welcome. Second, Adrian just called to tell me Stone is in satisfactory condition at Santa Sofia Hospital and under police guard."

"Thank God. Poor Stone. Does Adrian have any other suspects besides Mac?"

"None that I know of. Why? You sound weird."

I brought her up to speed on what Luke had told me about the person who'd dropped off Lily at the shelter.

Ashley spoke quickly. "That's great. It shows premeditation and introduces the idea of someone other than Mac as a possible suspect. From a legal defense standpoint, the more possible suspects, the better. What else you got?"

"We talked about motive."

"Uh-huh. Does Luke think money is the main motive behind Bunny's murder?"

"He does. But what upset me the most was that when we brainstormed other motives like jealousy, we both thought of Kaley."

Ashley audibly gasped.

"Are you still there?"

"Yeah."

"What's wrong?"

"That was another reason I called. Kaley's alibi for Stone's shooting. I looked up Kaley's yoga class and it's located off the Avenue, like she said, and does have a seven thirty class."

"Good. So that checks out."

"Not exactly. That class isn't held at that studio."

"Where's it held?"

"At the beach."

I gripped the steering wheel tighter. "You're kidding. Important little detail she forgot to mention."

"Did you tell her where Stone was shot?"

"No. Wait. I can't remember for sure. But I don't think I did. So why would she avoid mentioning the beach—"

Ashley breathed in and out audibly. "Unless she knew that would place her at the scene of the crime."

I gasped. "Wow."

"I know. There's something else. I checked the golf course. They normally open at seven."

"But?"

"They've been doing maintenance work this week and haven't been opening until ten."

I let out a soft whistle. "Another tidbit she failed to mention. So then neither Kaley nor Mac have an alibi."

"Hold up. That's all filtered through Kaley. I'd check with Mac first before you jump to conclusions."

My phone clicked. "Ashley, I've got another call. Can I call you right back?"

I picked up and it was Mac.

"Tory. There's been another one."

I was taken aback a bit. Was he taking the 'best defense is a good offense' move regarding Stone's shooting?

"I know."

Mac growled. "You saw it on Twitter?"

"What? No. I heard about it from Adrian. He was at my place when he got the call."

"What call?"

I sighed. "About Stone's shooting. Isn't that what we're talking about?"

He grunted. "No. Yes—I heard about that on the news. No, I mean there's been another leak of a story from the *Sentinel* that's circulating online."

"About what?"

"About Stone describing a suspect that looked like me."

"That's online? Why would anyone do that?"

"Yes. Or at least it was ten minutes ago. Clearly to pin Stone's shooting on me too."

"Where were you this morning when he was shot?"

"I went to Gaviota Grove for breakfast."

My head jerked to alertness. So Kaley lied. I couldn't wait to call back Ashley.

"Did anyone see you there?"

"Tory, it would be impossible not to be seen there. A lot of people saw me there. For one, your new tenant."

"Heath Grant?"

And why did my face get hot when I spoke his name?

"Yes. I met him there for breakfast. Call him if you don't believe me."

I needed to call Heath back anyway. I'd been putting it off because I couldn't decide whether or not I wanted to go to his damn dinner party. Why did he have to ask me? Just to torture me. He must have known all women were attracted to him. What the heck. YOLO. I might as well go. I'd call it networking for possible Hollywood clients to make myself feel less guilty for being attracted to not one, not two, but count them, three guys at the same time. Pretty sure that's not what a love triangle was supposed to mean.

After we hung up, I called back Ashley.

"I'm here at Jacaranda Gardens, pulling into the parking lot right now. There are about a dozen protestors on the street at the driveway entrance."

"Protesting what?"

"Let's see. One sign says *Stop Developers*, but I wanted to let you know that was Mac who called. And guess what? He said he wasn't at the golf course this morning—"

"Ugh. That's bad. So he doesn't have an alibi? And Kaley lied?"

"Yes, bad for Kaley because she lied. But good for Mac because he has an alibi. He had breakfast at Gaviota Grove this morning. And has witnesses."

"That's super. So that's one less crime to blame him for, at least."

"Exactly."

"Wait. Finish telling me about your coffee date with Luke. Apart from the Kaley stuff, how was it otherwise?"

"It was fine. I'll tell you more later."

"Are you still mad at Jake?"

"Pretty much. What about you and Adrian?"

"I'll tell you more later."

I chuckled. "Okay. I deserved that. I don't think it was a date exactly. I think he was just passing on some info to me. He acted flirty. But maybe that's just his personality. Or maybe any guy who shows me any attention I interpret as flirting. I honestly don't know anymore."

Ashley raised her voice slightly. "Or maybe he was actually flirting with you. No. I haven't had a chance to really talk to Adrian. He said he'll call me later. Oh, he did tell me that Bunny for sure was poisoned."

I exhaled heavily. "Does he know what the poison was?"

"Yes. The second lab results came back and confirmed it was a cardiac glycoside, oleandrin, that killed Bunny. It's a potent poison, and very bitter. He said it would take less than a teaspoon of oleandrin to kill someone."

I drew in a breath. "Oleandrin. That sure sounds like it must be derived from the oleander plant, right?"

"Yes. That's what Adrian said."

"I noticed oleander hedges behind the community garden next to the street. I've been meaning to research their toxicity more but haven't had the chance."

Ashley breathed into the phone more loudly. "The big mystery is why would Bunny willingly eat something that tasted so bitter without immediately spitting it out?"

"Beats me. Okay, I'm inside the condo now, gotta go. Talk to you later."

I walked through the lobby and peeked into the manager's office to let Joey know I'd arrived, but he wasn't there.

I went back outside and strolled along the lavender-bordered sidewalk that surrounded the property. I circled all the way around to the community garden. The yellow tape was gone. It was as if a tragedy had never occurred there. I looked around at the plots. My gaze fell on the shrubs beyond the iron fence at the edge of the property. Oleander. The source plant for the poison the lab tests had identified. It looked harmless enough. Pretty with its long thin leaves and clustered flowers. The killer didn't need to have gotten it here. It was common in Southern California. But how the devil would the killer have gotten Bunny to take it if it had a bitter taste? And then I remembered—I'd seen oleander around Stone's apartment building too.

"Tory."

I jumped.

"So sorry."

"Joey. Hey." I fanned myself.

"I didn't mean to startle you."

"That's okay. It's just that this is a recent crime scene. Next time, if you could give me a heads-up, like calling my name from afar instead of kind of creeping up on me, I'd really appreciate it."

Although in fairness to Joey, as I stood next to him breathing in the sickeningly sweet smell of his hair pomade, the overpowering scent cloud that enveloped him also served as an early-warning system of sorts.

He blushed. "Sorry. Wasn't thinking. I just wanted to let you know Melinda Yang is here."

"Great. Thanks for letting me know."

Joey and I walked together to the street entrance of the community garden.

I turned to him. “You heard that Bunny Hare’s son got shot?”

“I did. So sad. You know he did some maintenance work here at the condo to prepare for its opening, right?”

“What?”

“Yeah. You saw him. He was the maintenance guy you were scolding.”

“*Scold* is a strong word, Joey. I don’t think I scolded him, did I?”

Joey nodded. “You scolded him about disturbing the crime scene and tampering with the evidence.”

“That was Stone?”

I thought back. I hadn’t really focused too much on the maintenance guy himself, more on what he was doing with the possible evidence.

I stopped. “I remember seeing him, but I didn’t realize it was Stone. Hard to tell with the mask and the cap he wore.”

I wondered whether Bunny knew he’d been there that morning.

We resumed our journey toward the street.

Joey dipped his head. “That’s right. That was Stone Hare. Glad he’s going to be okay.”

I nodded. “I understood he was estranged from his mother. Did he mention anything to you?”

“I’d only met him a couple of days before that. We didn’t talk about anything other than work-related stuff. As I told you, today is my first official day. Although, honestly, it doesn’t feel like it because I’ve been living in the condo for several days now.”

“That’s right. So then maybe you can help? Did you see anyone strange hanging around? Or fighting with Bunny? I’m sure the police already questioned you.”

“Yes, they did. Sergeant Gomez in particular was curious about the days leading up to Bunny’s murder.”

I bet he was.

Ernie still owed me one. I’d suggest a meetup to pick his brain.

Joey and I exited the garden’s rear street gate.

Melinda Yang and her team, like the protestors, had positioned themselves on the street behind Jacaranda Gardens. Her update was very brief and focused on the protestors.

I ambled down the sidewalk back to the community garden gate.

Melinda spotted me and broke into a wide smile. "Hi, Tory. Nice to see you again under slightly better circumstances today."

"Great piece. I was watching your segment from behind the oleander."

"Funny you should mention oleander. My source at SSPD told me the autopsy results revealed Bunny was poisoned with oleandrin. My producer wants me to follow that lead. You're a landscape architect. You're familiar with plants. Just the person to help me. Don't worry, it won't be live. I don't even know if I'll use it, but since you're here we might as well."

She motioned to her cameraman and before I knew it, she was questioning me on camera. I basically just regurgitated what I'd googled and what Ashley had told me.

Afterward I walked out to my car with Joey. "Anything you forgot to mention to Sergeant Gomez? I know him and probably will be talking to him soon."

"Oh. No. Nothing else."

I halted. "Who did Stone Hare hang out with on his breaks, if anyone?"

"Like I said, I've only been here about a week, but from what I could tell, he seemed like a loner."

I turned to head to my car.

Joey raised his voice. "Except . . . he did go to his car to eat lunch sometimes, and I saw a woman drive up once and join him."

I spun around. "You did?"

"Yeah. I'd forgotten that."

"What was she like? Would you recognize her if you saw her again?"

"Hard to say. I was inside the lobby. So not the best view. But she looked attractive from a distance. Shoulder-length blonde hair. Seemed to have an average height and build, maybe on the slender side? They did hug so I assumed it was his lady friend."

"What kind of car did she have?"

"A nice one. Looked like a late-model Mercedes."

What would Stone be doing with a rich girlfriend when he couldn't afford rent? In a Mercedes, no less.

And then I stopped in my tracks.

The McGregors had two Mercedes. And Kaley had shoulder-length blonde hair. Was Stone seeing Kaley? I felt dizzy, like I'd just spun around a dozen times. What if Stone and Kaley were having an affair? My first thought—Kaley really got around. My second thought—I wondered if this new revelation had anything to do with Bunny's murder.

I thanked Joey and got in my car and headed to my office. Back at my desk, I called Heath Grant and he verified Mac's alibi. I also accepted his dinner invitation. Heck. I was already confused about everything. Why break my streak?

CHAPTER 18

The rest of the day flew by. I caught up on my work emails and finished two proposals with looming deadlines, one for Santa Sofia's Natural History Museum's Arboretum and Botanical Garden and another for a winery. After I finished my most pressing matters, I decided to swing past the hospital to see if Stone was able to accept visitors.

Santa Sofia had two hospitals located within its city limits: the smaller St. Matthew's Hospital, and Santa Sofia Hospital, which was a midsized facility compared to the larger Santa Sofia Medical Center located about five miles south of town, a regional hospital serving Santa Barbara County.

I crossed the Avenue and drove a couple of miles to the quiet neighborhood where Santa Sofia Hospital was situated. I turned into the entrance, which was flanked by a simple yet elegant landscape design of sunken troughs filled with gravel and succulents. I continued along a perimeter road, passing the lane that led to the Emergency Department, and continued straight to the parking lot in front of the main five-story hospital building.

I walked through glass doors to the hospital entrance. The first thing I saw was a long, curved desk under a sign that read *Reception and Information*. It was manned by three women, each of whom had their own station marked by plexiglass dividers. I went to the middle desk and asked if Stone Hare was allowed visitors. I knew the hospital had a one-visitor-at-a-time policy.

The woman looked up Stone's name. "He has a visitor right now."

I slumped my shoulders.

She placed a clipboard and pen on the raised counter in front of me. "If you like, I can take your name and cell phone number and you could wait in your car in the parking lot until his visitor leaves."

I stood up straighter. "That would be great. Thanks."

I couldn't believe my good fortune.

"I'll call you when his visitor has left."

I walked back to my car with a spring in my step, excited by the prospect I might be able to definitively rule out Mac in at least one crime. I figured once Stone learned Mac had a solid alibi, his recollection of his assailant's description might change, and we might get a clearer lead on the real culprit. I listened to some Stray Kids while I pondered whether I'd made the right decision by accepting Heath Grant's dinner invitation. My thoughts kept coming back to Mac. What if Stone told me he was a hundred percent certain it was Mac who shot him? I couldn't imagine that my gut feeling could be so wrong about Mac. And what would be the implications for Mac's alibi and the people who vouched for him, like Heath Grant? I wondered who else might have wanted to harm both Bunny and Stone.

After I'd listened to one song, I googled Scarlett Hare's boyfriend, Denny Wargo, to see if I could find anything incriminating about him that might indicate Scarlett's possible motive to get rid of her mother and brother. I found an old news story about him. Denny Wargo had owned Wargo's River Ranch Barbeque Restaurant for eight years and had apparently been a high roller with shady connections who'd purportedly been swindling the Chumash Indian casinos in the area for double that amount of time. He'd been married and divorced twice.

I propped my chin in my hand and gazed out the windshield. I was betting Scarlett's energies were most likely focused on the path of least resistance for securing her financial status, working on becoming wife number three rather than killing her mother and brother.

Next, I googled the environmental groups Bunny had been involved with. All were well-regarded, well-funded, and got high rankings on Charity Navigator, so the likelihood of anyone from one of these groups having a motive to get rid of Bunny to get any funds she might have designated to them in her will seemed slight.

Which reminded me, I needed to ask Luke if he'd gotten any closer to finding out who Bunny's beneficiaries were.

I stared into space considering all of this when I did a double take. The sight of a woman jogging from the hospital entrance to the parking lot in high heels was comical enough to have gotten my attention. But what really made me look twice was her outfit, the same outfit she'd worn as a server at Wargo's. It was Scarlett. Had she just visited Stone? She'd told me they were estranged. Maybe it had taken a near-death experience to make her give him a second chance. She looked in my direction, but I doubted whether she had seen me. How would she even know my car?

My phone vibrated. It was a text from the hospital saying I could visit Stone. It must have been Scarlett who'd been visiting Stone. It would have been too much of coincidence to be otherwise.

I didn't have to wait long for her to leave. She peeled out of the lot like a Grand Prix racer, her car's tires screeching. Then a thought occurred to me. Why was she speeding? And why had she been running, and in heels? With her car out of sight, I ran as fast as I could to the hospital entrance, my head filled with crazy thoughts. Like what if Scarlett had just offed Stone? Maybe she'd come to finish him off, having missed the first time. Maybe that's why Stone was so certain Mac had been the shooter, because Stone was afraid his sister might finish him off if he squealed on her, and Mac was already a murder suspect and pinning the attempt on him would have been at least halfway plausible.

I picked up my pace. My heart felt like it was beating out of my chest.

I arrived at the front desk out of breath and panting. "Hi, I'm here to check on Stone Hare."

The female clerk gave me the side-eye.

"To visit him, I mean. You just texted me."

"Oh, right." She checked her clipboard. "He's in room 4052.

Elevators are to your left."

I accepted the visitor badge she handed me and jogged toward the elevators, hitting the Up button when I reached them. An elevator door instantly opened to reveal an empty car. I rushed in and pushed *4*, my heart pounding as the elevator seemed to take forever to reach the fourth floor. The elevator jolted gently to a stop and the doors opened. I turned my head quickly back and forth, searching for room number guides to figure out the way to room 4052. Down the hall to the right, I saw an SSPD officer standing outside a room with his back to me. That must be Stone's room.

I trotted toward him, my heels clicking on the linoleum tiled floor loudly enough to make the cop turn around. I was surprised to see it was Ernie Gomez. Now that my former nemesis had morphed into an almost normal human being, I no longer recoiled at the sight of him.

Ernie tipped his head. "Hi, Tory. Good to see you."

I panted. "How's Stone? Have you checked on him lately? Is he okay?"

"Yeah. I just poked my head in the door after his last visitor. I asked him how his leg was doing, and he gave me a thumbs-up."

I leaned against the wall, sweating, and gripped my chest. "Thank God. I'm here to say hi to him. I won't stay long."

"Sounds good."

I started to go toward Stone's door. "Oh, by the way, Ernie. I've been meaning to contact you."

Ernie's eyes lit up.

"Ever since I spoke to Joey, the manager at Jacaranda Gardens."

The spark in Ernie's eyes dimmed a bit. "Oh, yeah. I interviewed him."

"Right. About that. Did you come across any evidence implicating anyone other than Mac in Bunny's murder? I'm happy to report that I spoke to Mac, and he has an airtight alibi with credible witnesses for Stone Hare's shooting. So, if you guys are thinking the same person who shot Stone also murdered Bunny,

I think that eliminates Mac. What's your current theory?"

I held my breath, waiting for Ernie's answer, hoping the police believed both crimes to have the same perp. Because then Mac would practically be free and clear of any blame. But as for his wife, Kaley, she was another story.

"It's still an active case. We're still gathering evidence. We'll follow up on any person of interest who can provide an alibi. Officially, we're saying Bunny's killer and Stone's assailant may or may not be one and the same person." He lowered his voice. "But between you and me, it makes the most sense to think it's the same person. Coincidences can happen, but two members from the same family, a few days apart? Unlikely it's different perps."

My body relaxed hearing that news. Now I hoped Mac's alibi really checked out, and it wasn't just Heath vouching for him because they were friends. If it did, I felt he would no longer be a prime suspect. And I didn't even have to twist Ernie's arm to get the information. I was loving his personality makeover.

"What about that paper cup I saw stuck in the hedges? Any prints on that? Or analysis of the contents? It must have been empty but maybe a trace of something showed up?"

"What cup? I don't remember a cup as evidence?"

"I saw it while all your CSI guys were on the premises. I assumed they got it. I didn't want to touch it and contaminate it."

And then I thought of Stone and his rake and trash bag.

"You guys checked all the trash cans, right?"

"Of course. We collected it all. Now, whether we've gotten around to analyzing it all is a different matter."

"Well, that cup seems like promising evidence to me. I'd get on that right away, if I were you."

He gave me a mock salute. "Yes, ma'am."

"Anyway, I hope you can eliminate Mac as a suspect soon."

"I'll keep you posted."

"Thanks."

I knocked on Stone's door, which was ajar.

"Hello?" I pushed open the door and walked in.

Stone, who was sitting in a chair with his leg elevated on a stool and crutches next to him, turned to look at me.

"Oh, you can get up and about. That's great. How are you feeling?"

"Hey. I remember you. You were my mom's friend. Better, thanks. On pain drugs, so that's cool."

"Yes. Tory Benning. I don't want to stay long or bother you. As I might have mentioned, Mac McGregor is a suspect in your mother's death and he and his wife swear he wasn't involved and asked me to help prove his innocence."

"Yeah. I remember."

"So, it was understandably disturbing to hear that your description of your shooter fits a description of Mac McGregor."

The corners of his mouth were turned up slightly and he had a slight glaze in his eyes that gave me the impression he literally was feeling no pain. Stone looked stoned.

"Yeah, like I told the cops. It all happened real quick like. I wasn't expecting someone to pull a gun on me. He came up on me from behind. As soon as I saw the gun he was in my face and I knocked his arm, which probably saved my life, but then in our struggle for the gun on the beach it went off and that's when I went down with my leg wound."

"Then what happened?"

"He picked up the gun and ran away."

"Thank God he didn't try to shoot you again."

"Yeah. Guess he freaked out. He just took off." He extended his arm to make his point.

I tilted my head to the side. "Were there any witnesses?"

"Nah, just me. It was a deserted part of the beach."

"Did he say anything to you?"

He shook his head. "Nah."

I shifted my weight. "So, have you gotten a lot of visitors?"

He hesitated before responding. "No. I'm kind of a loner."

"Surely Peter or Scarlett have visited you?"

He lowered his head. "Nah. I'm kind of estranged from my family, like I told you the other day."

I nodded. "Yes. I remember. And you're sure the shooter was an older man?"

"Yep. In a hoodie. If there're any cameras around the beach they probably wouldn't help because of the hood."

I found it odd that he would mention cameras.

"But you got a good look despite the hoodie?"

"More or less. He was wearing a mask. But it looked like Mac to me."

So now his assailant was wearing a mask too. Yet still he was ready to ID Mac.

"Oh, you know Mac?"

"Nah, only from that time in the community garden. But I remembered what he looked like."

"Okay. Well, thanks so much for your time. And hope you feel better real soon."

Ernie was down the hall when I exited.

I strolled over to him. "Say, Ernie, has Stone had a lot of visitors today?"

"No, just his sister. Why?"

"Oh, just curious. Okay, thanks."

Thanks for confirming that Stone lied. As I power-walked out of there my head was swimming with questions. Why did Stone deny that Scarlett had just visited him? And why was he throwing Mac under the bus?

I got in my car trying to sort out my thoughts. I turned on Stray Kids as background music to calm myself down so that I could analyze things in an orderly fashion. That's when a silver Mercedes caught my eye as it drove into the half-empty lot, glided right past me, and parked an aisle away. Emerging from the Mercedes was Kaley McGregor, dressed casually in cropped leggings, tennis shoes, and a jean jacket. She looked around. It seemed her gaze lingered on my car for a few seconds, as I tried to slink down in my seat. Then she bustled into the hospital. Hmm. I wondered whether she was here to visit Stone. And if so, why was Stone so popular all of a sudden?

I called Ashley. "Thanks again for being there for the window repair guy. I really appreciate it. How about I buy you dinner?"

"Adrian just called. We're going to catch a quick bite then he has to work. I can come over after."

"Oh. You guys are on again?"

"We were never off. We haven't had a chance to talk. He's been working twenty-four-seven and I've been slammed too. Hopefully, we'll have a chance to talk over dinner."

"Okay. Good luck. See you later."

"And Tory?"

"Yeah?"

"I'll take a rain check on your dinner offer."

I laughed. "Of course."

CHAPTER 19

On my way home I stopped by the *Sentinel*. Maybe Peter could shed some light on Stone's newfound popularity.

He was walking to his car as I pulled up. I parked and got out of my car.

Peter strolled toward me. "Hi, Tory. What brings you here today? Let me guess, more questions."

I laughed. "Yes, actually. Just a few brief ones. I just went to visit Stone and I saw Scarlett there, leaving from a visit. And then later, when I left, I saw Kaley arriving, I'm assuming to visit Stone too."

His head jerked at the mention of Kaley.

"It was my understanding that Scarlett and Stone were estranged from each other and Bunny. I guess his injury brought them back together?"

Peter stopped and adjusted his glasses. "I wouldn't know. As I told you the other day, I have little interaction with them."

"I'm still bothered about that rock with the note you said you got the night before."

Bringing up the note didn't seem to register a strong reaction in Peter either way. I didn't know whether the light blue lenses of his glasses were vision-related or just to make him look cool but, regardless, it made it difficult for me to read his expression accurately.

"Why did you say it was left there the night before their fight on TV? Couldn't it have been left there that morning, after Mac said 'this isn't over' on TV?"

He looked down at his feet. "Why would it matter?"

Why would it matter? I blanked out. In my eagerness to be

Columbo I'd momentarily forgotten my point. I made a mental note not to ask a suspect a question I didn't know the answer to myself.

"Why would it matter? Really, you're asking me why it would matter?"

Peter gazed at me intently. "That's right."

I inhaled and exhaled slowly. And then I remembered.

"The timing of when the rock was left at your house would matter because if it was left in the morning, it's highly unlikely it could have been left by Mac since he was at the community garden all morning. However, if the note was left the night before, it suggests the note was left by Mac, or someone who could predict the future. Because what are the odds that two different people would think of the exact same comment? Not very likely. Assuming the killer isn't Mac, the real killer could have seized the moment to plant the note on your doorstep after hearing Mac say 'this isn't over' that morning on TV to further implicate Mac. Do you see how the timing could be crucial?"

Peter shifted his weight. "Yes. Since Mac couldn't be in two places at once, at the TV interview and at my house immediately afterward."

"Exactly. And since we can assume that Bunny didn't notice the rock with the note on it when she left in the morning, or else she would have mentioned it in the interview, I think we can also assume the rock and note were placed on your doorstep sometime after Bunny left but before you did."

Peter ran his hand through his hair.

I crossed my arms. "Where were you exactly when Bunny was killed? I remember seeing you at the community garden after the interview."

"What are you implying exactly?"

"I'm not implying anything. Simply asking a question."

"I watched Bunny on TV at home and then dropped by the community garden afterward."

A thought flashed in my brain. I remembered my online search for the symptoms of oleander poisoning. I had a hunch.

"What were Bunny's long-haul Covid symptoms? You mentioned the other day that she had lingering symptoms?"

"Initially she had headaches. But more lately stomach issues."

"Nothing else? You mentioned loss of smell before. Did that linger? And did she lose her sense of taste too?"

He snapped to attention. "Why, yes. She had both of those from the start. We expected them to dissipate. But she claimed they never did. She was worried about not smelling smoke if there was a fire."

"Or tasting oleander if she was being poisoned."

Peter shot me an alarmed look.

I compressed my lips. "I think we just discovered why it was possible to kill Bunny with a bitter-tasting poison like oleander."

All the color had drained from Peter's face. "Someone capitalized on her health situation in order to kill her?" He sighed heavily. "Look, I have to go. I have a lot to do today. I'm meeting with Adrian later and hope to get some closure."

Closure? On what? I wondered.

I opened my car door. "One more thing. I was surprised to see Kaley McGregor visit Stone at the hospital. Do you know how they knew each other?"

His whole demeanor changed when I mentioned Kaley. If looks could kill, I'd just been annihilated.

Peter's brows furrowed and his face turned dark red. "I don't see any reason to drag Kaley into this." He moved closer to me.

Whoa. Where did that flash of anger come from? After he snapped at me, I took a step back, trying to will the hairs on my arms to stand down. Was he being protective of his girlfriend? Or bordering on homicidal craziness?

He held my gaze as if he was going to say something but sighed heavily instead. Then he abruptly turned and headed to his car.

I drove home feeling mixed emotions. I still felt stung by Peter's flash of anger, reminding me I needed to be more careful. I didn't want to set anyone off and be the next victim. But also, I felt hopeful. Perhaps Peter planning to meet with Adrian later was a sign he'd seen the futility of denying he killed Bunny. Was that why he was meeting with Adrian? Was he going to confess?

Iris and Lily were waiting for me by the door when I returned home, both barking their little heads off. Otis strolled out from my bedroom after a few minutes to see why the Poms were making such a commotion. I checked out the window repair in my office and was happy that my fortress was once again secure. After we went outside and romped around in the backyard, I grabbed my phone and took some photos and videos of Iris and Lily and sent them to my aunt Marian and to my aunt Veronica and uncle Bob. After our photoshoot, we all came back inside for dinner.

I wrapped a piece of salmon in parchment paper and stuck it in the oven. I microwaved half of a sweet potato and some green beans. After everything was ready, I sliced a lemon from my backyard tree and squirted it on my salmon.

I hopped onto a barstool and dug in. After I'd eaten a few bites, I scrolled through Instagram. My phone pinged. It was a reply from my aunt Veronica. She loved the photos of Lily and wanted to know if she and my uncle Bob could pop over quickly to see her.

I texted her back. *Yes, please!*

I hadn't seen my aunt and uncle much lately because of social distancing. We'd had one or two get-togethers outdoors, but mainly we stayed in touch by phone, text, and FaceTime.

A few minutes later my doorbell rang. My aunt and uncle were charmed as soon as they laid eyes on Lily, who ran circles around them as they were still walking inside.

Aunt Veronica crouched down to pet Lily, peering at her through her round tortoiseshell glasses and smiled. "Oh, my goodness, Tory. She's such a little doll."

"Isn't she? So affectionate too."

Uncle Bob, looking like he'd added a few extra pounds to his already portly waistline, leaned in with a half hug and pecked me on the cheek. "Funny thing. As soon as we pulled up, a car that was parked on the street just took off like a street racer.

Made a racket with its tires screeching."

I froze. "Really? What kind of car?"

Aunt Veronica studied my face. "Something wrong, dear?"

Uncle Bob set down the plastic container he was holding on my hall table. "Your aunt baked these today. Chocolate chip." He furrowed his brow slightly. "It was a Mercedes. Should we be concerned? Someone bothering you?"

"Yes . . . no . . . I don't know. It's just that I've noticed a silver Mercedes following me a few times lately. Once when I was with Jake in his car. Once with Ashley in her car. And once or twice outside my house before." I shuddered. "Then there was the rock through my window."

Shoot. As soon as the part about the rock left my lips, I knew I'd revealed too much.

Aunt Veronica shook her highlighted hair. "Oh, my goodness. A rock? Did you call the police?"

"Yes, of course. Adrian and Jake even spent the night here the night it happened."

Uncle Bob scratched his mostly bald head. "Why would someone throw a rock in your window? Neighborhood kids?"

"No, I'm afraid it's more than random vandalism. I was targeted."

After ten minutes of bringing my aunt and uncle up to speed and trying to calm them down, I felt like I'd succeeded in convincing them I would be careful and keep in close contact with Adrian and Jake, especially if anything else occurred.

"You know you're always welcome to stay at our place for as long as you want until this all blows over and an arrest is made."

I hugged them both and told them I would think it over.

Uncle Bob sighed. "Rumor has it they're closing in on arresting Mac McGregor."

I tilted my head back and forth. "I hope not, because I don't think Mac is the culprit."

Aunt Veronica rested her hand on my shoulder. "Tory, please don't endanger yourself by getting involved."

Too late for that. I knew I was getting warm. I couldn't rest until I found Bunny's killer.

After they left, I curled up on my living room sofa with Iris, Lily, and Otis. I wondered whether Ashley was going to make it over. It was getting late. When my phone buzzed, I thought it was her. But it was Jake calling. I debated whether to pick up, but remembering my promise to my aunt and uncle to keep him and Adrian up to date, I finally did.

"Glad I caught you."

"That car was outside again. My aunt and uncle saw it when they dropped by. They just left."

"That's not good. Make sure all your doors are locked."

"I always do."

"Good. Do you have some time to talk right now?"

"I guess."

"Great. I'll be right over."

That wasn't what I had in mind. At all. But he'd hung up, and ten minutes later he was at my front door.

He hugged me. "So glad we can finally talk."

I strode back into the living room, inwardly rolling my eyes. "Sure. But what's to talk about? I saw what I saw."

Jake followed me. "You're still mad."

I paced from one end of the room to the other. "Mad, no. Disappointed, yes. I don't mind seeing other people. We never spoke about exclusivity exactly. But I would at least like to have been told in advance instead of happening upon you all like I did."

Jake let out a loud exasperated sigh. "But that's just it. It wasn't like it was a double date."

I put my hands on my hips. "Sure looked like that to me."

He touched my arm. "Look, you know me. I wouldn't do anything to hurt you . . . in fact, quite the opposite."

I shoved my face closer to his. "Then why would you go on a date and let me stumble upon it like that?"

"It's not what it seems." He bit his lip and shook his head.

"What?"

He inhaled and exhaled loudly.

"I promised I wouldn't tell you."

"Promised who?"

He tilted his head down and then looked up at me like a puppy. A very cute puppy, I had to admit. With dreamy blue eyes.

"Okay, I get it. If you promised, you can't tell me who. Got it."

We sat next to each other on the sofa. Iris and Lily scrambled up and sat between us. Jake pet them both and then patted my hand.

I cocked my head. "If you promised someone, that someone must be Adrian. Because who else could it be, correct?"

He gazed deeply into my eyes.

"Can you just nod if I'm correct? Technically, you're telling me nothing."

He laughed. And nodded.

"That was a nod, right? Not just a tick?"

He laughed again, and his eyes twinkled at me.

"Good. Okay, so if Adrian didn't want you to tell me, it could be for one of two reasons. One, he didn't want Ashley to find out. Is that it?"

He didn't react.

"Okay. Or he didn't want you to tell me because it was related to a case, right?"

He nodded.

I loved this game. It was like Twenty Questions, only with higher stakes.

I leaned back. "I can't believe you'd promise Adrian something like that. Where's your allegiance to me? You know I'm careful and can be trusted."

"Look, Tory. I know that. Adrian knows that too. It's just that he wants to do everything by the book because as Ashley could tell you, you can have the right suspect but not sufficient evidence to prosecute them."

I crossed my arms. "I'm careful though. I want the right person to be prosecuted, convicted, and locked up more than anyone."

We both sat immersed in our own thoughts for a few minutes.

Jake cleared his throat. "So, when I spoke to you when you were on your way to your father's house, you said something didn't feel right about us."

I nodded. "And that was even before you decided to exclude me from the investigation and go on double dates."

I stole a glance at him.

He looked downward. "So, what's the matter?"

"Well, for starters, when I thought you'd been cheating on me, I went ahead and accepted an invitation. A dinner invitation. For tomorrow night."

"Okay."

"From a guy."

"I figured that part out."

"So there's that."

"This is someone you're interested in? Who you're attracted to?"

I honestly didn't know the answers to his questions.

"It's Heath Grant. The movie star."

Jake glanced at me. "I know who he is. We saw him at Gaviota Grove, remember?"

"Oh, yeah. I forgot."

Lily had crawled up Jake's chest and started to lick his face.

Jake emitted a deep chuckle. "How'd you meet him?"

"He's the new tenant for my father's house."

He leaned back and nodded his head slowly. His shoulders drooped.

"But don't worry. It's not a date. Like going out to a restaurant. He's cooking dinner himself at the house."

"That's supposed to make me feel better?"

I giggled. "Oh, no. Not just the two of us. He's throwing a dinner party."

Jake sat up straighter. "So, is this your way of telling me you don't want an exclusive relationship?"

"I don't know. Honestly, I'm feeling really confused. I loved hanging out with you before the pandemic. I really did. And I love talking to you. But I don't know whether I'm . . ." I took a deep breath. "I don't know whether I'm afraid of getting closer with anyone, not just you, or maybe just you, I don't know. I'm afraid of investing in someone and loving them, only to possibly lose them again. Like what happened with Milo. It's scary."

"It's always scary."

"I know. But your line of work, you follow criminals, you interact with dangerous people. The probability of you getting hurt just seems higher than normal."

"A lot of my work is routine stuff."

"But not all. What about you? How do you feel after the pandemic? About seeing me?"

"I did a lot of thinking during the lockdown. That's what I've been wanting to talk to you about. It made me realize that life is short."

I did a double take. His tone had changed, and he suddenly seemed more businesslike. He seemed detached and matter-of-fact. Was he breaking up with me? After all my worry and revealing my feelings to him? I felt so embarrassed.

He sighed. "Too short to spend it wasting time."

He *was* breaking up with me. I felt my eyes filling with tears.

"I wanted to let you know—"

I stood up. "Stop right there. You don't have to ramble on. I get it."

"You do? How do you know?"

"Body language. See how your arms are folded. You're closing yourself off."

He unfolded his arms and chuckled. "Keep your day job. You'd make a terrible body language reader, if such an occupation exists. Tory, I don't know where you're getting some of your wild ideas. Jumping to conclusions. That's not the Tory I know when you're trying to solve a crime."

My phone pinged. It was Ashley. *Sorry for the delay. I'm on my way.*

"Ashley is on her way over. She went to dinner with Adrian and had planned to be here earlier. Guess their *talk* went longer than expected." I made air quotes.

Jake raised his eyebrows and look bewildered. "Okay, I'll be quick then. I just wanted to tell you—"

The doorbell rang. I peeked out the window and opened the front door for Ashley.

"That was quick."

Iris and Lily had run after me and were barking and wagging their tails.

Ashley laughed as she petted them. "Yeah, I actually texted you after I parked. I was watching this shady car that went super slowly past your house."

Jake appeared in the hallway. "What's this about a car? Again?"

Ashley's mouth opened in surprise. She glanced at me. "Oh, I'm sorry. I didn't know you were here, Jake."

Jake hugged Ashley briefly. "On my way out. Nice seeing you, Ashley. Please make sure you two stay out of trouble. I'll keep my eyes open for the car. What was the make of the car? Did you happen to catch the license plate?"

Ashley turned to me. "You're not going to like this."

I rolled my head to one side. "Let me guess, a silver Mercedes?"

She nodded. "Yep." Her gaze turned to Jake. "It happened too quickly for me to get a license plate number. By the time I had my phone out they'd driven away."

Jake frowned. "So how many times have you seen the same car hanging around here?"

"I don't know. A handful of times?" I hung my head. "But it's been more frequently lately."

He dipped his head and looked up at me. "A handful? That's precise." He rolled his eyes. "And you think it's the same car that followed us from Gaviota Grove?"

"That's what I'm assuming."

Ashley grimaced as she picked off some dog hair from her dark gray pants. "Honestly, I can't be sure it's the same car that followed us from Wargo's. Yeah, it was silvery, but there are lots of shades of silver . . . or shades of gray." Ashley giggled.

Jake tilted his chin up. "Okay, I'm out of here. Let's find a time soon to finish our conversation." Jake hugged me and went out the door.

Ashley's eyes widened. "What was that all about? What conversation? Did he tell you about their 'double date'?"

"We started to get into it. But them he clammed up. Because Adrian swore him to secrecy."

"Well, Adrian explained it all to me, and he must have forgotten to swear me to secrecy, so let me tell you what he told me."

My head snapped to attention. "What? Really? Tell me."

We strolled down the hallway in the direction of my living room.

"Turns out they *were* both working. They were trying to get dirt on Scarlett from two off-duty servers from Wargo's."

"Adrian suspects Scarlett?"

Ashley fluffed her hair. "He was checking her out as a possible suspect. But after Stone was shot, and Scarlett apparently had an alibi, his attention refocused on Mac."

I spoke softly. "So Jake and Adrian aren't dating those girls?"

Ashley smiled and shook her head. "Nope."

"Then why didn't Jake just tell me that?"

Iris and Lily both pawed at me to be picked up.

Ashley scooped up Lily. "I don't know. But I do know this little munchkin is so sweet."

I picked up Iris and we all went into the living room. After several minutes of playing with the dogs, a thought occurred to me.

"Hey, I have an idea."

"Why do I have a bad feeling right now? Didn't you just hear Jake tell us to stay out of trouble?"

"I heard. This isn't anything bad. It's just surveillance."

"Surveillance. Of whom, may I ask?"

"Kaley."

We moved to my leather couch, where we curled up at opposite ends.

I adjusted a cushion. "I still think something is off with her. The way she's given me mixed messages about Mac. Like help him, but then the next minute he and Bunny were archenemies. And her lying about not only her alibi but about Mac's. Why would she do that unless—"

Ashley wiggled around to get comfortable. "She's guilty of something."

"Exactly. My plan is to see if we can catch her in the act of stalking me. Now that Jake is gone and you're out of your car, let's see if she comes back to stalk me."

"But she already did, assuming that was her I saw."

"I know. But I was thinking tomorrow night. I have Heath's dinner party. But after that we can wait outside so that we're prepared if she drives by, and we can take a photo of her and her car."

"What if she comes while you're at the party?"

"I was thinking maybe you can take the early shift. And then I can relieve you when I get back."

"I don't know. Let me sleep on it."

Ashley rose to go.

"Don't go. Stay here tonight. You can play with Lily some more."

Ashley looked at Lily for a few seconds. "Okay. Done."

"Oh, good. Slumber party."

We got ready for bed. As I double-checked to make sure the doors were locked, I peeked outside and there was a car parked at the curb in front of my house. My heart started beating quickly.

"Ashley, the car is there again."

"No!"

"Uh-huh. I'm going to lock and unlock my car with my fob from inside. See if that scares them off." My Lexus beeped as I locked and unlocked it.

The other car's headlights turned on and it sped away.

I leaned my back against the front door with my arms outspread. "Okay. That's it. New plan. We can't wait till tomorrow. We need to get more proactive. And now. I think we should have an early morning stakeout. Lie in wait in your car. Then when the car comes again, whip out our phones and take photos."

Ashley crossed her arms. "Don't you mean if, not when? No

guarantee they'll return. How early in the morning are you talking about?"

I thought for a moment. "I don't know. When it's still dark out."

"That's not morning, that's nighttime."

"Okay, how about when the sun rises. Around five thirty."

She stepped back and raised an eyebrow. "Are you sure this is necessary?"

"It is. Because then we can give the photos to Adrian, and he'll see that Mac isn't the only suspect."

"What if it's Mac?"

"It isn't. He was at Gaviota Grove when the car first followed me and Jake. They're coming daily now. I think they're trying to intimidate me. What have we got to lose?"

Ashley deadpanned, "My beauty sleep."

"Oh, come on, Ashley. A stakeout will be fun. We can bring snacks."

"Go on."

"Aunt Veronica brought me a whole container filled with her chocolate chip cookies tonight. We can take those."

"I do love her chocolate chip cookies. Sold."

"You're easy." I patted her shoulder. "We ride at dawn."

CHAPTER 20

I'd set the alarm on my phone for five thirty. When the ringtone sounded, I felt as if I'd just fallen asleep. I twisted around in the sheets and fumbled for my phone on the bedside table. I hit the screen to stop the bleating bell and swung my legs out of bed. I'd purposely slept in sweatpants and a sweatshirt so it would make it easy to roll out of bed and be ready to go. I remained seated while I pushed each foot into my Allbirds, felt loafers as comfy as slippers that softened the blow of getting up with the chickens.

I gently tapped on the guest room door to wake up Ashley. No response. Iris was by my side, tracking my every move with a nervous intensity, seeming to wonder what was going on. Lily was lying on her side, still asleep.

I knocked a little louder. "Time to get up," I whispered so as not to startle her.

Ashley answered in a groggy voice, "Okay. I'm up."

When I cracked the door open, Ashley was putting her shoes on.

She yawned. "Be with you in a minute." Ashley had also slept in a sweatsuit I'd lent her.

While I was waiting for Ashley, I went into the kitchen and made some coffee and poured it into two travel mugs.

Ashley padded out and took one of the mugs. "Ah. Thank you."

"Grab a water bottle. Here are the cookies."

"Yes. Let's not forget the only reason I've agreed to this folly." Ashley snatched the cookie container. "You realize I normally only get up this early for British royal weddings and South Korean competition show finales featuring the Stray Kids, don't you?"

I pulled a sad face. "Yes. I'm aware you're making a special exception for me and that you don't sacrifice your beauty sleep lightly. I'm very grateful for your service."

We stopped at the front door. I peeked out at the street. It was empty except for my neighbors' cars.

"Good. The coast is clear. Make sure you have your phone."

We trotted out to Ashley's black BMW, which was parked on the street, our eyes alert. Once we were inside with the doors locked, we both sighed. We put our coffee mugs in the center holders and the container of cookies on the console.

"Let's keep down as low as we can get." I slumped into my seat.

Ashley adjusted her seat so that it leaned back more.

I wiggled around in my seat to get more comfortable. "Now's a good time to review all we know about Bunny's murder and Stone's shooting."

"Oh my God." Ashley scrolled through her phone.

"What?"

"Ernie sent me a text last night."

"What did he want."

Ashley turned to me. "To give us a tip. He heard at the station they were close to arresting Mac for Bunny's murder and Stone's shooting in the next day or so."

"What?" I sipped my coffee. "Don't they know Mac has an alibi for Stone's shooting?"

"Maybe they're still checking that out. And maybe that's why they haven't arrested him yet. Can I open these?" Ashley pointed to the cookie container.

I nodded. "Of course you can. You're probably not wrong about checking alibis. Hopefully, Heath will substantiate Mac's claim he was at Gaviota Grove. But still, that they're considering an arrest means we have to step up our investigation too."

Ashley selected a cookie and bit into it. "Um, these are so good. Chewy. Okay, so let's go over the list of suspects. Who's your current favorite? Still Peter?"

"I alternate between him and Kaley. Or Peter in cahoots with Kaley. It still seems like a variation of *Strangers on a Train* to me, only they're not strangers, and only one person is murdered."

Ashley snickered. "So not at all like *Strangers on a Train*."

I chuckled. "It so is, if you look at how killing Bunny and pinning her murder on Mac gets rid of both of them for Peter and Kaley."

Ashley tilted her head. "Yeah, I still don't know if that's like *Strangers on a Train* because they all know each other, but I'll go with it for now because I'm not wide awake. Peter gets rid of a wife who won't divorce him, and Kaley not only gets rid of her rival but gets rid of her spouse, too, by putting him in jail."

I broke off a piece of a cookie and popped it into my mouth. "Then there's Scarlett, who's shady as they come. But she supposedly has an alibi for Stone's shooting."

Ashley reached for another cookie. "Anyone else? Like any *Sentinel* employees, environmental protestors, or campaign people?"

"You know, once Stone got shot, I eliminated all of those. I think the motive for Bunny's murder was more personal and intense. I mean, not only was she poisoned, she was hit on the head. Someone really wanted her dead."

"Yeah, about that. That's puzzled me this whole time. What, was she not dying fast enough? Did the killer get impatient? Seems so bizarre."

I nodded. "Yeah, that's always bothered me too. Unless . . ."

Ashley's brown eyes widened. "What?"

"What if it was a different person who hit her? Not knowing she had already been poisoned?"

Ashley picked a large crumb off her sweatshirt and ate it. "You mean like Peter hit her, not knowing Kaley had already poisoned her? Or vice versa?"

I sipped my coffee. "Although Peter told me he was at home and watched Bunny on TV."

Ashley tapped her coffee mug. "Maybe that's what he wants

you to believe. Do we have proof?"

I broke off more cookie. "I'm pretty sure Adrian has asked neighbors for surveillance videos on the day of the murder to check Peter's story, no?"

"Yep. You're probably right." Ashley drank some coffee. "What about clues?"

I popped the piece of cookie into my mouth. "So far, there are quite a few. Let's see if I can remember them in the same order I heard about them. The first was the supposedly leaked editorial. Depending on whether it was real or fake has different implications. And then there was the glove that Mac thought belonged to Bunny that he showed me the night before Bunny was murdered. Then the day she was killed the police found supposedly the same glove, plus a spade with blood on it, under a tarp in Mac's plot, and I spied a man's gardening glove in Mac's car. Peter supposedly found a rock with a note on it saying 'this isn't over' on his doorstep, similar to the one thrown through my window days later. And there's the paper cup I saw stuck in the oleander hedge, probably later picked up by the cops in a trash bag that Stone carried as he swept the grounds of Jacaranda Gardens. Am I forgetting anything?"

Ashley smacked her lips. "Wow. That's a lot of clues. And no bullet from Stone's gunshot wound, I'm assuming? If it was only a graze, correct?"

"I don't know whether they found the bullet. And yes, almost too many clues, if you ask me. Knowing Mac as I do, I never thought he was capable of murder. Despite his impulsiveness and lion's roar, he's also very smart and kindhearted, harmless as a kitten. But then when so many clunky clues started to pile up, all implicating Mac, it struck me as staged. I've always believed Mac was being set up."

Ashley sipped her coffee. "Oh, by the way, I forgot to tell you. Adrian told me he finally got the note Peter found and that his analysts have determined that both notes were written by the same person."

"Doesn't surprise me. I assumed that all along."

Ashley turned her head. "I see headlights. Get down."

A car drove by without stopping. As soon as it passed, I raised my head. It looked like a gardener's pickup truck.

I sighed loudly. "False alarm."

"So why was Jake at your place? To talk about the double date?"

"That and something else."

"What?"

"I think he's going to dump me."

"What? Are you crazy? He adores you."

"Does he? He got super serious and was trying to be nice, but I just had a weird feeling."

"Based on what exactly?"

"Body language."

Ashley laughed. "Since when have you been good at body language? I mean, you can be pretty adept at reading people when it comes to crime-solving. But romantic relationships are a whole different arena."

"Yeah. You might be right about that. He told me I misread him. But based on his intense demeanor, it was something serious. So, he's either dumping me, which I admit would be weird since we weren't really together, at least lately—"

"Or he's going to propose."

I shoved her shoulder. "No. Get out. We'd only dated seriously for a couple of months before the pandemic hit."

"You never know."

"Trust me, I know." But did I? I'd had that feeling earlier in the week.

"What's the latest with Luke? Have you heard anything more from him?"

"No. I need to check and see if he found out anything more about Bunny's will." I checked the time. It was six twenty. Early for a text. But I didn't care.

I texted him. *Have you found out anything regarding Bunny's will yet? Let me know. Thanks.*

"And you're still going over to Heath Grant's for dinner tonight?"

I grinned. "Sure am. They're all so different."

"And hot."

"That never hurts."

We both laughed.

"I know. I can't believe I have chemistry with all three."

"Tory, you little hussy. I'm pretty sure when people refer to love triangles, they don't mean one woman involved with three guys."

I chortled. "I know. I had the exact same thought. Great minds think alike. So, what about you and Adrian? What's going on now with you two? You sounded satisfied with his explanation of the double date."

"I am. We're going to continue our talk over lunch." Ashley grabbed my arm. "But, oh, I can't believe I forgot to tell you this. Everything has been so chaotic that it slipped my mind. You know Tate the firefighter?"

"Yeah. Tate Robinson. He introduced himself to me at the community garden. The one from the Secret Maze. But I could have sworn I'd seen him at the Christmas tree lot too."

"What about Trey? Do you remember him?"

"What? That's what I thought Tate's name was, but he corrected me."

Ashley's eyes were dancing with merriment.

"Why?"

"They're actually two different people."

"What do you mean? Like a split personality? Oh no, Ash. That's a red flag. You don't want to date anyone with multiple personalities. Like that old mystery drama *The Three Faces of Eve*."

"Funny you should mention that, but no, they're not one guy with multiple personalities."

"Okay, so they look identical, but they're two different people. You mean they're twins?"

Ashley grinned broadly. "Not exactly. They're brothers."

I chuckled. "Huh. Really?"

Somewhere in my brain a fleeting idea sparked. Something to do with two different people looking identical. But a second later, the thought had evaporated.

"Yep." She held up three fingers. "And there're three of them. The third one is Tristan. They're triplets." Ashley was beaming as if she'd just won the lottery.

"Get out. Identical triplets?" I gave her shoulder a gentle shove. "Tate had mentioned he was at the Secret Garden with his bros. I didn't know he meant it literally."

"Yes. Apparently all three were at the Firefighters Fundraiser. Makes sense because they're all firefighters. No wonder I kept thinking I was running into him everywhere—it was different brothers. They're practically identical. Not totally. But clearly, they look a lot alike since I can't tell them apart yet."

"How did you find out?"

Ashley cackled. "I googled and the three of them turned up. Apparently, they also have a band, and they produce their own music. I listened to a couple of their songs. They're actually pretty good."

I poked her in the arm. "And you have the nerve to tease me about love triangles. Ha! Pretty sure it doesn't mean dating triplets either."

We both cracked up. Our laughter was interrupted when we saw headlights.

Ashley whispered, "Someone's coming."

The car passed us and then pulled over to the curb across the street and parked. It was a silver Mercedes.

Since I was in the passenger seat, I had a better vantage point than Ashley. I squinted to read the license.

I got my phone out and took several pics. "Yay. Got it captured."

"Make sure you get parts of the street so we can prove to Adrian it was parked on your street."

It was starting to get lighter. I hoped light enough to prove the car's location.

I took more photographs. "Mission accomplished."

"Great. Now what?"

"Maybe you should start your engine? And see what they do?"

Ashley bit her lip. "Are you sure? What if they get out and have a gun?"

"Be prepared to floor it and drive straight to the police station if that happens."

Ashley put her seat belt on. "Okay. Buckle up, buttercup. Here goes."

I fastened my seat belt. "I've got my phone poised to take a close-up if they turn around."

But they didn't turn around. As soon as they saw Ashley's headlights go on, the car took off.

CHAPTER 21

After the car sped away, Ashley and I sat dumbstruck for a few seconds.

Ashley glanced over at me nervously. "Should I try to follow them?"

"Oh God, no. It's still early and there aren't many cars out yet. They'd know we were following them. I hope it was light enough to see the license plate." I checked my phone to look at the photos I'd taken. "Yay. The photos look good."

"Great. Then let's go back inside."

Clutching our water, coffee, and cookies, we jogged back to the house, looking behind us at the street every other second. We were greeted by all three animals at the door. It was seven ten. Breakfast time. But first, I let Iris and Lily out in the backyard. While they frolicked, I did a couple of stretches on the patio to ease my tension. Then I walked around the perimeter of the backyard to get my blood circulating after sitting in the car for so long and to burn off the jitters.

When the dogs and I returned, Ashley had changed back into her own clothes and had made more coffee.

She sat at my kitchen counter, munching on a cookie. "These really are good. One of the best chocolate chip cookies I've ever had."

I pulled up a barstool. "It's Aunt Veronica's secret recipe. I think she puts oats in them to give them that chewy texture. Maybe a little bit of banana for the moistness? I don't know. Every time I ask her for the recipe, she kind of diverts the conversation." I chuckled.

"That's too funny." Ashley took a sip of coffee. "I have to slow my roll. Seeing a stalker in action triggered my stress eating and my craving for comfort food. Can you send me the photos of the Mercedes and the license plate, please, so I can send them to Adrian?"

"Okay. Maybe also tell him our stakeout was for self-defense purposes, so he doesn't get mad at me. Couch it in terms of me wanting to protect myself instead of trying to interfere in his investigation."

I grabbed my phone on the counter, forwarded the photos to Ashley, and noticed a new text. "Okay. I just sent them all to you. And looks like Luke responded to my text."

"Thanks. Good thinking about the approach to take with Adrian. Even though we're all on the same team, we don't want him getting all pushed out of shape. What did Luke say?"

I read Luke's text. "He wants to meet for breakfast if I'm free. What should I tell him?"

Ashley focused on her phone while she typed a message to Adrian and sent him the photos.

After a few minutes she looked up. "Meet him. Tell him you're free as a bird." She laughed.

I grinned. "You know what he meant."

Ashley winked. "You never know."

"Ha, ha. Very funny. He meant available to meet, not whether or not I'm single and ready to mingle."

Just as Jake had said. He could be as corny as Ashley and I were at times, making me feel a pang for his silly humor.

Then I slapped my forehead as I remembered his text. "Oh my God, Jake *is* breaking up with me. His text told me he was 'single and ready to mingle.' I can't get over the writing was on the wall all along."

"You mean the writing was on your phone all along."

I gave Ashley the stink eye. "Not helpful."

Ashley pouted.

I stood up. "I've got to get ready."

I threw on a pair of black jeans and a black top and brushed my teeth. After I brushed my hair, it didn't look half bad, mainly straight with a few random loose waves, so I decided to wear it down.

Twenty minutes later I was looking for a parking space outside Clementine's Bakery. I found one and saw Luke sitting outside at a table. In an abundance of caution, many restaurants like Clementine's had decided to restrict their service to outdoor dining since it seemed Covid-19 surges would be with us for a while, ebbing and flowing like a roller coaster every couple of months or so. This appeared to be the new normal.

Luke stood up and pulled out a chair when he saw me. He was wearing a light blue shirt with the sleeves rolled up and jeans.

"Hi." I gave him a little wave. "What's up? You said you have new information?"

"Yes, I do. And I thought it would be easier and safer to do it in person."

"Safer?"

"Yeah. Finding out all this stuff has made me realize, once again, you can't believe everything someone tells you."

I wondered why he didn't answer my question about safety more directly. Was he in danger? Were we in danger? And more importantly, was I in danger?

Luke's piercing gaze was unnerving. I was all for eye contact, but he was killing me with his lingering stares. In a good way.

We studied our menus for a few minutes and gave a server our orders.

I unwrapped the silverware that was rolled up in a paper napkin. "So tell me what you've found out."

"First of all, I have a confession to make."

"Okay."

"When we first met and I told you Bunny had hired me to investigate her kids, that wasn't really true."

I leaned back in my chair. "Oh."

"The truth is she did hire me, but it was to follow Peter because she suspected him of having an affair."

"Well, she was right about that. And I kind of figured that was all part and parcel of you conducting a thorough investigation anyway. Why didn't you just tell me that?"

He straightened out his fork and knife. "Because it was a way to let you know I was working for her without revealing the true reason, which would have violated my confidentiality agreement."

"So you decided to lie to me."

He raised his eyebrows. "That's a harsh way of putting it."

"Okay. How about you bent the rules a bit. Is that better? I've been known to bend a few rules myself, in the pursuit of justice, of course."

"I knew you might be a good resource, given your experience looking at cases from a layperson's perspective. And it didn't hurt that you were personally involved with the people I was investigating."

"Then why are you telling me now?"

"Because I don't want you to get hurt. Whoever killed Bunny showed they're getting more desperate by shooting Stone. I thought it better to let you know that Peter was the person who concerned Bunny most."

Was this the danger Luke had alluded to earlier? Great. Out of all the suspects, Peter had been the one I'd had the most contact with.

I gulped. "Thanks?" My voice quavered slightly. "Better late than never, I guess, to be brought into the circle of trust."

And so much for his previous "Justice League" invite.

Luke chuckled as he stretched his long arms in the air and straightened up. "I tracked down Bunny's probate attorney."

I leaned on the table. "You did? Did you find out who her beneficiaries are?"

Luke nodded. "Uh-huh. Peter inherited most of Bunny's fortune, the rest goes into a trust for journalism scholarships at UC Santa Barbara's Department of Communication."

"And her kids?"

"Nothing."

I sat back in my chair. "I'm not really surprised. I'd found an interview with Bunny where she said she didn't believe in leaving her kids money. She thought giving her kids money undermined their motivation."

Luke pointed at me. "But get this, her lawyer also told me that recently Bunny had asked him to draft a new will where her kids would be the main beneficiaries and Peter would be excluded totally."

I leaned in again. "Really? Why? Because unmotivated kids were a lesser evil than a cheating husband?"

Luke drummed his fingers on the table. "I guess."

The server delivered our coffee.

I added some milk to mine. "Did her kids know Peter was the main beneficiary?"

"I think so. Apparently, Scarlett had come along to one of the lawyer meetings with Bunny. So, I think it's safe to assume Scarlett knew that Bunny was going to change her will to benefit Scarlett and Stone and disinherit Peter."

"Interesting. That would be an incentive for her kids to want to keep Bunny alive, not kill her."

Luke sipped his coffee. "Exactly. Bunny's lawyer told me she hadn't changed her will yet. She was waiting to see what my investigation found out."

"Peter is still the main beneficiary then?"

"Correct."

I pushed away from the table. "That means that Peter was the only one who had a financial motive to kill Bunny. That's been my theory all along."

"Don't be so quick to pat yourself on the back. There's more." Luke tapped his coffee cup. "At her last meeting with her attorney before she was murdered, Bunny had told him she wanted to not only drop Peter as a beneficiary, but that she no longer wanted to add the kids."

I straightened up. "Another change of heart? Why?"

"She told him she was convinced someone in her family was trying to kill her."

I leaned on the table so hard I nearly overturned my coffee. "What! She believed someone in her family was trying to kill her? Did she say who? I wonder what gave her that idea. She told that to her attorney? Why on earth hasn't the attorney come forward?"

Luke shook his head. "No, she didn't say who. Apparently, the attorney already told all of this to the police."

I rested my chin in my hand. "Oh, really."

I wondered how long Adrian had known all of this. Maybe that's why he and Jake were asking questions at Wargo's about Scarlett. It all made more sense now.

"Wait a minute . . . so Bunny hired you to find out more about Peter having an affair. Did she tell you anything about someone trying to kill her too?"

"No. But her last meeting with her attorney was on the day before she was murdered, and she asked him to draft a new will excluding her whole family. She'd scheduled a meeting with me the afternoon of the day she was murdered. I'm guessing she was going to share her theory with me then."

"Had you found any evidence of either Peter or her kids plotting to murder her?"

"No. Wherever she got the idea that one of them was trying to kill her, it wasn't from me."

"Hmm." My eyes fixed on a smoothie just delivered to a woman at the next table. "I don't see the kids having a motive to kill her if they knew they weren't beneficiaries. But Peter, on the other hand . . ."

Luke leaned closer and nodded. "Listen to this. Bunny's probate lawyer said Peter had given him a call the day before she was murdered too. Peter thought Bunny had gotten paranoid, maybe as a side effect of Covid. He said she'd acted differently after contracting it. Almost as if she were still hallucinating like she had when she had it."

I wondered now if she had, in fact, taken Mac's cabbage.

The server delivered our breakfast. We'd both ordered eggs Benedict. We ate a few bites in silence.

"This is so good." My eyes wandered to two tables away. Someone else had ordered another breakfast smoothie, making me feel slightly guilty for indulging in such a huge breakfast. And then a thought occurred to me regarding Bunny.

"You knew that Bunny had long-haul Covid symptoms, right?"

Luke nodded.

"Did you know she still hadn't gotten her sense of smell or taste back?"

Luke dabbed his mouth with his napkin. "Yes. Bunny's lawyer told me that Peter had mentioned Bunny's sense of taste and smell were still shot. And she had brain fog too."

"Seeing all these smoothies go by made me think of that smoothie Bunny had the morning she was killed. I bet the poison was in her smoothie. If we found out where she got the smoothie, we might be able to figure out who poisoned her."

Luke cut a bite of his eggs Benedict. "Yeah, I already figured that out."

I fiddled with my sandal strap. "Well, thanks for letting me know."

He paused from eating. He licked his lip and stared at me.

Oh, boy.

"Not that you need to report to me or anything." I laughed nervously.

My face was on fire. *Just. Stop. Talking.* I lowered my head and focused on cutting a very precise slice of Canadian bacon and egg.

Luke drummed his coffee cup. "I didn't mention it because, honestly, I only figured it out recently myself when I learned she'd lost her sense of taste."

"Oh. That's fine then."

Again, his gaze lingered, and he licked his lip.

Close your mouth, sir.

I took a deep breath. "I wonder if Peter saying she had brain fog was an attempt by him to gaslight Bunny? Making it seem like Bunny didn't know what she was talking about when she said someone was trying to kill her. Or wanting to cut him out of her will."

"You mean like in the movie. Anything is possible, I guess. But she always seemed sharp to me so I don't think Bunny would have fallen for that."

"Maybe not enough to make her wind up in a mental institution, but just to make her think she was imagining it and to doubt her own perceptions."

"That's why she hired me. So that I would provide an objective perspective."

I ate a bite of egg, bacon, and English muffin. "Peter could be lying about Scarlett bringing her mother smoothies. Maybe it was Peter who was giving Bunny smoothies."

Luke nodded. "Or maybe Scarlett brought the smoothies and Peter poisoned them."

I dabbed my mouth with a napkin. "Peter had a motive as long as he was in the will. But what was Scarlett's motive?"

Luke looked at his plate and then at me. "I don't know."

I twisted my mouth to one side. "Me either. I'm stumped."

Luke set down his fork. "Maybe Scarlett poisoned her mother and then tried to kill her brother too."

"But why?"

Luke rested one hand on the table. "Maybe Stone figured out that Scarlett had poisoned the smoothie, and she wanted to silence him before he snitched on her?"

I rested an elbow on the table. "But Scarlett wasn't at the community garden that morning, was she? How could she poison Bunny if she wasn't there? Also, I'm pretty sure she had an alibi."

"Hmm. Unless she gave it to her earlier. I need to double-check her alibi."

We both resumed eating our breakfasts in silence for a few minutes.

I set down my fork. "But Kaley was there at the community garden. I still think she and Peter might be in cahoots. And maybe they decided to kill Bunny for her money before Peter was disinherited."

Luke seemed to be considering what I said. "Maybe. But the other thing I found out—"

My fork clanked as I knocked it on my plate. "There's more?"

"Guess who invested in Peter's production company?"

"I don't know. Who?"

"Heath Grant."

I gasped out loud. "You're kidding."

My worlds were colliding.

CHAPTER 22

After I left Clementine's, I went straight to my office.

I called Ashley. "What's up?"

She yawned. "Nothing much. I'm dragging because I've been up since five thirty to support my best friend, but other than that I'm okay. How was breakfast with Luke?"

"A very grateful best friend. Thanks again, Ash. The breakfast was fascinating."

Ashley drew in her breath. "Oh. Do tell."

"Not like you think. About Bunny's murder."

I quickly summarized my conversation with Luke to Ashley.

"Wow. So you still think Peter is the person with the strongest motive."

I looked out my window at trees swaying in the breeze. "I do, yeah. Don't you?"

"I guess. But if Heath and a group of other investors had just infused Peter's production company with financial backing, I don't really see money as Peter's motive."

I considered Ashley's words while tapping my desk. "Maybe it wasn't about money only. Maybe it was because Bunny wouldn't give Peter a divorce. Maybe it was Peter's girlfriend who wanted to get rid of Bunny."

"Kaley? You still suspect her?"

"Yeah. My gut tells me something's up with her. Between her mixed messages about Mac, her lying about her own alibi and Mac's for Stone's shooting, I don't know. Something just seems off there. Coupled with Peter's jumpy demeanor. They both seem suspicious to me.

"And, like Peter, she had the means, motive, and opportunity.

Oleander is common. Bunny was her rival. And she could have slipped the oleander into Bunny's smoothie relatively easily if she enlisted Peter's help, either knowingly or unknowingly. Calling it a vitamin supplement or something. Making it seem like she was trying to help Bunny."

Ashley yawned. "All true."

I put my phone on speaker and stood up and walked over to the window. "Maybe she acted alone. Maybe with Peter. I don't know. But she's acting shady for some reason."

Ashley cleared her throat. "Just remember curiosity killed the cat."

I stared at my phone. "Thanks? I can always count on you to increase my level of already high anxiety."

"Hey, that's what friends are for." Ashley laughed. "Are you getting excited about the dinner party at Heath Grant's?"

I paced around my office. "Excited and nervous both. I don't know who or how many others will be there. Like I know nothing, except the house, which is mine. So yes, it'll be a little weird."

"I'm so curious who else will be there."

I leaned against my desk. "Me too. What are you doing tonight? Seeing Adrian again?"

Ashley breathed into the phone. "As a matter of fact, I am. He couldn't break away for lunch after all. Hopefully, we'll be able to finish our talk over dinner. Like you, I'm feeling a bit shell-shocked after the last year. It gave me time to rethink and reset. To reevaluate my life and my goals. In terms of work, I realize how much I want to keep doing pro bono work, like my work with the Justice Program before the pandemic. Nothing beats the feeling of helping others who otherwise wouldn't have the means to hire an attorney. But the problem is, I've been so busy lately, especially with the pandemic backlog, that I haven't had the time to do pro bono work. So, I've been thinking of possibly hiring an associate lawyer to help me so that I can."

"Wow, Ash. That sounds like an excellent idea. I'd love to do more pro bono work too. Especially after my visit to the shelter. If all the proposals I've submitted lately pan out, I might be in the same position of needing to hire another landscape architect to help with the load so I can continue doing pro bono projects too. But I don't want to jinx anything by jumping the gun."

Ashley sighed. "Speaking of work, I better get back to doing some."

"Me too. Plus, I need to research oleander. If it was in the smoothie like I think, I want to see what the symptoms of oleander poisoning are. And then figure out who gave Bunny the oleander-spiked smoothie."

"Good luck and be careful."

I grabbed a bottle of water and hopped on my computer, ready for a deep-dive google search for oleander. I found that all the parts of the plant were extremely toxic, and even a small amount could be lethal.

Someone could have easily added leaves, stems, or flowers of the shrub into a blender when making a smoothie. It supposedly had a strong bitter taste, but since Bunny had not yet regained her sense of smell and taste, she probably wouldn't have been able to detect the bitterness.

In terms of symptoms, oleander poisoning had many possibilities: weakness, irregular heartbeat, blurred vision, stomach upset, dizziness, depression. Depression and loss of appetite were most often seen in chronic overdose cases. I wondered if Peter's assumption that Bunny had stomach issues and foggy brain from Covid was wrong. What if it was a symptom of her being poisoned with tiny amounts of oleander? But as I researched further, I learned that it was so extremely toxic that even a tiny amount might have been fatal, leading me to the conclusion that Bunny must have ingested oleander for the first time on the day she died.

I sat back in my leather chair and rested my feet on the big wooden desk that had been my father's. Maybe Peter or Kaley or someone at the *Sentinel* had known that Scarlett brought Bunny the shakes and then tampered with the one she had that day. Or maybe Scarlett had poisoned it herself and had given it to Bunny before she got to the garden. Hmm.

By three I was starting to get drowsy and made some tea, then continued to go down the oleander rabbit hole online for another hour. At four I stopped by the Benning Brothers Nursery across the street to pick up a plant for Heath before heading home. I picked out a small gardenia with several blooms on it, found a planter to fit it in, and by four forty-five I was back home, watching Iris and Lily play in my backyard. Lily had made an incredibly seamless transition into our little family. Bunny must have shown her a lot of love because she was a very good dog. She was already house-trained and socialized, the wonderful benefit of many senior rescue dogs.

I fed the dogs and Otis and then took a shower. I hadn't worn much makeup lately so now I felt a little went a long way. Some brownish gray eyeshadow, a bit of eyeliner, smudged, and eyebrow pencil. I brushed some blush on the hollows of my cheeks and mixed some light coral M.A.C. lip pencil with a bit of rose-colored lip gloss. I wanted to seem hip but not trying too hard, as if I was starstruck, so I went with black slim-fit pants, a lowcut black tank top and a Splendid LA black jacket I'd found for a steal online at Nordstrom Rack. I tried to replicate the fashion pony Philip had styled and it didn't turn out too bad, but I decided in the end to sweep my hair up into a messy bun instead. Hoop earrings and a simple gold necklace and diamond pendant finished the look. I sprayed a bit of Hanae Mori perfume on my wrists and rubbed it on my neck around my ears. I was red carpet ready. Or rather, ready to have dinner with someone who'd walked the red carpet many times.

Iris and Lily followed me as I led them in dance to the backyard as I sang "Who Let the Dogs Out," a song that Iris had learned to associate with going outside, and now Lily already seemed to know what it meant. Our little dancing procession alleviated the jitters starting to build in anticipation of Heath's dinner, at least temporarily.

Once back inside, I patted all three pets. "Be good. I won't be gone too long. See you later."

All three looked back at me with wistful yet resigned expressions, or perhaps it was with relief, knowing they could now get some peace with me gone as they toddled off to their beds to nap.

The drive up to my father's house in Sycamore Canyon was gorgeous any time of day, but at dusk it was particularly stunning. As the road wound up into the hills I caught breathtaking glimpses of the twinkling lights of Santa Sofia below, and beyond, the darkening horizon with the lighted pier and the majestic reds, pinks, and purples of the sinking sun reflected on the ocean.

When I turned into my father's driveway and pulled up to the house, Heath's navy Bentley was the only car I saw. I parked next to his car. My heart was beating fast, and my stomach felt fluttery. Was I the first one here or the only guest? I pulled out my phone and immediately checked the text he'd sent with the time and date of the dinner to make sure I hadn't gotten the day mixed up. But it was the correct night and time.

I sighed heavily and checked my hair in the mirror and gave myself a pep talk, as you do. "You can do this. Don't be nervous. He's only won the title of sexiest man of the year twice. No big deal."

I grabbed the gardenia and walked along the drive in my high-heeled sandals. I rang the doorbell and Heath answered. He looked as dashing as ever in jeans and a crisp white shirt, loafers without socks, and a warm smile.

"Howdy. Right on time."

"Oh, good. I thought maybe I'd gotten the time wrong, and I was too early because I didn't see any other cars here." I handed him the gardenia. "This is a housewarming gift for you."

"Thanks. How thoughtful." He gave me a quick hug. "I told the others to arrive between six thirty and seven. I thought it'd be fun to get a chance to chat with you alone first, since I'll be busy cooking once everyone else gets here. I hated the thought of going through the whole night without having had a chance to get to know you a little better. Can I offer you something to drink?"

He put the gardenia on the hall table, and I followed him into the kitchen.

"A glass of wine would be nice."

"Red or white? Let me warn you, I've invited vintner friends of mine tonight. They own the Grey Lane Winery in Los Olivos."

"Oh, I love their wine. White wine, please."

"I happen to have their 2019 Chardonnay already open."

"Sounds perfect."

He poured wine into two elegant crystal wineglasses that looked like they were from Crate and Barrel. He grabbed a wooden board with cheese and crackers, and we moved into the living room. We sat in armchairs that faced each other at opposite ends of a coffee table.

I sipped my wine. "Very nice. Who else have you invited for dinner?"

"The Grey Lane Winery couple I mentioned. And the head of an entertainment company you'll probably recognize since it's an everyday name, and her entertainment attorney husband."

So far two couples. I was beginning to wonder if I was Heath's date. Wonder, hope. Semantics.

He sipped his wine. "And the McGregors."

"Oh, really?"

I wondered if I should share my theory that Kaley had been following me. Or wait until I'd gotten confirmation after Adrian ran her license plate. Heath had said he was old friends with Mac. I wondered what he thought of Kaley.

"Do you see Mac and Kaley a lot socially?"

"Whenever Mac comes to LA we try to get together. To be honest, I hardly know Kaley." He paused. "Jonq had pegged Kaley as a gold digger."

Jonquil "Jonq" Ryde was Heath's stunningly beautiful and talented ex-wife. An actress herself, she was more well-known in England for her work in the theater than here in the States.

He blushed. "Sorry to bring up my ex. Habit. And after all, we were together for all of two years, with the last year spent apart due to the pandemic. She was stuck in London, and I was in LA."

His eyes twinkled at the "two years" part. But they dimmed

when he mentioned their separation due to Covid. I liked his humor and his sensitivity. Each time I talked to him he'd seemed much more normal and down-to-earth than I'd have ever expected from a famous actor.

My phone pinged and I reached into my purse and snuck a glance, not wanting to appear rude. It was Ashley texting me that the license plate belonged to Kaley McGregor. I felt my face heat up and my heart pounded.

"Something wrong? You look flushed."

I took another sip of wine. "What? No. I'm fine. It's probably the wine. I didn't eat lunch."

Heath smiled slightly.

I chuckled, showing nonchalance on the outside, but I was panicking on the inside. The person who'd been following me was joining us soon for dinner. The same person who I suspected might be a murderer or a co-murderer. How should I behave? Let her know I was on to her? Probably not the greatest idea if she was the murderer.

I took another sip of wine. "Sorry to hear about your divorce."

An outright lie. Blame the wine.

Heath blushed again. "Thank you. We were living in two different countries. Our relationship just kind of petered out."

Hearing "petered," my thoughts returned to Peter and Kaley.

I plucked my phone from my purse. "Sorry, but I just remembered I need to text a friend about something. It'll just take a second."

I texted Ashley. *Kaley is going to be at this dinner party tonight.*

Heath jumped up. "My cue to fetch more wine."

In response, Ashley texted me back an emoji that was screaming in fear. She wasn't helping.

Heath came back with another bottle of wine. His hand touched mine as he steadied my glass while he topped off my wine. He looked into my eyes and smiled. My heart fluttered.

He sat down on the sofa perpendicular to my chair and then sprang up. "I forgot the berries. Let me go get them."

I texted Ashley back when Heath left the room. *Thanks for the reassurance*. I added an upside-down face emoji.

Heath returned with a small platter of raspberries, blueberries, blackberries, and strawberries. He tilted the platter toward me.

I took a strawberry and bit into it. "Mm. Delicious. So sweet."

"Farmers Market. The best."

The doorbell chimed.

Heath checked his watch. "Looks like the other guests are a bit early."

He trotted out of the room and several seconds later laughter pealed from the hallway. The next minute Heath returned with two men who he introduced as Kenji Grey and Alistair Lane, owners of Grey Lane Winery and Vineyards. Both looked to be, like Heath, in their early forties. Kenji wore a wide-brimmed straw hat and a collarless, unstructured jacket over expensive-looking distressed jeans. Alistair had his long-sleeved white shirt buttoned all the way to the top. He wore tie-dye long shorts and Birkenstock sandals. Both men greeted me warmly with deep head nods and wide smiles. Once Heath mentioned we were drinking their Chardonnay, they acted like shy children, telling me they hoped I liked it.

I took a swig of wine. "Love it. How do you all know each other?"

Heath brushed my leg as he walked past me to lower himself on the couch. Accidentally or intentionally, I couldn't tell.

Kenji lifted his hat for a moment to rearrange its fit. "We're business partners with Heath. Like so many celebrities have already done, we're jumping on the tequila bandwagon."

I took a sip of wine. "You have your own brand of tequila?"

"Yes. The launch will be this fall."

The doorbell rang again. Heath jumped up and headed to the front door. Voices sounded and the next minute a couple who looked to be in their late forties walked in. Heath introduced the woman as Jennifer Townsend. I'd read about her. She was a role model for career success, working her way up from a PA position to the head of a famous production company in record time, and she looked the part with her expensive clothing and impeccable hair and makeup. She now headed an internationally renowned entertainment company. With her was her husband. Heath introduced him as Ned Steller, a short, stocky bald guy with a beard, and partner in the big entertainment law firm of Steller, Klein, and Zanderman.

We bumped elbows playfully and Heath took care of making sure everyone had drinks. When the doorbell rang again, I tensed up. Time for another swig of wine.

Heath answered the door, and this time came back with Mac McGregor. No Kaley in sight. I exhaled.

Mac hugged me, and then turned to Heath. "Kaley's coming in her own car. She sends her apologies. She called to tell me she was running a little late. She'll be here soon."

I felt like I'd gotten a reprieve and had time now to calm myself down and figure out how I was going to relate to my stalker. I sipped my wine.

Once Mac had a drink, Heath announced what he had planned to cook for us. "Bouillabaisse. All ingredients fresh from the pier. I have everything all set to go."

My phone buzzed. I peeked at it discreetly. It was from Jake. I'd told him I was having dinner at Heath's. Why on earth would he bother me here. I didn't like that at all. And why call? Just text. I ignored it.

The doorbell rang. Kaley had arrived. I swigged my wine. I felt like I was playing a drinking game, only instead of jovially taking a shot every time someone said a particular word, I took a sip of wine every time I felt nervous. Only the stakes had risen, the game was murder, and there were only so many more sips I could take before I became inebriated.

Kaley greeted everyone. When she saw me, she had a startled response, like a newborn who hears a loud noise. I've had a lot of responses to my presence in the past, but this was a first. Maybe she'd figured out we traced her car and that was a guilt startle. She sat next to Mac.

Heath was now describing a salad that we'd start with, detailing all the ingredients from the Farmers Market.

My phone buzzed. If it was Jake again, I was going to be really annoyed. But when I checked my phone, the missed call was from Luke. What did he want? I'd get back to him later.

Heath had started to describe what he'd had in store for us for dessert. My phone buzzed again. This time it was Adrian calling. I assumed he wanted to tell me that the license plate was Kaley's. Old news. Ashley was my inside source.

"Aren't you the popular one?" Heath gazed at me intensely with a slight smile.

"Sorry. I missed that last part. Did you say a Sweet Lady Jane's triple berry cake?"

Jennifer spoke. "Yes, Ned and I picked it up in Santa Monica right before we drove up here. We had it in a giant cooler with ice packs."

I smiled. "My favorite cake in the world. And with all the fruit, somewhat healthful."

Jennifer giggled. "I know. Right?"

My phone buzzed yet again. Heath glanced at me. This was starting to get super annoying. It was Ashley. I bet Adrian had asked her to call me about Kaley's car. Why didn't she tell him I already knew?

My phone pinged.

This time it was a text from Ashley. I nearly blacked out when I read it.

Peter Yusem is dead.

CHAPTER 23

I shot up from my seat. "Sorry. I need to call someone back." Two thoughts immediately popped into my head as I ran unsteadily into the hallway to call Ashley. There goes one of my prime suspects. And there goes one of the best-sounding dinners ever.

Ashley picked up immediately. "We've all been trying to get a hold of you. Why don't you pick up your calls?"

"I told you I was at Heath's. What happened to Peter?"

"He was in a car accident."

"Oh, no! When? Where?"

"Adrian called to tell me about an hour ago. He said he tried calling you too. Peter apparently lost control of his car on one of the steep curves on Sequoia Highway and drove off the road and down a cliff."

"Had he been drinking?"

"We don't know yet. Adrian went to the scene of the accident. He said he'd let me know when he found out more."

"Was anyone else with him?"

"Don't know anything more than what I just told you."

"Got it. I'm horrified. Oh my God! Wait until Kaley finds out. She'll be devastated. Should I tell her?"

"No. That's why we were all calling you. Until Adrian finds out more and takes a look at the accident scene, we're all sworn to secrecy. Peter's ID hasn't even been confirmed yet."

"But it was his car for sure?"

"Yes, they ran his plates already."

The sound of a footstep startled me. I whipped around and Kaley was at the end of the hall heading to the kitchen. I wondered if she'd heard me mention her name or Peter's.

"Tory? Are you there?"

I lowered my voice. "Yeah, I'm here. Just saw Kaley lurking around."

"What are you going to do?"

"I don't know. I can't possibly stay here at Heath's dinner party now—"

"Why not?" Heath was so close to me I smelled the alcohol on his breath.

I must have jumped three feet. "Jeez. You scared the daylights out of me. Why did you just creep up?"

"I wasn't aware that I'd 'crept.'" He smiled.

I told Ashley I'd call her back and turned to Heath. "Someone I know has been in an accident. I need to go. All those calls I was getting were my friends trying to let me know."

Kaley loomed in the background looking inquisitive.

I turned to Heath. "I'm so sorry. But I really have to go."

"Let me walk you out."

We walked toward the front door.

"I'll fill you in another time but, short version, a couple of days ago someone threatened me. Threw a rock through my home office window. Now someone who was also threatened just died in a supposed car accident." I made air quotes. "A little too coincidental for my liking and frankly, it has me in a tizzy."

"Oh, no." His lips parted and his face became more somber. "That sounds horrifying. Are you going to be okay? You can always stay here if you're afraid. Scout's honor I'll behave like the most professional bodyguard ever, for real. I've had to learn a lot of martial arts for my movies and have to say I hold my own with the professional stunt artists. And after all, it is your house."

Whether it was genuine thoughtfulness (which I thought it was) or a come-on line, I just felt a draw to Heath at that moment that was almost magnetic. Especially the way the soft light from the simple wrought iron chandelier hanging in the entryway illuminated his face, making his light green eyes seem more luminous in the dim light.

"Thanks for the offer. That's very thoughtful of you. I'm going to ask a friend of mine to come over to my house and spend the night. I'm friends with her boyfriend and he's a cop, so maybe she can persuade him to come over too."

"Are you sure you don't want to stay for dinner? You can leave right after you sample my bouillabaisse."

"No, that's so sweet though. I just feel like I need to leave now."

"Understandable. Don't worry about the dinner. We'll do it another time. Do me a favor and let me know when you get home, so I don't have to worry about you."

The way he looked at me when he said that made my heart flutter.

"I definitely will. Thanks."

He hugged me at the end of the front path. A strong bear hug that made me feel safe. My heart was beating so hard it felt like it was going to burst out of my chest. Was it the emotions Heath's embrace released in me or the intense anxiety I was feeling about Peter's death? Probably both.

When I got to my car there was a note under my wiper. I opened it and sucked in air as I read it. It was from Kaley McGregor. She said she knew who had murdered Bunny and shot Stone, but she was afraid the police wouldn't believe her because she was their prime suspect's wife. A shiver went down my back. She wanted to meet me to get my advice on what to do.

Hmm. Then why had she practically recoiled just now when she'd seen me? That didn't make sense. And why had she seemed surprised to see me if she'd just left a note on my car?

I heard a noise and I flinched. I felt goose bumps on my arms. I stopped reading midway through and looked around quickly to make sure someone wasn't lurking in the bushes. Was Kaley watching me read her note from some shadowy corner or from a window inside? I opened my car door, bustled inside, and locked the doors before I read the rest of Kaley's note. She asked me to meet her later tonight at the beach.

I couldn't think of anything less inviting than meeting someone who had been stalking me at an isolated beach. But at least it was a woman, and maybe if she had some proof of who the killer was, this might prevent Mac from being arrested and charged, as Ernie had warned was imminent.

I started my car and reread the note. She wanted to meet at nine. My dashboard clock said it was eight forty-five. I had no time to dally if I wanted to get to the beach by nine. Plus, Kaley was probably making her own excuse to leave the dinner party herself by now. Whatever she had to tell me, she wanted to do in private. And last thing I needed was to run the risk of Heath seeing me hashing it out with one of his dinner guests in his driveway. He seemed to regard me as a gracious landlord so far, and I didn't want to tarnish that image. Before I backed out of my parking space, I texted Ashley to update her, and turned down the driveway to the street.

Ashley didn't respond. I didn't have the time to wait for her response. But at least she could check my whereabouts, if need be, with the Find iPhone tracker app. Ashley and I both had our Find iPhone app turned on since Milo had been murdered. We both communicated with each other a lot, especially in sketchy situations, but the app added a nice backup.

I navigated Sycamore Canyon's twists and turns more slowly than normal, thinking of Peter's dreadful accident the whole way down the hill. As I descended into Santa Sofia, the streets around the Avenue were mostly free of major traffic. I turned on the Promenade, the street that parallels the beach, and arrived at the designated rendezvous right before nine. Kaley had asked me to meet her north of the Santa Sofia pier, at a spot called Devil's Beach, named because of the hidden rocks close to shore that had claimed the lives of several unknowing surfers over the decades.

I made a turn into the small empty parking lot above the beach and parked but left my motor running.

I texted Ashley. *Any news?*

The next second Ashley called me, and I picked up right away.

"Tory! Are you crazy?"

"Why are you screaming?"

"Because I just saw your texts. Why would you go alone to an isolated beach, at night, to meet someone who might be dangerous?"

I had to admit my little drinking game had probably given me more bravado than I normally had.

I cleared my throat. "That's why I told you. So you'd know what I was up to. It's called the buddy system. Besides, remember I took that self-defense class."

"For a week."

"Not my fault if the pandemic cut it short."

She sighed. "Please be careful. And don't overestimate your prowess."

"Thanks for your vote of confidence."

"Anyway, I just got off the phone with Adrian. Peter had been at Gaviota Grove. He was on his way to meet Adrian at the police station. His brakes failed. He called Adrian and said they felt defective but then the phone went dead. Adrian thinks that's when they must have completely failed."

"You're kidding me. I can't imagine how terrifying that would be without brakes, picking up speed." I shuddered.

"Adrian thinks it's probably foul play. Peter was on his way to tell him something he'd found out related to Bunny's murder and he told Adrian he was afraid his phone might be tapped so he wanted to meet in person."

I gulped. "Really? Wow. That's what I was afraid of." I started to tremble.

Adrian was usually conservative so he must have had sufficient evidence to make him think it'd been foul play.

My voice quavered. "Well, at least Mac was at Heath Grant's when it happened, so he has an alibi. Same for Kaley. Even though she got there later. I guess that lets them both off the hook?"

Ashley breathed hard into the phone. "Not necessarily. The brake tampering had to have occurred sometime between after he arrived and before he left Gaviota Grove. Hate to burst your bubble, but Adrian said Peter had spent around three hours at the grove. Someone had all that time to tamper with his brakes. Being at a dinner party several hours after the car had probably been tampered with isn't much of an alibi."

I sighed. "You're right. Sorry. If I'd thought for a minute, I would have realized that. This has upset me on so many different levels. Death. Murder. My prime suspect eliminated."

"Literally."

"And now, all of a sudden I feel like I'm in jeopardy myself. Like there's this crazy person running around willing to kill anyone who gets in their way."

Ashley snickered. "You're just figuring that out now? They threw a rock through your window and said stop nosing around."

"I know. But that was when only Bunny had been murdered. I didn't realize we were dealing with a maniac who knocks people off like a serial killer to shut them up."

Ashley exhaled loudly. "You think that's why Stone was shot?"

"Probably. That's why he has a police guard. In case the killer tries again."

Ashley coughed. "Had a police guard."

"Wait. What?"

"Adrian told me that Stone's been released from the hospital. But I'm assuming they're still guarding him, right? Especially now that Peter is dead." Ashley exhaled loudly. "Maybe I should spend the night at your house tonight."

"Not going to lie. I was just going to ask you." I saw headlights turning into the parking lot. "Okay, looks like Kaley is here. Send out the troops if you don't hear from me."

"Stop. Are you scared for real?"

"Not really. Okay, maybe a bit. But I'm curious as to what her theory is."

The silver Mercedes pulled into a space nearer the street. Kaley McGregor got out of the car and walked toward the beach.

I got out of my car. "Kaley. Hi."

Kaley turned toward me and gasped when she saw me. That same reaction she'd had at Heath's. As I approached her, her eyes widened, and she started to edge back to her car. Her face registered everything except that she was happy to see me.

"Hi. What's up?"

She scanned the parking lot nervously. "I was about to ask you the same thing."

"I'm here because of the note."

She studied my face. "Me too."

I chuckled. "Obviously. Since you arranged it."

"Arranged what?"

"To meet me here."

Kaley gasped. "I arranged it?"

I was sensing a "Who's on First" vibe, and I didn't like it.

Headlights of a car entering the parking lot made both of us turn our heads. Another silver Mercedes pulled into the lot. For a moment I felt slightly woozy and disoriented. The car parked and Scarlett Hare got out and walked toward us.

I started toward her. "Hi, Scarlett, what on earth are you doing here?"

It was then I noticed Scarlett was holding a gun.

Kaley's voice was trembling. "Why do you have a gun, Scarlett? What's wrong?"

I looked around to see if there was anything I could protect myself with. Nothing but some trash bins. If I'd been smarter, like Kinsey Milhone, I'd already be hidden in one of them at this very moment, and armed with a gun. But no, I stood defenseless save for the mace in my shoulder bag, which I'd never used before and wasn't even sure I knew how to anyway. There were always my shoes. I didn't know whether the high-heeled sandals I was wearing were better than other options I might have worn. What they lacked in heft they gained in sharpness. I could see them gouging out an eye.

While my reaction was to weigh my fight options, Kaley seemed to be focused on flight. She started to trot toward her car.

Scarlett waved her gun at Kaley. "Get back over here. Next to

Tory."

Kaley dropped her shoulders and shuffled toward me. When our gazes met, amid the alarm, there was now a glimmer of solidarity, as we both realized in an instant of clarity that we'd been lured to the beach under false pretenses and were once again on the same team.

"Why did you trick us? Clearly, Kaley didn't write this." I held up the note.

"You're smart as well as pretty. Such a shame you're not long for this world."

Kaley gripped my wrist.

Scarlett sneered. "Don't act like you're upset my mother is dead, Kaley. You and Peter were one of the reasons she had to be killed."

Kaley started to tremble.

"That's right. Own it. When my brother discovered you and Peter were having an affair, he blackmailed Peter, thinking Peter would pay up to keep him quiet and not tell our mother."

I shook my arms a little, but Kaley wouldn't let go of me. "But Peter didn't pay him, did he?"

Scarlett shook her head. "He did at first. But then he got funding for his production company from la-dee-dah friends like Heath Grant and realized he didn't need our mother's money as a safety net." She looked at Kaley. "He didn't care if we told our mother about his affair with you anymore."

I shifted my weight, trying to stop my shaking. "So he stopped making blackmail payments?"

Scarlett nodded. "But the silver lining was that once our mother caught wind of the affair, she planned to change her will and leave everything to me and Stone. But then the private detective she'd hired to spy on Peter found out stuff about my boyfriend and his gambling debts."

My heart pounded harder when she mentioned Luke.

Scarlett aimed the gun at Kaley. "My mother would never have found out about Wargo's debts if it hadn't been for your stupid affair. But once she did, she changed her mind about leaving everything to me and Stone and planned to change her will again. She was going to cut us all out, me, Stone, and Peter."

My voice quavered. "That's when you decided to kill her."

Scarlett sneered. "That's when we knew we had to get rid of my mother before she changed her will, while Peter was still the heir, and while Stone and I were still stipulated as contingent beneficiaries if Peter died."

Kaley managed to squeak out a question. "But why did you bring us here?"

I gulped. I'd figured it out. Was Kaley that dense? Clearly to kill us both. Hence, the gun. Probably stage it as a murder/suicide to tie up all the loose ends. And by loose ends I meant witnesses with knowledge about the murders Scarlett had committed.

Scarlett smiled wickedly and shot me a glare. "She doesn't know about Peter?"

Kaley squeezed my wrist more tightly. "What about Peter?"

Scarlett snickered. "He's dead. Yes. Your poor little boyfriend Peter met with a nasty accident. Failed brakes, I believe."

Kaley snapped her head in my direction. "Is that true?"

I nodded.

Kaley screamed like a madwoman. Half werewolf howl, half war cry. Then she lunged at Scarlett like a flying monkey. Scarlett was caught off guard and not prepared for Kaley's superhero leap and lost her balance. Kaley kicked Scarlett behind the knees. As Scarlett's knees buckled, Kaley pounced again and dragged her down. This was my opening. I lurched toward Scarlett, my gaze focused on her gun, and dove toward her arm, grabbing the wrist of her hand with the gun with both my hands, and aimed her hand upward with my outstretched arms. Scarlett had a tight grip on the gun, but she was also trying to fight off Kaley, who was acting like a hungry monkey brawling over food, willing to fight to the death. We all grunted and swore as we rolled on the sandy ground. The whole time we struggled I tried to keep the gun aimed upward, like the hand on a compass that always points north. Scarlett let out a blood-curdling shriek. Kaley had bitten her ear and Scarlett let go of the gun as she instinctively grabbed her ear.

I swooped down on the gun, picking it up gingerly, and took off toward my car. I stumbled a few times and fell once as I tried to put as much distance as possible between the gun and Scarlett. Everything felt as if it was in slo-mo and my legs suddenly felt as if they had lead weights tied to them as I lumbered to my car while Kaley and Scarlett grappled on the ground. When I finally reached my car, out of breath and my heart ready to bust out of my chest, I opened the door and locked myself in. I was trembling so hard I could barely function, but I managed to get my phone out of my purse and call nine-one-one. The dispatcher told me to stay on the line. I turned on my engine, ready to run over Scarlett, if necessary, but Kaley appeared to be beating the heck out of her. Whatever strength and body control she'd learned in her yoga classes had paid off.

I heard sirens almost immediately, and the next minute a convoy of cop cars plowed into the lot. A blur of uniformed officers piled onto the beach. They soon separated the fighting women and cuffed Scarlett.

I got out of my car when I saw Adrian.

My voice sounded tinny and tiny. "Thank God you're here."

He ran over and gave me a quick hug. "You have Ashley to thank. She knew something didn't feel right."

Then I saw Jake. He ran over to me. His hug was longer.

CHAPTER 24

Two nights later I was driving up the winding road in Sycamore Canyon to my father's house again, aka Heath Grant's place, with Ashley in the shotgun seat. The last time I'd driven on this road I'd been headed to a beach meeting with Kaley McGregor, filled with anxiety and fear. In the span of a few hours so much had been revealed.

We drove in silence, each of us deep in our own thoughts. I wondered if Ashley was still processing the sequence of events like me.

I navigated each curve more carefully than usual. I couldn't help thinking about poor Peter Yusem on his last fateful and fatal ride on Sequoia Highway, frantically pumping his failed brakes as his car gained speed, realizing too late that Scarlett Hare, or more probably Stone Hare, had tampered with them.

Since her arrest, we'd learned that when Scarlett accompanied Bunny to visit her probate attorney, she'd found out that she and Stone were contingent beneficiaries if Peter died. That's when she'd hatched her plan to murder her mother and Peter. I shook my head. It would have been helpful if Bunny's probate attorney had revealed that key detail to Luke initially. Thank God Adrian had seen the actual document.

Since Scarlett knew she and Stone were contingent beneficiaries if Peter died, she had always planned to get rid of Peter eventually, but the plan was to wait long enough so the police wouldn't connect his murder with Bunny's. But once Scarlett learned Peter was going to the police with incriminating emails he found, she moved up the timing.

I tapped the steering wheel. But that had all been for nothing, since Adrian had already suspected the siblings and had requested warrants for their phones, where he ultimately would have found Scarlett's searches for oleander poisoning.

Just like Luke Barrett had told me, Bunny's suspicions about her kids were correct. Their only motivation was money. Scarlett's relationship with Denny Wargo, a con man and gambler, didn't help. Wargo had been her downfall, encouraging her evil plot, and she pulled her impressionable younger brother into it with her.

As if reading my mind, Ashley broke the silence and said, "Man, those were some cold-hearted siblings, huh?"

"True. But Scarlett was the mastermind. Stone basically followed her orders."

Ashley snickered. "Until he didn't. Scarlett must have been so mad when baby brother had a temper tantrum and knocked his mother out cold with his rake. After all of Scarlett's meticulous planning, Stone's impulsive behavior nearly ruined Scarlett's whole scheme to frame Mac for Bunny's death."

I glanced over at her. "I know. After Scarlett had so carefully plotted Mac's setup, from stealing both Bunny's and Mac's cabbages, to texting Mac from a burner phone, the planted glove, the phony leaked *Sentinel* editorial, threatening notes, and delivering her mother the oleander-spiked smoothie, only to have Stone mess it up."

Ashley whistled. "I'm impressed by how fast they pivoted and regrouped to plant new fake clues related to a head wound—the blood-stained glove in Mac's car and the bloodied spade under Mac's tarp—to keep suspicion on Mac."

I grimaced. "I'm still blown away that Stone was willing to let his sister actually shoot him in the leg in a staged murder attempt. He literally took one for the team to further incriminate Mac in Bunny's murder by implicating Mac as his assailant."

Ashley sneered. "Scarlett was probably like 'that's what you get for not sticking to the original plan.'"

I cleared my throat. "By the way, Joey now has promised to do more thorough background checks on everyone he hires for

Jacaranda Gardens. Stone slipped through the cracks because he was Bunny's son. A more careful inspection of his past would have raised some red flags."

I still marveled how Scarlett had gone to such lengths to prevent herself from being a suspect, from giving Stone all the dirty work, down to wearing a blonde wig when meeting Stone in his car at Jacaranda Gardens.

"Stone was the one who threw the rock through my window too. And who'd brought Lily to the animal shelter."

Ashley stretched her arms up, her gold bangles clinking. "And Scarlett lured Kaley to the hospital?"

"Correct. By leaving another fake note on her car impersonating me. The note asked Kaley to meet me there. Scarlett hoped Kaley and I would run into each other at the hospital in another effort to create mutual suspicion, doubt, and distrust. I'm amazed it worked for a while. It made me suspect Kaley of murdering Bunny and shooting Stone."

Ashley smoothed out a wrinkle in her beige blouse. "Yup. Then there was the whole thing trying to scare you by following and stalking you in a silver Mercedes to make you think it was Kaley."

I nodded. "For sure. But I'm a bit annoyed with myself for not picking up on the possibility that there might have been more than one silver Mercedes. I think once I realized both Kaley and Mac each owned a silver Mercedes, I never thought beyond two identical cars, and that maybe another person drove a third Mercedes, like Scarlett.

Ashley crossed her legs, her beige pants draping elegantly. "Hey. Don't beat yourself up. Was it actually Scarlett's car or did she rent it with the intention of confusing you?"

"That I don't know. But putting counterfeit plates on it that matched Kaley's was an evil stroke of genius."

Ashley bit her lip. "I still can't get over how Scarlett was a master at mind games. The way she made Kaley have second thoughts about trusting you. What a waste to use that talent for crime. She would have made a great defense lawyer."

I chuckled and shuddered at the same time. "Totally. Scarlett had devised a brilliant scheme using anonymous notes to make Kaley suspect me of bad faith. That instead of helping clear Mac's name, I was really trying to implicate him because I was the real killer. Casting suspicion on me because I was a landscape architect and oleander would have been my murder weapon of choice. Scarlett was intent on twisting Kaley's opinion of me and making her doubt me, which accounted for Kaley's increasing nervousness around me."

Ashley reached over and squeezed my shoulder. "All I can say is that thank God Scarlett's plan to stage a murder and suicide scenario to explain how you and Kaley would be found shot dead on the beach was thwarted."

I patted her hand. "That makes two of us."

I turned into the long steep driveway of my father's house. "I wonder who else Heath invited? That power couple I met the other night said they'd driven up from LA, giving me the impression they were only here for the weekend. But maybe the winery owners will be here."

"Adrian's invited."

My head jerked. "Is he coming? How does he know Heath?"

"Adrian said Heath reached out to all the people involved in solving the crime. He's impressed with how the residents of Santa Sofia came together and worked as a team."

My stomach gurgled in anxious anticipation. "Did Adrian mention whether Jake had been invited?" I parked at the far end of the parking area and turned to look at Ashley.

She glanced at me. "Jake will be here."

I took a deep breath. "Great. When were you thinking of telling me that minor detail?"

Ashley held her hands out and shrugged. "I thought I just did."

We both giggled.

I unbuckled my seat belt and smoothed out my black top and pants. "You know this is going to be awkward for me. He was on the verge of breaking it off with me the last time I saw him at my house."

"Don't overthink it, Tor. It's a thank-you dinner, not a showdown."

"Easy for you to say. All you have to worry about is Adrian. Oh, wait. I forgot. And the triplets." I glanced over at her, struggling to hide a smile.

We both dissolved into laughter.

"Please refer to them by their names. 'The triplets' makes it sound like you're referring to a musical theater act, like the Infant Phenomenon in *Nicholas Nickleby*."

I laughed. "I'm sure they're used to it. What are their names again? Trey, Tate, and . . . ?"

Ashley unbuckled her seat belt. "Tristan."

"Isn't that them?" I tilted my head in the direction of an incredibly handsome Black guy who'd just driven up in a Jeep with two passengers who looked equally hot.

Ashley's eyes widened as if she'd just been confronted by a bear.

"That's them. What am I going to do? I'm so embarrassed."

"I must say you do have great taste. All three of them are gorgeous." I watched with appreciation as they got out of the Jeep, each walking with of a swagger. "And cool."

Ashley slumped in her seat. "Did they see me?"

"I don't think so. They're looking at their phones and chatting with each other. Okay, they went inside already."

Ashley opened her door. "Gah. What'll I do?"

"Just be your normal charming and vivacious self. Two of them know you from crime scenes they were called to. They're probably happy to know you're alive and well." I caught her gaze. "Don't overthink it."

She gave me the side-eye. "Okay. Touché. I deserved that. I now understand the stress of juggling boyfriends."

I opened my door. "It's definitely a tough balancing act if you like them all."

Ashley and I got out of the car as another car drove up.

Ashley gave me an impish grin. "Well, look who's here."

I did a double take when I saw Luke Barrett wave to me from his car. He parked and jogged over to me.

He smiled broadly, revealing his cute dimples, and threw his arms around me. "Great to see you. How are you?"

I straightened out my top, which had gotten squished when he practically lifted me off my feet. "I'm okay, thanks. Still a little shell-shocked after having a Glock aimed at me, but okay, considering. Thanks again for calling the cops. Between you and Ashley, the whole SSPD was there in no time."

He patted my arm. "Yeah, I'd been following Scarlett follow you for several days. When I saw her headed to the beach and your car, I knew it was time to call in the squad."

I pulled back. "Wait, you'd been following her following me for days, you say? It wasn't just that night?"

Luke nodded. "Right. I wanted to catch her incriminating herself, so we'd be able to keep her in jail once arrested."

Ashley read my face accurately and said "Oh boy" under her breath.

I crossed my arms. "So you knew I was being stalked by a murderer and didn't tell me."

Luke's cheerful smile dimmed, and he blushed. "That's accurate."

I shook my head. "Don't you think that would have been useful information for me to have?"

Ashley sidestepped toward the front door. "Shall we go inside?"

We all walked toward the front door. Luke, looking annoyingly handsome in a gray shirt and gray jeans, lightly put his hand on my back.

I turned to him. "I don't understand why you didn't give me a heads-up. It's not as if you were working for Bunny any longer, obviously."

"But I *was* hired by someone else to find out who killed her."

I stopped abruptly. "You were? By who?"

Luke smiled slightly. "By our generous host today, Heath Grant."

Once again, my worlds were colliding.

I clutched my chest. "Heath Grant? Why on earth would he hire you?"

A deep theatrical-sounding voice answered. "Because Bunny was married to Peter Yusem, the owner of the production company I'd just invested in. I certainly didn't want to be doing business with a murderer. Everyone always suspects the spouse."

I spun around to see Heath Grant, looking even more attractive than usual in dark jeans and a light lavender dress shirt that brought out his tan skin and light green eyes.

He hugged me. "Hey. Glad to see you happier than the last time I saw you."

The door was open, and we all walked in. Heath made sure each of us had a drink in our hand in a matter of minutes. He poured me a glass of Cabernet and I drifted off into the living room. Ashley and Adrian were sitting next to each other on a couch laughing. One of the triplets was talking to Luke, one to Kenji and a third to Alistair.

Heath brushed past me laden with two platters of cheese and fruit from the kitchen to the living room.

Luke sidled up to me holding a gardenia. "This is for you. I'm sorry for not telling you about Scarlett. I wanted to tell you. But honestly, I was on her tail the whole time. I wouldn't let you get hurt."

My heart melted. I held the gardenia to my nose and breathed in its seductive scent. "You picked this in the front of the house, didn't you? They're one of my favorite flowers. That's why I planted them here."

He smiled. "Mine too. Even though I had you covered the whole time, I wasn't worried about you. I'd read about your past encounters with dangerous individuals. I sensed you were a strong woman who could take care of yourself."

His brown eyes gazed into my soul. I gazed back, falling under his spell.

Ashley whispered in my ear as she breezed past me, "Jake just got here."

My gaze roamed the room until I found him standing in the doorway. Looking good. He raised his chin in acknowledgment when our gazes met and smiled slightly. I had the sudden thought that maybe I was dreaming this whole event.

I turned back to Luke. "I understand your perspective but—"

Luke brushed his hair back from his face, exposing his perfect bone structure. "I knew there was going to be a 'but.' To make it up to you I'd love to take you out to dinner as a peace offering."

"I'd like that." I looked around for Ashley. "I need to talk to Ashley for a sec. I'll be back."

I found Ashley in the kitchen refilling her wineglass.

She looked at me nervously. "I need fortification. Adrian is chatting with all three of the triplets right now."

"I thought you didn't want to refer to them as 'the triplets.'" I smiled.

Ashley's gaze drilled into mine. "Really? I'm expressing a cry for help and you're correcting me?"

We both guffawed.

"I can think of worse problems. Just saying."

"Speaking of problems, Jake is heading our way."

The next moment I got a strong back hug that ended with Jake's arm slung over my shoulder.

"Hi." I faced him and looked into his eyes and then away, dreading the "it's not you, it's me" conversation.

Jake dropped his arm and turned to Ashley. "I'm so glad you had the wherewithal to alert Adrian once you found out Tory was meeting Kaley. Thanks to you, the cops got there before Scarlett's evil backup team joined her. Adrian said Stone and Wargo were spotted parked on the Promenade not far from the beach."

Mac and Kaley McGregor had arrived together as we were chatting and walked in our direction.

"You're very welcome. I'm just glad no one got hurt." Ashley flicked her hair at Jake and turned her gaze to Kaley as she approached us. "Although I heard Kaley got pretty banged up and has some nasty battle scars."

Kaley smiled at Ashley. "Only a few bruises that are already healing, thanks."

Peter's death had devastated Kaley, yet the person who comforted her the most in the last few days was the person she'd betrayed, her husband Mac. Go figure. Mac and Kaley had been through a lot together and had decided to remain friends, although they hadn't decided whether to stay married. Mac strode over when he spotted me.

"There she is." He patted me on the back. "Thank you again, Tory, for being a loyal friend and believing in me, even when the going got tough. And for keeping a cool head when I couldn't."

"Aw, thank you, Mac. I'm sorry you had to endure all the stress of being a suspect. Been there, done that."

Kaley turned to me and gave me a high five and then pulled me in for a hug. "Tory, what can I say? I think we make a good team, don't you? Thank you."

"I'm the one who should be thanking you. You saved my life when you jumped Scarlett."

Kaley patted my shoulder. "Thank God you took her gun away from her."

Heath joined us. "Tory, I was just talking to Alistair and Kenji. Expect a call from them. They're interested in hearing your landscape ideas for their winery renovation."

"Okay. That sounds good. I'll look forward to talking with them."

Jake, who had drifted away, had circled back. "Hi. Can I grab you for a second?"

"Sure." I raised my eyebrows to Ashley as Jake took my hand and led me outside to the back patio.

His gaze met mine. "I've felt awful since we ended without talking about what I've been wanting to talk to you about for days now."

"Okay."

I braced myself. I knew being dumped by Jake was going to hurt, even though we hadn't officially been together. Even with the dashing movie star Heath Grant, and the romantic PI hunk

Luke Barrett, to fall back on.

Jake inhaled and exhaled heavily. "Okay. First let me say I know how hard it was for you to lose Milo. I know because I was right there alongside you as you searched for your missing husband and then his killer. And I certainly never intended on causing you more grief by making you think about all that again, especially since you've come such a long way emotionally in coming to terms with your grief."

"Thank you for acknowledging that, Jake."

"But that being said . . ."

I knew it. Just when I was toying with the possibility of more of a commitment, he was going to make it a nonissue. Ah, well. Admittedly, I was on the fence. But still, I wanted it to be my decision. Or at the very least, a mutual decision.

"I wanted to make sure I talked it out with you in advance to make sure it was okay with you."

Huh? "You wanted to make sure I was okay with it?"

Jake nodded. "About me buying a house in Santa Sofia. That's what I've been wanting to discuss with you. Not only because it would mean we would be living in the same town, that's a longer conversation, but because I didn't want it to trigger unhappy memories."

"I don't understand."

He hesitated. "I found a place on the beach. I know Milo's condo was on the beach and that's all a part of your relationship with him. I want to respect your feelings. If you feel you can't handle another boyfriend who lives on the beach . . ."

He turned red when he realized the "b" word had tumbled out of his mouth, and I wasn't referring to "beach."

My face heated up. "That's the important talk you've been wanting to have?"

He nodded. "Yeah. What did you think I wanted to talk about?"

I took in a deep breath. "Honestly, I thought you were going to tell me you didn't want to see me anymore."

"What?" He gave me a quick hug and then pulled back, and

his blue eyes gazed into mine. "How could you possibly think that? You know I'm Team Tory forever."

I melted from his gaze. "Oh, it was easy, given my twisted way of protecting myself from further sorrow."

Jake kept his hands on my arms. "You're way off if you think I'm trying to break off seeing you anymore. I've been saving my money and wanting to invest in real estate for a while now. Santa Barbara has become so outrageously expensive. I know Santa Barbara isn't that far away, but with traffic, and our busy lives, I thought I can just as easily work here in Santa Sofia as from Santa Barbara. And PI work is pretty flexible."

I felt light-headed. I had read the situation wrong. Not totally wrong. At first, I'd thought he wanted a bigger commitment. But this was so much more sensible and gradual.

I smiled. "It sounds like a great idea, as long as you don't expect anything to come of it necessarily, in terms of our friendship. It would be a lot of pressure if you moved here with expectations that our relationship would necessarily get more serious."

He dropped his arms. "Totally agree. No pressure whatsoever. I just wanted to get your reaction. It's just removing one barrier to seeing where our relationship goes, or if it goes at all. But might as well give it a chance unimpeded by obstacles like not living in the same town."

Heath came out onto the patio. "How are you doing with your drinks? Can I get either one of you something? Kenji and Alistair brought a glorious selection of their Grey Lane Chardonnays and Cabernets."

Jake and I followed Heath back into the kitchen.

I turned to Jake. "I'm fine with it. Go for it. Beach living is great. My house is only a couple of blocks from the beach, and I love it. Great for running and walking dogs."

"Are you sure?"

I nodded.

"Great." He gave me a side hug.

Heath's bouillabaisse did not disappoint. It rivaled the bouillabaisse served at Sadie's Seafood Café, and that was saying a lot. Combined with sourdough baguettes and a green salad with avocadoes and artichokes, it was a sublime dinner with the best company. And the Grey Lane wines we sampled were superb. For dessert there was a pear and almond tart, fresh fruit, and triple berry crème brûlée in small ramekins whose tops Heath caramelized himself with a kitchen torch for dramatic flair.

By the time we all finished eating it was nearing eleven. Ashley was going to get a ride home from Adrian. I decided to make my getaway and say my goodbyes as the crowd of guests dwindled to avoid any possible awkwardness involving my three love interests, who were not only all in the same place, but socializing with one another and, apparently, becoming fast friends as I looked on.

Help.

I walked out to my car in the chill night with a spring in my step, feeling grateful and appreciative for how the last couple of days had all gone down. Not only had justice been served in Bunny's and Peter's murders, but there'd been a silver lining in that very dark cloud, with Bunny's Pom finding a forever home with my little fur family, starting the next chapter in her life along with her new name.

I also felt grateful for the men in my life, not just Uncle Bob, who was my rock, and some of the guys in my trusted Benning Brothers crew, but also for the men who were potentially shaping up to play larger romantic roles in the days ahead. I hadn't yet sorted out all my feelings about my romantic future, but I was hopeful. Heath was hot and glamorous, Luke was hot and intense, and Jake was hot and sweeter than ever.

But having three possibilities was a good kind of problem to have. After Milo had been killed, I felt as if my life was over, and I'd never love someone again. Attracted to someone? Heck, yes. But love? I highly doubted it. Plus, I'd had the additional fear that if I were lucky enough to find love, what if I lost it again?

I inhaled and exhaled deeply as I stood by my car door. Maybe I should focus on work for a while and only date casually. Given the number of potential projects I'd lined up, free time might turn out to be zero anyway.

As I beeped open my door, I noticed a note tucked under my windshield wiper blade. I inhaled sharply. Not again? But this time it was an envelope, with my name on it. I grabbed it and got in my car and instinctively locked my doors.

When I opened the envelope and read the note, my heart pounded.

It said, "Looking forward to spending more time together."

It was unsigned. Except for a drawn heart.

BOOKS BY JUDITH GONDA

Murder in the Secret Maze
Murder in the Christmas Tree Lot
Murder in the Community Garden

ABOUT THE AUTHOR

Judith Gonda is a mystery writer with a penchant for Pomeranians and puns, so it's no surprise they pop up in her amateur sleuth mysteries featuring landscape architect Tory Benning. As for the hot buttered lobster rolls, black tea, and California wine that also pepper her pages, they can be traced to her growing up in Connecticut, London, England, and the San Francisco Bay Area.

Trained as a Ph.D. psychologist, she taps the knowledge gained from her time spent conducting research at USC, heading a human resources department, and running focus groups as a jury consultant to inform her characters and plots.

Judith currently resides in Southern California with her architecture professor husband and her two rescue Poms/surrogate daughters. Her two human daughters, a landscape architect and a TV writer, live nearby. All, along with crime stories in the news, have inspired her books.

To learn more about her upcoming releases, please visit her website at judithgonda.com.

www.ingramcontent.com/pod-product-compliance
Lightning Source LLC
LaVergne TN
LVHW100523110826
845146LV00002B/758

* 9 7 9 8 9 9 4 1 4 6 4 5 3 *